Woman at the
GARAGE SALE

GARAGE SALE MYSTERY SERIES
SUZI WEINERT

International Standard Book Number 13: 978-1-60452-168-9
International Standard Book Number 10: 1-60452-169-6
Library of Congress Control Number: 2020944461

BluewaterPress LLC
2922 Bella Flore Ter
New Smyrna Beach, Florida 32168

http://www.bluewaterpress.com

Editing by Carole Greene

Cover Art by Jake Eatmon and Mike Eatmon.

DEDICATION

To my intellectually curious,
well-read and supportive sister,
Margo Gibbs,
for encouraging my writing experience.

And

To my resourceful editor,
agent and great friend,
Carole Greene,
for sharing my
Garage Sale Mystery Series adventure.

CHAPTER 1

SATURDAY

J ennifer Shannon froze at what she saw. Then her heartbeat quickened as she stared at the unusual object. Photos she viewed online only yesterday rushed to mind. Impossible, but this looked just like that Chinese ritual wine goblet. She felt its magnetism draw her closer to the cluttered garage sale table. She eased her way through the ring of shoppers around the display, who picked up and examined whatever caught their fancy. Her breath caught as another shopper's fingers trailed across the goblet's rim, hesitated, and then moved on.

Sudden movement on her left warned another rival readied to pounce on her find. As she sprang into action, her hand shot forward in an impulsive wild grab, a fraction ahead of this opponent's equally clutching grasp. Her fingers clamped on the goblet's edge and gripped tight, then whisked it through the air into her protective arms. Pulling it close, she cradled it against her chest.

Her opponent's bitter, angry voice caused her to look up sharply.

"How *dare* you?" snarled the well-dressed, mustached man. "I wanted that."

To de-escalate, Jennifer chose politeness. "Sorry, but I've searched a long time for this. Otherwise, I'd offer it to you."

"You don't understand," the man growled. "I deal in *antiquities.*" His condescending voice matched his haughty expression. "I have a client, a *collector*, who needs this piece to complete an important set. You just want it because it's..." he sniffed dismissively, *"different."*

Jennifer bit back a feisty retort. Why further this conversation headed nowhere? She started to move away.

"Wait!" The man reinvented himself, now with syrupy friendliness and artificial smile. "My apologies," he oozed. "Sorry we got off on the wrong foot. Here's my business card, proving I'm who I say I am. You chose something here today that interests me. Whatever price they quote you, I'm willing to buy it from you at double that amount." A confident grin accompanied this irresistible offer.

"Sorry," Jennifer said. "It's not for sale."

Sputtering at this affront, he shouted, "All right, I'll triple the amount."

"No thanks."

Furious now, he eyed the object in her arms as if about to snatch it. She gripped it tighter.

The man gave a strangled cry of rage, causing other salegoers to eye them warily. With a menacing expression, he moved close and seethed through clenched teeth. "You'll regret this." Then he spun around and stalked away, fists clenched.

Only when she assured herself this obnoxious man had left the sale did her protective arms unfold. She rotated her find to examine it from all angles, and grinned. Yes, the very goblet she wanted for her living room's Asian collection. The museum-quality bronze original of this convincing reproduction would date from the Shang Dynasty around 1600 BCE. She tucked the treasure firmly under her arm, absent-mindedly stuffing the man's card in her pants pocket to free fingers for more shopping.

She circled the sale again. The owner should have called this an "estate sale" because of the quality and quantity of unusual merchandise. No formal rules distinguished "estate" from "garage" sales. The distinction largely reflected a seller's choice. She'd attended so-called "estate" sales selling crummy household merchandise, contrasting with today's "garage" sale displaying fascinating, one-of-a-kind items.

Moving among the tables, she collected some "smalls" and nodded to "regulars" she recognized. Like her, they made the weekend rounds of McLean's garage and estate sales. Their passions differed—first edition old books for some, vintage postcards for others, or postage stamps on those post cards. Some hunted military paraphernalia, Fostoria or other glass, certain china or silver patterns, button collections, and so on. Or like her, alert to eye-catchers for her own home, or filling family or friends' requests. Sometimes she scooped up underpriced articles to consign profitably at a local consignment store, or to sell on Craig's List or e-Bay.

At least ten buyers shuffled ahead of her in the purchase line at this well-attended sale. Awaiting her turn, she took a final look around. Her scan passed then snapped back to a woman on the other side of the yard. Hadn't she seen this same woman at a few other sales? She looked somehow so familiar. As the purchase line inched forward, Jennifer tried not to stare at her. Where might she have met her? A store clerk, fellow parent, a distant neighbor in her housing development or member of one of her various clubs? Nothing fit.

Yet she felt she *knew* that face. She watched the woman move to another table of merchandise; hands clasped on her purse shoulder strap rather than fingering merchandise, as buyers typically did. But maybe nothing appealed enough for the woman to examine.

And Jennifer felt further drawn by the woman's expression... not just lost in thought, but something else. She looked as if she were about to burst into tears.

Jennifer felt a surge of compassion for this distressed person, but then chastised herself. Had she correctly interpreted the woman's bleak expression, or was it her imagination? Hubby Jason laughed at her efforts to "read" strangers, but she couldn't stifle her natural inquisitiveness about what explained people or things she saw. She stared at the woman. Why so familiar?

"Is this all you have today?" The Seller's question jerked Jennifer back to the garage sale.

She set her selections on the cashier's table. "Yes. Great sale today—such variety."

Seller smiled, checked tags and totaled the price. Producing cash, Jennifer pointed to the Chinese vessel in her hands. "Do you know anything about this?"

"My parents brought it back from a trip to China about ten years ago. Mom died six months ago, and Dad passed last month. Now my sisters and I face the nightmarish task of downsizing their entire household. They were world travelers and, as you can see," she indicated the many tables, "collected *lots* of mementos. But sorry, I know nothing else about this one. A fancy metal cup, is it?"

"Wine goblet, I think." Jennifer glanced at the line of buyers behind her and hurried to ask something else. "This may seem an odd question, but do you happen to recognize the blond woman over there? Perhaps someone from your neighborhood?" Their eyes followed Jennifer's pointing finger... but the woman was gone. Jennifer glanced left and right, to no avail. "Oh, sorry. Guess she left."

Seller paused. "You mean the one with the long blond hair?"

Jennifer brightened. "Yes." Buyers jostled impatiently behind Jennifer as the Seller shuffled through bills in her apron pocket for Jennifer's correct change. "No," she said, "I don't know her, but I noticed her, too. I thought she looked...unhappy."

Surprised, Jennifer said, "Funny, I had the same reaction." Their eyes met, but the next buyer inched forward, gently nudging Jennifer to move on. And, like that familiar-looking woman, the moment was also lost.

CHAPTER 2

Two weeks earlier, on the last day of school, Arnie Anderson stepped off the Langley High School bus. He grimaced as he hurried in the side door of his Great Falls home, praying to avoid his hated stepmother. He couldn't forgive his father for marrying Magda only six months after his real mother died. How could the man degrade his mother's memory that way? Even if Magda had warmed to Arnie, his mourning would have challenged them both. But Magda instantly disliked him as much as he resented her.

How he missed his own mother. She'd called him her "happy surprise" baby, who arrived ten years after his two siblings. He was 16 years old when she died, last year. His deep sadness over her passing felt like physical pain. With his father traveling on business and his siblings grown and flown, Arnie remembered cherished time and closeness shared with his mother when she was still healthy and they were often the only two at home. This bond increased during her terminal illness, when he was the only family member regularly at her side. He loved her and she doted on him.

"You're wonderful," she'd told him. "Smart, good-looking, and dearly loved by your mother...and father," she quickly added.

He thought about his older siblings, Jim and Anne, who'd graduated from college to live and work elsewhere. Magda tolerated them, perhaps because they visited only on occasional holidays. Not a threat to her new territory. But she plied her instant animosity toward Arnie in a myriad of effective ways.

Arnie knew his siblings missed their mother too, but Jim and Anne recovered faster, distracted with their own friends, activities, and jobs. Like them, Arnie excelled at school and earned good grades, but unlike them, he had few friends and only one activity besides classes: drones.

He eased inside the house and tiptoed up the servant staircase to his room on the second floor. His fingers tightened on his door handle, knowing in a few more seconds he'd slip to safety inside his room. But then a sound caused his teeth to clench...her dreaded shrewish voice.

"There you are," she crowed, appearing behind him. "Guess who got out of your room again today? Sent my cat allergies through the roof. Don't forget, the maid skips your room each week now, because Toby runs out when she opens your door. Also, from now on, limit your laundry washing to Saturdays, so I escape cat dander from your clothes and sheets." She paused. "And about the stench in your room. I expect you to clean Toby's litterbox every day. I won't tolerate a smelly house. And I've stopped lugging those heavy cat-litter bags home from the store. Find your own way to buy it and get it here." Her voice rose. "Better yet, get *rid* of that disgusting animal."

She started to walk away but turned abruptly, her expression smug. "I also put a lock on the pantry door so the maid can't steal anything. Consequently, you won't have access there either. Your food from yesterday is on your refrigerator shelf and there won't be any more until you eat it." She hustled down the hall, leaving Arnie speechless at his door.

He entered his room cautiously, foot ready to block Toby's possible escape. But the cat, snoozing on the rumpled bed, opened his eyes. Seeing Arnie, he stood and stretched. The boy removed his backpack and sat heavily on his desk chair. He slumped forward, cradling his head in his hands, trying to stanch his rising anger. When the cat slid against his legs, he reached down to pet it. "I can't take much more of this, Toby. What do I need to, like, *do* to get Dad's attention? Burn down the house? Shoot up the school? Kill myself?"

Toby jumped onto his lap, rubbing a furry cheek against Arnie's hand. "I can't undo Dad's insane new marriage. And I can't go back and change him into, like, the Dad I wanted—the kind who played catch or took me camping or taught me tennis. Now he's, like, harder to reach than ever at the very time I..." His voice trailed away.

Cradling the cat against his chest, he remembered eking out a few precious minutes alone with his father last month when he tried to compress his frustration into the fewest words. "Whatever else Magda tells you, she's mean to me every day," he told his father. "You're, like, not here most of the time so you don't see it. It's...it's that Cinderella story, Dad, but I'm the step-kid getting dumped on. I can't please her. With Mom gone and you traveling, I'm, like, alone here except for Magda. Couldn't you and I spend some time together, just the two of us? It feels like I'm...disappearing."

But his father's face had turned stern. "Listen, Arnie, I married Magda mostly for you—someone to run the house and make it a home for you while I'm away. Don't you like having meals on the table, clean laundry, and tidy surroundings? I sure do. I work hard for this big house and the perks that go with it, like your school. There isn't a better high school than Langley, but to qualify to go there you must live in certain areas of McLean. Hey, you have your own computer and TV and cell phone. Don't you feel any gratitude for all this?"

"But...it isn't, like, what you said. Magda makes me invent my own food from stuff in the pantry that she just locked. And she gives me, like, only one laundry day a week to wash my own stuff. I clean my room because she, like, told the maid not to. She criticizes everything I do. She hates me, Dad, and Toby, too. And when you come home from trips, she takes all your time. It's like you forget me. I know you're, like, busy and you work hard, and thanks for the neighborhood and school...but if you could, like, just give me some of your time..."

His father shrugged, impatient. "Cut the crap, Arnie. Man-up. Learn to get along. Life at our house is new for Magda. You know she had no children of her own, so she's trying to work out a relationship with you. Just humor her. Look, you know I'm on the road to provide all this for you, and when I finally get home, don't you think I earn some peace and female companionship? You're too big to need a daddy, so stop sniveling and spend more time with kids your own age."

"But..." Arnie's fists clenched. He could blow up, yell at his father, tell him what a loser Dad he'd become. But would that draw them closer or drive a final wedge between them?

His father turned away, calling over his shoulder, "Now run along and do your homework—or whatever it is you do."

Back in his room, Arnie had stared out the window, gazing across their meticulously groomed lawn, garden and trees. Could he funnel his anger into something positive? He knew the energy had to go somewhere, because bottling it up could tear you apart before you exploded. Yet only negative solutions sprang to mind, like hitting or burning or cutting or killing. What startled him was the satisfaction he felt while imagining vicious ways to strike back at Magda. It seemed so right. Yet, somehow, he knew it wasn't.

He stared again out the window. Movement caught his eye—a big dog had wandered into their yard. Wait, wasn't that Hercules from down the street? The kids who lived next door to the animal said the owners shouldn't have a pet because they didn't walk him or play with him. He lived in their fenced yard 24/7 during the summer. One kid said in wintertime they kept Hercules in a cage indoors.

The German shepherd found a way out of his fence periodically, roaming the neighborhood until someone reported him. Arnie gave Toby a wary look. "What if I have you out for a walk and that dog gets out?" He rubbed his pet's neck. "Don't worry, Toby. I'll protect you, no matter what happens."

The dog wandered out of view and Arnie refocused. Think positive. As he stared through his window, a breeze rustled the trees and bushes below. This combination seemed to connect him for a moment with nature's timeless, soothing rhythms. As if a breeze also swept through his mind, he pulled out a notebook and began to write.

> *Dad,*
>
> *To cause you and Magda less trouble, I need a way to be more on my own. I need a car. You gave a car to Jim and Anne when they reached my age, so I'm not asking for something special. With a car, I could get a job. With a job, I would have money. With money, I could buy Toby's food and litter and my own food. I'd only spend nights in my room at home. Please do this for me.*
>
> *Love from your son, Arnie*

He read the letter several times before folding it into an envelope, where he wrote his father's name and office address— lest Magda intercept and destroy it.

CHAPTER 3

After attending three garage sales, Jennifer cut short her morning jaunt and drove home, eager to compare her Chinese goblet to her research. After pulling into the garage, she carted most of her buys into the kitchen, surprised to find her husband concocting a sandwich.

"Honey," she said, "I thought you planned tennis this morning."

"One of our doubles team couldn't come and the other two decided on singles. You know I get winded playing singles now. Plus, I want to finish my workshop project. So here I am."

"Too bad, hon. On the other hand, you love building things, so it's win-win." She sat heavily in a kitchen chair and closed her eyes.

Jason felt concern. "Jen, you went to garage sales this morning, right?" At her nod, he put down his sandwich. "You usually come home excited, talking about what you bought." He studied her. "What's wrong?"

"Oh, Jay. This summer's challenge is finding the right senior residence for Mom. Easy-peasy, I thought, but no. She's teamed up now with Veronika, which is great—they're wonderful friends, both in their late 80s. But now they envision fancy apartments in some senior Taj Mahal that I doubt exists around here. I want her happy and feel responsible for helping that happen—especially after uprooting her from Florida so I can watch over her here."

Jason nodded. "We rented the Donnegan's house across the street for her for only three months, and one of those months has passed.

"And when she leaves, they plan to sell it, which ramps up the pressure. If I don't find a place she likes by then, I guess she'll have to move in with us and store her furniture while the search continues."

Jason kissed her forehead. "If anyone can find a solution, it's you, my Jen." He headed toward the garage.

She gave him an appraising look. "Wearing your workshop outfit?"

He glanced down at his tennis whites. "Ah, good point." He turned instead toward the stairs, just as Becca thumped down from her bedroom and rushed into the kitchen, where Jennifer still slumped in the chair.

"He's at it again, Mom. Another drone outside my window this morning. Fortunately, I was dressed so he didn't get an eyeful. This *must* stop. I'm going to talk to Gerry's parents... unless you want to. I'm serious about this, Mom."

"Gerry...the neighborhood boy? That Gerry?" Jennifer asked.

"Well, not really a boy any more...he's seventeen, only four years younger than me. Their family lives next to Mrs. Ogleby, the Hoarder."

"Now, Becca, that's just a rumor."

"Confirmed by the Conner girls, who sold her Girl Scout cookies. They said she tried opening her front door just a little, but when she let go to sign the cookie order, the door eased open by itself. They saw the hallway behind her crammed floor-to-ceiling with newspapers, magazines and *stuff*."

"Someone actually got a look?"

"Yes, so back to Gerry, Mom. We need to stop him. He sees what his drone's camera sees. He's a peeping-tom." She remembered college psychology classes. "Maybe even early symptoms of a deviant personality."

"I hear you, but let's not go too far. Maybe he's just a kid with an exciting new toy, discovering what it can do."

Becca sighed. "*Mom*, he got it for Christmas. Now it's June. He's had it *six months*. And it's not just me...how about everybody else he spies on? Are you more concerned about a kid's right to play with his intrusive toy than you are your daughter's right to privacy?"

"No, honey, of course not. Just trying for perspective." Jennifer considered the situation. "Have you mentioned this to him?"

"Oh yeah. You know I walk or jog the neighborhood most days, so I see a lot of neighbors. Sometimes I stop to talk. I often see Gerry and his friends flying drones in the pool parking lot or the community park. I act friendly and interested in their drones. Then I spill how I feel about a drone looking in my window. Last, I play the Golden Rule card."

"The what?"

"How would *they* feel if someone spied through *their* windows?"

"How does that go?"

"They stare at the ground. Act nervous. They're teens. They try anything until they're called on it. Having their drone spying through my window after they *know* it annoys me makes me crazy."

"I see your point."

"Like Business 101: first you talk to the person causing the problem, so he has a chance to correct it. If that doesn't work, you go up the ladder. So I talked to the boys first. Since that failed, next step is to talk with their parents, which I'm perfectly willing to do it, unless you want to."

Jennifer considered this. "You've thought this out. Good for you, Becca. But one of these days you'll move out of this neighborhood to start your own life, whereas I'll still live here. Peace with my neighbors is always desirable…," she glanced at Becca's determined face, "…along with fair play, of course. So, why not let *me* talk to his parents."

"Your choice, but please, Mom, today—ideally this morning."

Jennifer fingered the Chinese goblet. "Okay. Meantime, have you visited Grammy yet?"

"Mom, she rents the house right across the street and spends half her time over here anyway. But, no, I haven't checked on her today. You want me to dash over?"

"Well, she *is* 87, and until I find senior housing for her, she's in my direct care. And she *is* someone we all love and worry about."

Becca put her arms around her mother. "You're right," she stepped back, "but isn't the residence-search almost over?"

Jennifer sighed. "It got harder when she and Veronika dished up new expectations. I've found many senior places offering enough services but only small apartments—especially in older buildings. But the one we'll see today is newer. Maybe we'll get lucky this time." She didn't look convinced. "I just hope Grammy's lucid long enough to make her own choice. Otherwise, that falls to me."

Becca sighed. "Back in Florida, when we envisioned this for her here, it sounded easy."

"BTW, thanks again, Becca, for flying there and staying weeks to help me rescue Grammy and bring her here."

Becca smirked. "Guess the message is: be very, very nice to your children, like me."

Jennifer's eyebrows arched. "Why?"

"Because we'll choose your retirement home if you can't."

CHAPTER 4

Saturday morning, Arnie grinned as he raced his cat down to the driveway. "Look at this, Toby. I can't believe Dad got me a car. A used car, sure, but it's only, like, twelve years old." They circled the vehicle. "Still looks good and runs fine. Mileage sucks, but with my new job I think I can, like, keep gas in the tank."

Arnie opened the door. "Come on. Let's go for a ride." Toby leapt inside and Arnie settled into the driver's seat. The boy's smile reflected the new freedom this car offered, but also a surge of warmth he'd felt in the jaw-dropping moment when his father said, "Here's a hundred bucks to get you started. You're an okay kid."

Jolted by surprise and starved for affection, Arnie spontaneously hugged his father, but the man pulled away, clapping Arnie on the back. "Don't get any tickets, kid." Hungry for his dad's attention, the boy processed this incident as a rare expression of his father's love.

"Wow," Arnie cried, revving the motor and guiding the car onto the street. Excited at the options this car enabled, he pulled into the empty parking lot at Scotts Run Park—to think. Once parked, he stroked his cat's luxurious fur. "Here's the plan, Toby. Nights I'll sleep and shower at home. Days I'll work, eat at fast-food places and use that cheap coin laundry. I'll use bathrooms at work or the library or McDonald's." His smile faded as he studied his cat. "But what about you? You're okay with me in my room at night, but who knows what Magda could do to you when I'm not around."

The cat nuzzled his hand. "You can't stay home, but you can't stay in my car on hot summer days while I work. Even if I park in the shade, the heat could zap you. I need to figure this out since with Mom gone, you and Dad are the only ones left who even care about me."

Suddenly, he felt alarm. What if he *couldn't* fit his beloved cat safely into this gypsy life he planned? The unthinkable crossed his mind. If he couldn't keep his pet safe, who could he find to care for or even temporarily adopt Toby? Forget animal shelters with unknowable futures for their animals.

His cherished cat purred on the seat beside him. "You need me." He lifted Toby onto his lap and his voice cracked. "and...I need you." His arm circled the cat and he buried his face in Toby's fur. "What are we going to do?"

As his helpless inaction grew from frustration to anger at his unfair predicament, he focused on Magda. She personified his cursed situation, from the locked pantry to threatening Toby to monopolizing his dad's time. How could he undo the Voldemort-grip she exerted on his father? If Harry Potter triumphed over Voldemort, could he destroy Magda? He mimed pulling a magic Hogwarts wand from his pocket, waved it toward home, and shouted, "*Magda dissolvium.*" He grinned. But this imaginary victory's relief evaporated fast. The bewildered boy again gazed outside the car window to the parkland's wooded hills arching toward the sky, as if the answer to his problems lay somewhere among those trees.

Toby's expectant meow drew him back to reality and a glance at his watch. Oops. He needed to get to his friend's house for Saturday drone activities. He guided Toby from his lap to the passenger seat, drove to Gerry's neighborhood and parked down the block so as not to annoy his friend's parents. He whistled as he walked and Toby followed him down the sidewalk "just like a dog," his mother used to observe.

"Young man. Yoo-hoo, young man. Would you please help me for a minute?"

Arnie looked up. A woman on the front porch of the house next to his friend's home waved at him. He pointed to his chest. "You mean me, ma'am?"

"Yes, you. Would you mind lifting something heavy for me?"

He turned toward her porch. "Ah, well I...sure. I'll help if I can."

"What's that following you?"

"My cat. We're...we're taking a walk."

"Haven't I seen you around? Aren't you friends with the boy next door?"

"Yes, ma'am."

"Well, if you're going to help me, come along then."

Closer now, he noticed how much she resembled an older version of Magda—same dark eyes, black hair, round face and cross expression. He and Toby followed her around the house to her detached two-car garage shaded by an oak tree. She passed the building's car doors to unlock a side door. The dim interior brightened when she flipped the light switch.

Half the garage contained a car; the other half held dusty old furniture piled with stuff stacked every which way. She pulled out a stepstool. "These four boxes go on this top shelf."

Arnie grabbed the first heavy box, teetered up the stool, fought for balance as he lifted the box waist-high, then shoulder-high and finally over his head onto the shelf.

"Whew." He stretched his shoulders as he climbed down. "What's in there?"

"Books, but heavy, like bricks."

"You got that right." Arnie panted before repeating the drill with the remaining boxes.

"Thank you, young man." The woman smiled. "I want to pay you for doing this."

"Not necessary, ma'am." But then a sudden wild idea flashed through his mind. Did he dare? "But...but instead would you please let my cat stay here in your garage during the daytime this week while I, like, work at my job in McLean? He's a good cat and I have a litter tray in my car, so no accidents. I'd take him home with me every night."

The woman's brow furrowed. Her frowning face studied the boy.

To fill the silence before she said no and too embarrassed to tell the truth, Arnie invented. "My...my brother's new German shepherd terrorizes my cat when I'm not there. I brought Toby with me today to protect him. But now I realize I can't leave him in my hot car during my shift at the grocery. I promise I'd take him home with me every night."

As her frown intensified, his heart sank, so he blundered on. "He wouldn't bother anybody in your garage and it's only to protect him for a week while I figure out a better solution."

She shook her head. "No, I'm sorry."

As his frustration rose, he tried hard to keep this bottled anger from exploding out of control. Again, he focused on how much this woman resembled his hated stepmother. He tried one last time, his exasperation growing. "But nobody uses your garage. You wouldn't even know Toby's there. I helped you. Can't you, like, *please* help me keep my cat safe?"

"You don't understand. I can't help you. You seem like a nice, polite boy and I'd like to, but I can't."

Arnie's desperation escalated toward full blown anger— anger over his father's indifference, Magda's cruelty, Toby's safety and now this woman's selfishness. As rage took over, he barely heard the woman say, "Here, come to the back door with me so I can pay you for helping me."

Losing the fight for control, he followed her up the back-porch steps. She raised a warning hand. "Wait here. I'll be right back with my purse."

As she disappeared into the house, billowing anger overwhelmed him. Instead of waiting outside, he stepped inside the back door and did something else.

CHAPTER 5

Becca tapped her fingers impatiently on the table. "Mom, thanks for agreeing to confront Gerry's parents about my drone problem."

"Well, 'confront' is too strong, but I will tell them the drone can't invade your privacy. Surely, they'll agree."

"If they don't, there's Plan B."

"Plan B?"

"Involve the police. Don't cringe, Mom. Gerry and his parents need to know I mean business. The police are my last resort. I'd explain to the cops I tried solving this myself the nice way. They'll understand they're the next step."

Jennifer sighed. "I hear you, honey. But let's hope Gerry's parents solve this first."

Becca gave a crafty smile. "How about a fair trade? I'll check on Grammy while you talk to Gerry's parents. Deal?"

"Deal."

"Bet you can't get out the door for your visit before I can," Becca teased, her hand on the front doorknob.

Jennifer sighed with resignation. "Bet you're right," and followed her outside to walk down the street.

As she strolled along the sidewalk, Jennifer drew in the appealing, balmy June morning. Blue sky arced overhead, ribbons of colorful flowers curled amid pleasing landscapes in the yards she passed, and lush manicured lawns stretched toward houses from the sidewalks. The pride this community's residents took in their property showed, same as thirty years ago when she and Jason had bought their house here.

Sun warmed Jennifer's skin as a stray breeze lifted wisps of her hair. Perfect day for a stroll. Maybe she'd coax her mother to walk this afternoon. Exercise made sense, whatever one's age.

She still marveled at "Grammy's" decision to exchange aging-in-place risks at her Naples, Florida, home for nearness to Jennifer's family here in McLean. A brave decision for her mother, and a huge relief for Jennifer, who found protecting her mother's fragile elder years difficult from that distance.

As she passed Ogleby's house, Jennifer noticed no outdoor hint of this woman's alleged hoarding. But maybe, like many neighbors along the street, she hired a landscape service to regularly trim and mow the outside for a monthly charge.

At the curbside mailbox marked "Wilberforce," she turned into their walkway and rang the bell. The door opened. "Hi, Connie. It's Jennifer from down the street."

"Jennifer. Good to see you again. Won't you come in?"

"Yes, thank you."

Connie led them to her kitchen. "Do you mind visiting with me in here while I bake cookies? Would you like one from this batch just out of the oven?"

"Can't resist the pleasant aroma of baking. Thanks." Jennifer picked one and took a bite. "Mmm, delicious. Looks like you're making a lot of them today."

"We're celebrating Gerry's school awards with a little family party tonight."

"Oh?"

"Yes, two awards. A plaque for Junior Class President and a medal for outstanding junior scholar. He had the highest grade-point average of anyone in his class. We're so proud of him."

"I can see why."

"These days some kids his age get involved with drugs or bad friends. We're lucky so far."

Jennifer cleared her throat, wondering how to pursue Becca's mission. "What about his drone?"

"That, too. He's president of the high school's drone club, with about 25 members. Drones are the new rage and he's into them. He thinks they do a lot of good and have a big future."

Considering her task here, this caught Jennifer off-guard. "A lot of good?"

"Yeah. Gerry says real-estate companies use them for property overviews and land surveys. He says they're also used for roof inspections, storm damage surveys, construction photos and counting crowds. And, of course, great for group photos like family reunions, weddings, team pictures, and..."

But her words cut short as Gerry and another boy his age rushed into the house. Gerry shouted, "*Mom,* quick, call the cops. We...we think she's, like, *dead.*"

CHAPTER 6

C onfusion clouded Connie's face. "*Dead*? What...?"

Excited, Gerry spoke fast. "Mrs. Ogelby. Next door. The Conner girls asked us to, like, drone her upstairs windows to see if she packed those rooms with stuff same as her downstairs. I just did and, Mom, the drone saw her, lying on the floor." He shivered. "Nobody could look that way unless they're, like, dead."

"Quick, show me the pictures."

He activated the drone screen and they gazed at views inside the second-story window of the house next door. They saw stacks of junk piled high on and between furniture. The camera zoomed in on the window of another junk-filled room where a woman lay on the floor amid the hoarded clutter, her eyes open, arms out-flung and mouth agape. A trickle of blood oozed across her forehead.

Connie and Jennifer gasped at this arresting scene. Gerry winced and his companion paled.

Gerry pointed. "See that ladder tilted over her? Bet she fell off it trying to, like, pile more stuff on top of what's already there."

Connie reached for the phone. "You're right, Gerry. Something's very wrong. I'm dialing 911."

Finishing the call, she turned to Gerry. "A patrolman in the area should be here in a few minutes." She looked toward her neighbor's house. "That poor soul."

"Okay, Mom," he said, eagerly. "Arnie and I will, like, wait for him on our porch."

No sooner did they reach the porch than a police cruiser's flashing blue-and-white lights whipped around the corner of their street and stopped at their mailbox.

Connie and Jennifer hesitated on the front porch as Gerry and Arnie bounded out to meet the patrolman. The women couldn't hear the trio's conversation, but pantomime told the story as the cop and youths exchanged animated words. The patrolman studied the drone's pictures, and Gerry pointed to their neighbor's upper window. The three hurried to Mrs. Ogleby's front door and exclaimed at finding it unlocked. Gerry and Arnie heard the cop speak into his lapel microphone. They heard the words "backup" and "supervisor." A second police cruiser came minutes later. The two patrolmen shook their heads when the boys followed them inside. The cops entered the house alone while the boys fidgeted on the porch.

Then a Fire and Rescue van arrived. Two medics hustled inside the Ogleby house. Fifteen minutes later they emerged, climbed into their vehicles and the F&R drove away.

The patrolman walked Gerry and Arnie back to their own porch. They exchanged names. "Mrs. Wilberforce, these are two alert boys. I need to write up a report on this. May we go inside?"

"Is she....?" Connie asked.

The patrolman took out a notebook. "Yeah. Medics say looks like she died a couple hours ago."

"You're leaving her there?"

The cop studied her, deciding how much to say. Until they ruled out suspicious death, the woman's body was part of police evidence. "The homicide detectives will be right along. They want the situation as undisturbed as possible to determine what happened. Meantime, let's get this report underway. I'll talk to some other neighbors when I finish here."

Connie's eyebrows rose. "Homicide? But..."

"Just routine procedure, ma'am, to evaluate any unattended death."

Jennifer rose, clearing her throat. "Connie, you're obviously busy now, so I'll be on my way. Maybe we can talk again soon?" She turned to Gerry. "Well, young man, this gives new meaning to Neighborhood Watch." She nodded to his friend, who hadn't been introduced. "And you are...?"

He smiled and extended his hand. "Arnie Anderson, ma'am."

Jen walked home slowly, preoccupied by this tragic neighborhood event. As she approached her own house, an uncomfortable realization caused her to stop short on the sidewalk. She had not even addressed, never mind solved, her daughter's drone dilemma.

CHAPTER 7

Jennifer unlocked her front door. "Anybody home?" she called from the foyer. Silence.

She walked into the dining room and called again.

"Out here in the garage," came a muffled male voice.

She found Jason in his garage workshop, wearing plastic goggles and bent over a piece of wood. A red bandana, secured behind his head, covered his nose and mouth. He turned, pointing his whirring drill toward her.

Despite the tragedy of Mrs. Ogleby's death, Jason's incongruous outfit forced Jennifer to laugh. Looking confused, he turned off the drill.

"Is this a holdup?" she giggled.

The impatient bandana-muffled voice said, "I'm working here, Jen. What is it?"

She pointed. "Your new accessories?"

"I couldn't find a dust mask and I didn't want to breathe wood particles, so I improvised."

"Clever, Jay. You just surprised me." She produced a mirror from her purse, trying unsuccessfully to wipe the smile from her face. "Here, take a look."

He positioned the mirror and gave a grudging nod. "Okay, I see what you mean."

Her demeanor sobered. "Jay, I have something to tell you."

"I'm almost finished. Can it wait?"

"I don't think so."

He sighed and faced her but didn't remove his disguise. "Okay, go ahead."

She described visiting the Wilberforce house to discuss Becca's drone concern, and what happened there.

"Sorry to hear this, Jen. I remember back when Mrs. Ogleby used to walk around the neighborhood like a normal person. She really hoarded stuff?" Looking at his wife's troubled expression, he changed approach. "How are *you* handling this?"

"Such a shame. If only alert neighbors might have prevented this. *And* I didn't solve Becca's problem...."

"Did I hear my name mentioned?" Becca asked, walking into the workshop. "Grammy's here, too. It's lunch time so why don't we all move to the kitchen while Mom does some culinary magic?"

"Good idea." Jennifer smiled and led the female trio toward the kitchen.

Reluctantly, Jason removed his bandana, unplugged his drill and followed.

Jennifer retold the Ogleby story while heating soup and tossing a salad.

"We had a hoarder on my street in Florida," Grammy volunteered. "She'd lived there about thirty years. Hoarding's a psychological problem, you know."

Jason looked up. "Psychological?"

Setting the table, Becca paused. "Yeah, we learned about this in psych class. Hoarding's linked to anxiety, depression, loneliness and even OCD and ADD."

"And even *what*?" Grammy looked puzzled.

"Obsessive-Compulsive Disorder and Attention Deficit Disorder," Becca explained. "Hoarders feel embarrassed about the disgusting mess they create, so they keep people away. This isolates them more, making the hoarding syndrome spiral forward."

Grammy folded her hands in her lap. "I knew Barbara and her family. Her kids grew up in our neighborhood before moving away for college and careers. At first, they visited her, but then Barbara offered to visit them instead. This fit well since her kids had jobs and families, making their travel harder. So they didn't realize she hoarded at all, never mind how much, until her daughter made a surprise visit. What she saw stunned her."

Jennifer carried bowls of soup to the table and joined them. "What did her kids do when they discovered the truth?"

"They came by to ask if I'd noticed a change in her personality, and I had. I'd known Barbara for years; not close pals but always friendly. Soon after we first met, she told me how living through the Great Depression affected her parents. They taught her early not to waste anything she might ever need—string, rubber bands, newspapers, soap slivers, cardboard boxes, paper bags, tinfoil, leftover food, and the list goes on."

Becca nodded. "At first, she probably felt good playing into those old parental tapes."

Grammy continued. "Maybe Barbara controlled her hoarding until the children left. Or maybe her husband's death tipped her over the edge. But she changed from outgoing to hermit. When I went by on walks, she might wave to me from her window but didn't invite me in the way she used to. None of us knew she hoarded or how much until that daughter's unannounced visit. They got her professional help, but maybe too late, because soon after, they moved her to a facility, and within a few months they sold the house. I wonder what happened to her."

Jennifer folded her napkin. "Better than what happened to Mrs. Ogleby, I hope. Becca, what's wrong, honey? You look unhappy."

Becca sighed and hung her head. "Now my situation's worse than ever."

"Well, that's a segue." Jennifer touched her arm. "What do you mean?"

"Discovering the dead neighbor makes Gerry a drone-hero now. It's his green light to snoop windows more than ever."

CHAPTER 8

The simultaneous ringing doorbell and unlocking key at the front door signaled a family member arriving. "Hello. Anybody here?" called a voice from the foyer.

"Hannah!" Jennifer recognized her daughter's voice. "Out here on the sun porch."

A door slam, murmuring voices and shuffling feet brought Hannah's family into view. "Just dropping by to say hello," she said.

Jennifer relieved Hannah of her six-month-old son. "How's my grandbaby today?" she cooed to this baby, as she once had to her own five. Tickling his tummy evoked a beaming baby smile.

Jason bear-hugged son-in-law Adam and asked, "Zealand sleeping through the night yet?"

"Hah! We wish. Think we'll live long enough to experience that?"

Jason chuckled, remembering that parenting stage. "Hang in; you will. What's the family's police detective up to these days? Any excitement in Fairfax County?"

Adam sighed. "The usual craziness: crimes against people, property, and society. The weird things folks do defy belief. But right now, I'm on temporary loan to Homicide."

Jason looked puzzled. "What does that mean, exactly?"

"Fairfax County has Crime Scene detectives and homicide detectives. We're separate but work as a team. I was crime scene, but Homicide's short on people right now, and asked for me. It's great experience for me as a cop, except for the downer of dealing with homicides every day. Maybe you read about the body found at Scotts Run Park? We don't know how to read that one yet."

"Because..."

"Because the autopsy's inconclusive about foul play. Then we also had two murder-suicides, one where the guy took out two little kids along with the wife. And a carbon monoxide poisoning. Homicide investigates all unattended Fairfax County deaths."

"Doesn't every house have a carbon monoxide detector these days?"

"Hard to believe, but they're elective—building code doesn't even require them in new houses. Prevention campaigns help some, but not everybody salutes." Adam held out his arms, taking baby Zealand from Jennifer as she and Hannah joined them from the kitchen.

Grammy waved to the baby, rewarded with another big smile. "Are your cases the naturally occurring kind of monoxide?"

"Maybe you're thinking of radon gas. Carbon monoxide doesn't happen naturally—only as the product of combusting fuels like gasoline, wood, propane, charcoal and so on. Those new push-button-ignition cars can run silently enough for a driver to think the motor's off when it isn't. Or remote-starter cars that cool your car in summer or warm it in winter before you get in. But if that car's in your closed garage and you forget turning it on..."

Jennifer nodded. "At least with the old car ignition key-locks, you knew the motor stopped when the key came out."

Hannah nodded. "When you're juggling a crying baby, a diaper bag and grocery sacks, you might easily leave the motor on. After what Adam's told me, I make sure to turn off my car."

"Yeah," Adam continued. "Imagine: a driver parks in his garage, leaves the ignition on, closes the garage door like always and goes into his house. Meantime, the quiet-running motor churns out this colorless, odorless, tasteless lethal gas. If it's night and the gas seeps upward into bedrooms above the garage, those people fall asleep and never wake up. Then homicide investigators try to figure out whether those deaths are accidental, suicide or murder."

Jason looked puzzled. "If a person's carbon monoxided while deliberately sitting in his own car in his own garage, wouldn't that be suicide?"

Adam shifted in his chair. "Depends on circumstances. It might look that way, but it's also a relatively easy way to take someone out. No guns, knives, ropes or traceable poisons."

Jennifer looked thoughtful. "Then wouldn't that killer come from the victim's family? Who else has access to his garage?"

"Family, yeah...but maybe also a friend, boyfriend or girlfriend, neighbor, a clever enemy. The method is carbon monoxide asphyxiation, when gas builds up in the victim's bloodstream, replacing oxygen in red blood cells. As for the motive and opportunity, we look for suspicious involvement of others in the deceased's life."

Grammy stood. "When it comes to my great-grandbaby, I've had method and motive, and today I have opportunity. Adam, Hannah, may I hold little Zealand?"

Some six-month-olds cringe or cry at unfamiliar faces, but good-natured "Z" smiled at his great-grandmother as if he'd known her forever. When Adam passed him to Grammy, the baby stared at the loving eyes in her wrinkled face and melted, content, into her comfortable arms. Cuddling him close she whispered in his ear, "You're not just a baby—you're the beginning of a person."

CHAPTER 9

P umped by their pivotal role in discovering Mrs. Ogelby's death next door, Gerry turned to Arnie. "It's, like, awful that she died, but if we hadn't found her, she'd still be lying there in her house, maybe weeks... maybe *months*. So we made the difference."

Uneasy, Arnie nodded.

"This, like, proves the awesome good our drones can do." He grinned. "And we're the guys flying 'em. Great, huh?"

Arnie stared at the ground. "Yeah...yeah, it is. You're right. I'm sorry...I just have stuff on my mind."

"Like?"

"Just stuff..."

"Maybe I can help. You know it's safe with me. Sometimes just talking...."

"LUNCHTIME," Gerry's mother called from the house. The teens hustled inside and settled onto the kitchen island bar stools.

"BLT's and chips okay?" Connie asked.

Gerry grinned. "All-time favorites."

Arnie smiled. "Thanks, Mrs. Wilberforce."

Gerry's father, Matt, walked in. "Hello, boys. I just got home, but Mom texted me you had some drone excitement today. What happened?"

The center of his dad's attention, Gerry sat taller and talked around his sandwich. "You know Tessa and Willa—the Conner girls? They live, like, one street over that way." He pointed while taking a one-handed sandwich bite. "They've been after us for weeks to, like, learn more about Mrs. Ogelby's house after what they saw there...junk stacked to the ceiling. Their mother said hoarding sickness has cures and maybe she could help if we learned it's true."

Matt leaned forward with interest. "Go on..."

Gerry nodded toward Arnie. "First, we used a drone to look through Mrs. Ogelby's street-floor windows, even though anybody could, like, just walk up to *look* in those windows. A face at her window might freak her out, but she probably wouldn't even notice a drone. Closed curtains on most of her first-floor windows, but in the two open windows facing the back yard, we, like, saw exactly what the Conner girls did. So I phoned Tessa about the hoarded stuff, and she wanted us to find out if she hoarded upstairs, too."

"Everybody getting enough to eat?" Connie asked.

The boys nodded as they munched. Gerry swallowed. "Normally we wouldn't, like, peek in people's windows, but Tessa's, like, really cute and I..." he couldn't hide a blush, "I kind of like her." He covered his embarrassment, hurrying the conversation forward. "So...I decided to drone the upstairs for her."

His father prompted. "And..."

"Well, the house is basically square with three upstairs windows on each side, making twelve total upper windows. We started by the garage and found *her* eight windows later."

"When you saw the room with Mrs. Ogelby on the floor, what made you think she was in trouble?"

"Dad, I've never seen a dead person in real life, but lots on TV. Mrs. Ogleby didn't move. Her eyes didn't blink. Her mouth, like, hung open, and she fell in a weird position that wasn't normal. She looked...*dead.* You could see playback on my cellphone, but the drone's right here, so I'll use it." Gerry jumped up, retrieved the equipment and ran the camera playback for his dad.

Matt turned to Gerry's friend. "You thought so, too, Arnie?" Arnie nodded.

As Connie removed lunch plates, she put her hand on Arnie's shoulder. "You seem quiet today. Everything okay?"

Arnie fought the impulse to throw himself on the floor and scream his life's madness to these normal people. Instead he said, "Just stuff on my mind. Some family problems...but mostly my cat."

"Your cat?" The Wilberforce family exchanged looks. "What's with your cat?"

Too embarrassed to admit the truth, he retold the invented German shepherd story.

"Why, Arnie, that's easy. We're happy to help. We like cats. Why not leave Toby with us during the day while you work at the grocery? Why not bring his litter box and food in now before you two go off to your drone club meeting? We'll get acquainted with Toby before you take him home for the night."

Arnie couldn't believe his ears. What relief—Toby safe! And since he visited his friend Gerry almost every day this summer, if he'd written the script, it couldn't be tighter.

"You...you'd do this for me?"

Connie said, "You bet. Toby's lucky you care about him so much."

Arnie shifted his weight, coughing to hide a twitching lip. He stared at his hands, praying they wouldn't tremble.

If only somebody, anybody, cared about him the way he cared about Toby.

CHAPTER 10

As the Shannons finished their lunch, Jennifer turned to her son-in-law. "Did you hear about our neighbor Mrs. Ogleby today? Found dead in her house right down our street."

Adam shook his head. "No, but I'm off-duty today, so I wouldn't. What happened?"

Jennifer recounted the tale.

"Now that I'm on loan to Homicide, it will be easy for me to ask if her death seems suspicious. You know this teenager?"

Becca groused again, "According to Mom, Gerry's mother says he's a great student and heads a drone-hobby club. But what about the creep-factor when his drone looks in my bedroom window?"

Adam looked up. "That happened?"

Becca shrugged. "Three times this week. Really annoying."

Adam frowned. "He has no right to do that. It's illegal. You, on the other hand, *do* have the right to privacy. Not even police can use drones for surveillance without probable cause or a search warrant or surveying the primary residence of an arrested or wanted subject, or when an officer is in hot pursuit. But drones apply in dozens of other tactical support situations—detailing crime scenes and traffic accidents, helping find missing persons, surveying disaster sites like earthquakes, floods and storms, monitoring emergency or potential-emergency scenes..."

Jason's eyebrows lifted. "Like crowd-scanning for trouble on New Year's Eve at Times Square?"

Adam nodded. "Yes. Drones can even collect hazardous material samples or monitor radiation in a nuclear power disaster or a train derailment with toxic stuff in the railroad cars. They're fabulous tools."

Becca acquiesced. "Okay, okay. I get it. Drones have constructive uses. But what about my privacy?"

"Ah, that's the delicate side. Police doing surveillance or tailing suspects need probable cause, as I described before, or consent to justify use, and we're really careful because information not lawfully obtained can't be used in court to prosecute."

"So even police have no right to peek in my window with their dratted drone without a legal reason?"

"That's right."

"Gerry and his side-kick Arnie obviously don't know that."

"Want me to talk with them, or arrange for someone else to?"

Becca brightened. "*Yes!* Would you?"

"Sure, but not today, because it's best I do that in uniform. Better yet, I could arrange for a neighborhood patrolman to stop by for a little counseling. But you should also understand this kid's drone skills qualify him for prospective future recruitment by many employers, including the police force. Lots of professions are hungry for drones. Law enforcement competes with private industry to hire their know-how."

Hannah gently lifted a squirming Zealand from Grammy, who nodded her thanks. "Other professions like...?"

Adam reeled them off. "Real estate, security, disaster relief, monitoring livestock on ranches or crops on farms, insurance investigations, construction inspections, infrastructure evaluations and on and on...”

Jason gestured with his fork. “Sounds like an important new industry.”

“Absolutely. And we’re not even talking about the military uses.”

Jennifer turned to Hannah. “Change of topic. At a garage sale today, I bought a big mirror in an unusual frame that might work for your new house. You said to keep an eye out for decorator items. It’s leaning against the garage wall if you want a look.”

“Thanks, Mom.” Hannah finished lunch and left in that direction, carrying Z on her hip.

Jason turned to Adam. “How’s construction going on your new house?”

“We move in on Monday, but they’re still correcting some last-minute punch list items.”

“Let us know if we can help with your move.”

“Amusing Zealand a couple of days for us would make a huge difference. Then Hannah and I could concentrate undistracted on the move.”

“We’d love that assignment.” Jason smiled. “Jen, can we babysit a few days early next week?”

She checked the calendar on her kitchen desk. “I’m penciling it in now. Monday, Tuesday and Wednesday?”

“We’d sure appreciate it,” Adam said.

Hannah bounded into the dining room. “Mom, I love the mirror and I know just the spot for it, too. May I buy it from you?”

“Think of it as our house-warming gift to you and Adam.”

Hannah touched Adam’s arm. “It’s big. Want to measure if it fits in our car?”

“Here, I’ll take the baby,” Jennifer offered.” She pulled Zealand onto her lap as they disappeared into the garage.

Bouncing Z on her knee, Jennifer turned to her mother. "Grammy, remember we have an appointment today at three o'clock at the last senior residence on our list."

Grammy looked at her watch. "Yes, in an hour, and I'm ready. Veronika should arrive soon to go with us."

Though two years older than Grammy, Russian-born Veronika Verantsova had bonded with her when they met a month ago. Jennifer felt confident these two friends sharing relocation beat either one braving such a major change alone. Family support took a back seat to someone in the same trench. Jennifer giggled to herself. Ludicrous to compare these modern, comfortable senior facilities to trenches.

Adam and Hannah returned from the garage. "Yep, the mirror fits flat in the trunk."

"No, no." Jennifer raised a warning hand. "Always store and transport glass vertically. When it's horizontal, any invisible flaw could break the glass—especially when jiggled in a car. Remember glass repair trucks you drive past on the road. Their glass always sits vertically. And this even applies to protective glass on big photographs or watercolor paintings. Do you think you can reload your new mirror the safe way?"

Adam spun in his tracks, tape measure still in hand. "I'll find out." Hannah followed him. They returned triumphantly a few minutes later. "Loaded vertically." At the chorus of clapping hands, he bowed.

"Mom," Hannah marveled. "How do you know this stuff about glass?"

"Garage sales. Someone taught me, I taught you and now you can pass the knowledge forward."

CHAPTER 11

Veronika Verantsova arrived, greeted everyone warmly and caressed Zealand's plump cheek.

"How intelligent, this little one. I know because he didn't make a face at me." The others chuckled while she patted Z's chubby arm. He cooed back at her. "And Frances, my friend. There you are..." She hugged Grammy.

Jennifer indicated a chair. "Please join us, Veronika. I think you know everyone here from earlier family get-togethers."

Veronika nodded and sat down. "What brings you all together today?"

Hannah smiled. "We were on our way to one of McLean's fancy groceries and dropped by to see our parents on a beautiful June Saturday."

Veronika turned to Hannah. "Multi-tasking, eh? And hello to you, Adam—our family's brave policeman."

Adam stood respectfully and took her hand. "You're looking well, Veronika."

"I am, thank you." Veronika turned to Jennifer. "And how many garage sales did you visit today?"

"Only four, but many good finds anyway."

Grammy marveled, "If you add new things every weekend, why doesn't *your* house look like a hoarder's?"

Jason laughed a bit too enthusiastically. "Why do you think I call her half of the garage 'the warehouse'?"

Ignoring his remark, Jennifer explained. "I have a system. When I find something requested by friend or family, I deliver it within a week. If they don't want it after all, I consign it at a local thrift shop or save it for my own next garage sale. If I buy something for the house, I use it right away. If it replaces an item already there, I field that replaced item within a week."

"What did you bring home today?" Veronika asked.

"Let's see. A brand-new three-dimensional kite as an under-the-pillow gift for the next Grand who spends the night here. And the tall Oriental blue-and-white ginger jar over there, on the buffet. It blends with our dining-room color scheme and doubles as a flower vase for tall stems. Also, a big mirror Hannah wants. But the best find of the day is this." She held it aloft.

All eyes turned toward the aqua-color metal artifact about seven inches high. Three long, slender legs supported a bowl opening into a pointed flute on one side and a troughed flute on the other. The handle's side position indicated a righthanded drinker might lift the troughed side to his lips. Two short towers extended just above the flutes and mysterious etched symbols circled the bowl's exterior.

Hannah's nose wrinkled. "I get why you liked the ginger-jar vase, Mom, but this seems an odd choice."

Jennifer passed it around. "Can anybody guess what it is?"

"Made to hold something—maybe liquid or food, but why the long, thin legs? Not very practical," Adam mused.

Hannah hefted it. "Metal, but what kind and why?"

Veronika looked smug. "I know because I have one like it." She looked expectantly from face to face. "Can't guess? No, then may I tell them, Jennifer?" At her nod, Veronika announced.

"Jennifer found a Chinese Shang Dynasty ancient bronze ritual wine goblet."

"A *what*?" Jason sat forward. Veronika repeated.

"Isn't bronze a brownish brassy color? What's with the blue-green finish?" Adam asked.

Jason leaned forward. "I know that answer from engineering. Bronze basically mixes copper and tin. The Statue of Liberty is copper clad and originally looked copper color before turning blue green. Why? Because oxygen and air pollution react chemically with pure copper, just as they do with copper in bronze or brass. Nearness to saltwater or salt spray speeds that process."

Jennifer whisked out her cell phone, tapping the screen. "You're right, Jason. The Shang Dynasty reigned from 1700 to 1100 BCE." She did the math. "This one's surely a reproduction, so the manufacturer made it look old. But if it were an original, that patina would have oxidized for 3,500 years. This says these goblets were used for sacrificial rituals by the ruling elite, though details of those rituals remain unknown."

His detective experience alerted, Adam raised an eyebrow. "Secret rituals? Bet that spells trouble."

Veronika studied the goblet. "Yes, probably sinister rituals since they lived in a superstitious age when the ruling elite shamelessly exploited common people." She turned to Jennifer. "How do you explain your interest in Chinoiseries?"

"That's easy." She nodded toward Grammy. "Mom loved Oriental décor, so I grew up surrounded by it. I guess it took, because now I'm drawn to Asian pieces for my own home."

Grammy's eyes twinkled. "Perhaps in a previous life I lived in the ancient Orient. But during *this* life, your Dad and I toured several Far Eastern countries, and I studied Chinese art long ago in college. I just feel comfortable with things from that part of the world." She admired the teal wine goblet. "Some call this patina finish 'verdigris.'"

Veronika reached for the wine goblet. "Mine's the same or a close cousin. I don't know an original from a reproduction. At a garage sale, that doesn't matter, but if you pay top dollar you must trust your antique dealer for authenticity. And this brings up a topic about which I'd appreciate your advice, please."

Everyone looked toward Veronika. "Assuming Frances and I find our senior residence, then I'll move soon. My father gathered the furniture and art in my home today, most from Russia or Europe. When he died, I inherited the property, as-is. The place felt familiar and comfortable to me, so I didn't redecorate the upper floors. Those furnishings are even older than I am, which is saying a lot since I'm 89. Of course, I'll take some favorites to my new apartment, but downsizing means disposing of most. Who can I trust to sell them for me at a fair price?"

Jason looked thoughtful. "Is the larger question what you'll do with your equestrian farm and how that future affects your estate's house and contents?"

Veronika smiled. "Smart you are. Either a wealthy person wanting an estate will live in my house and enjoy the grounds much as they are now, or a developer will subdivide the property, perhaps converting my home into that community's clubhouse."

Adam shifted in his chair. "Have you consulted real-estate agents and developers?"

Veronika laughed. "They approached me for years when I didn't want to sell. Now I'm finally tired of my lonely life out there. I want my final years to include pleasant experiences with family," she nodded toward the Shannons, "and with dear friends." She touched Frances' shoulder.

"Have you invited appraisals from antique dealers in the D.C. metropolitan area?" Jason asked.

"Or maybe New York City's Sotheby's," Grammy suggested. "They're international and employ experts."

Veronika nodded. "You're both right. But auction success depends on motivated high bidders attending that day. Otherwise, valuable items may sell for too little."

Hannah asked, "Have antique dealers looked at your furnishings yet?"

"Yes." Veronika frowned. "A few locals, to get a feel for values. Most acted professional and shared their observations. Several offered to buy certain pieces on the spot. Only one, I didn't like at all—a Robert Radner. He was...an ill-mannered know-it-all." She gazed into space across the room. "You know how I sometimes see invisible things about situations...or people? As I did when Jen was in trouble with those terrorists? Well, this Radner's aura looked...*dark*." She gave an involuntary shiver.

Jennifer had witnessed Veronika's intuitive ability about people, never mind her occasional unbidden psychic vision. At least one such insight had saved Jennifer's life. She paid attention to this woman's extra-sensory impressions.

CHAPTER 12

S uddenly reflective, Jennifer let her attention drift. Looking around the room at familiar faces, she felt conscious of her blessings. Soon, at the July 4th family gathering, her three other children and their families would add more dynamics to this already lively group. An only child herself, Jennifer loved the excitement, camaraderie and fun of these big family events. Now, in their 60s, she and Jason "glued" them all together, but she hoped connections forged now would strengthen her family's closeness later after she and Jay passed on. Her precious loved ones. Nothing felt more important.

Tucking her hand into her slacks pocket, she touched something. She fumbled out a business card. Curious, she read it for the first time. "Radner Antiquities, Robert Radner, Owner." Vienna, VA address. She frowned. Hadn't Veronika just described this same man's dark aura, underscoring her own distaste for his rude manners? Memory from this morning's garage sale scrolled across her mind to his livid parting words: "You'll regret this."

The group's banter jerked her attention back to the present as she heard Veronika say, "I may sell some individual pieces to a few dealers who came last week. But their for-profit business means that their retail price at least doubles what they pay me, so they offer me as little as possible...more a wholesale price than what the items are worth."

Adam frowned. "Do you have security on your estate, Veronika? A houseful of valuable antiques on private property tempts certain criminals, especially now that your situation's known to dealers."

"Thanks for asking, Adam. I have a small staff: a cook, a driver/handyman and a nice live-in couple. She's housekeeper and he tends the grounds. No stable crew since I sold the horses. My live-in staff act as my daytime security force, although they aren't equipped to physically repel anyone. They'd call the police for intruders."

"And nighttime?"

"I hire a man to patrol at night from 11 p.m. to 7 a.m. He's from a security service recommended by several neighbors: Northern Virginia Sentinel Security Guards. Do you know it?"

"I've heard the name," Adam recalled.

"And my estate has an electrically operated gate-entry with a phone box to screen anyone arriving. That's also some protection."

Adam gave a thin smile. "Yes, but only for people who choose to use the gate. Is your property otherwise fenced?"

She considered. "A perimeter fence lines the property border, but it's only about four feet high."

"An easy to scale decorative fence, not a barrier fence?"

Veronika nodded, uncomfortable. "I'm afraid so. But suppose you're right. We're not dealing with Ft. Knox, here. Just a country home on a few acres."

"Quite a few acres." Grammy chuckled, trying to turn the conversation in a light-hearted direction.

Uneasy about her vulnerable security, instead of pursuing solutions, Veronika changed the subject. "Jennifer, you have a couple of eager senior ladies here, ready to find the perfect place for gracious aging. What residence-visiting adventure have you designed this afternoon?"

But before Jennifer responded, a chorus of voices intervened.

"We'll leave now, Mom...Dad...Veronika...Grammy." Hannah and Adam gave goodbye hugs before carting Zealand and his equipment out the front door.

"Me, too," said Becca, heading toward the stairs. "Happy home-hunting."

Jason stood. "And I'll move on to my workshop. Hope your quest goes well, ladies."

*****

Elsewhere in McLean at that moment, a dejected teen sat in his car, bolting a fast-food lunch before hurrying back to finish his shift at the grocery. He stared out the car window and, as the cat stretched in his lap to regain attention, Arnie confided his thoughts. "Why couldn't I be born into Gerry's family? Gerry's dad's interested in drones cause they're, like, Gerry's thing. And he spends a lot of time with Gerry and even his friends, like *me*. Heck, he takes me along on some of their father/son stuff—getting pizza or playing ball or shooting at the range. You should see me with those guns."

Arnie bit into his Big Mac burger and wolfed a few french-fries. When Toby's paw reached toward the sandwich, the boy blocked it. "Hey, I already fed you. Relax." He sipped his soda. "Since Gerry's my best friend, I can't let him find out what I did with my drone. We know not to spy in people's windows, but I just couldn't help it. That Becca, you know, she walks the neighborhood every day in those, like, tight workout clothes. She's...she's beautiful."

He downed the remaining burger in quick bites. "And she remembers my name whenever she passes Gerry's house and we're outside. When she asked us what grade we're in, she said she's just out of college...so that makes her, what... 21? That's only four years older than 17. Okay, it's a big difference now, but Magda's twenty years younger than Dad, so four years' difference means nothing, later."

Toby purred, eyes closed, as Arnie polished off the french-fries. "Yeah, she's a real woman and since I'm a man in the ways that count, I wanted to see more of her." He snickered at his own joke. "Get it, Toby? I wanted to see *more* of her." Practical again, he continued, "Gerry told me where she lives—the house down the street with an iron fence—so, it was easy to fly my drone past all the upstairs windows to find her room. Most people don't even notice a drone hovering outside their window unless they happen to look in that direction when it moves. But she did. Crappy luck, huh? Yeah, the picture shows her shaking a fist at it before she closed her curtains. Don't worry, I deleted it all. Gerry won't know."

Arnie finished his soda, crunched the cup and stuffed it into the fast food bag with the other trash. "I didn't catch her changing clothes the first or second time, so I tried again. Couldn't stop myself, even though it was tough with Gerry around. And especially after she, like, called us on it on one of her walks."

He sighed. "It's way too dangerous now. If Gerry knew it was *me* watching her, he'd freak, and he's, like, my only friend now, except for you, Toby. Besides, that cop says it's *illegal* to look in windows." A longing smile lit his face. "But it sure rocked while it lasted...."

CHAPTER 13

As they sat in the dining room, Jennifer opened her file folder and passed pages to Grammy and Veronika. She pointed to page one on her copy.

"Here's a little summary of our search. Last week you visited these two rental senior residences. Rentals offer cheaper entry fees and short-term contracts, making it easy for seniors to change their minds and move elsewhere. But their biggest apartments were much smaller than you want."

Veronika turned to Grammy. "Remember, they had no on-site health care facility, but you could hire caregivers to help in your own apartment."

Jennifer continued. "Page two describes how CCRCs offer contracts for services they offer and for various levels of care for your lifetime."

Grammy raised a hand. "CCRC?"

"Continuing Care Retirement Community." Jennifer checked her notes. "These are life-plan communities. CCRCs offer three levels of care: independent living, assisted living, and skilled nursing, which includes memory care and nursing care. But the kind of contract you choose decides which CCRC you join. Once you sign a CCRC life-plan contract, you're all set for the rest of your days."

Veronika's brow wrinkled. "Memory care?"

"...like dementia or Alzheimer's," Jennifer reminded.

Grammy read aloud from this page. "Contract 'A,' sometimes called Lifecare, is the most expensive because it includes unlimited assisted living, memory care and health services without extra fees beyond the initial buy-in and the regular monthly charges."

Veronika's finger followed her copy as she read aloud. "Contract 'B' is a modified version of 'A,' with similar services to 'A' but fewer automatic health-care services. If you need more, you pay that cost at market-rate."

Jennifer nodded. "Exactly. Now contract 'C' is fee-for-services. After the one-time enrollment charge and the continuing monthly maintenance cost, residents pay market rate for health-care service 'as needed' and their health care facility is right on campus."

Veronika looked confused, "So does each CCRC offer all three choices?"

"Unfortunately, no. The kind of contract you choose determines the kind of CCRC facility you buy into. But you gals have added something else: apartment size. Right now, only one CCRC in our area offers the big apartments you like, with sizes up to 2,000 square feet. So if size remains a priority, this narrows your local CCRC options to the one we'll see today."

Grammy brightened. "What's this place called?"

"Pebblebrook Manor, a contract 'C' senior residence in Ashburn, near Dulles Airport. They offer apartments up to 2,200 square feet and underground parking, which many senior residences don't have."

Veronika mused. "Isn't that only about a 30-minute drive from McLean, unless it's rush hour?"

"We'll find out by driving there today. Meantime, here's their brochure to study in the car. Notice the packet of apartment floorplans, some with porches or balconies. Each floorplan has an invented name, like Bentley or Cambridge so it's easy to refer to them. And we want to check their restaurants, transportation, fitness facility, entertainment, field trips, clubs and so on."

As Jennifer drove, the two women chatted in the back seat, discussing brochure features and amenities they liked.

Grammy pointed at a brochure page. "Look, hundreds of special-interest clubs to join."

Veronika added, "And entertainment bus trips to Kennedy Center, Smithsonian, local wineries and more. Also, musical groups and lecturers performing in Pebblebrook's own auditorium."

When they arrived, the gate guard provided a campus map and sales office directions.

"Beautiful landscaping," Veronika noticed as Jennifer pulled under the portico to drop her charges at the front door. By the time she parked and walked back to the sales center, an agent invited them into an office.

"Hello. Welcome to Pebblebrook Manor. I'm Alice Saunders." They introduced themselves. "How may I help you today?"

Grammy took the lead. "We're two women in our late 80s who don't want to age in place or live with family. Instead, we want a well-run senior residence with large apartments, good meals, social activities, and health care, if we need it."

Veronika nodded. "And we'd each like our own apartment to live alone, but our units close enough together to enjoy our friendship."

"Wonderful. Thanks for considering Pebblebrook Manor." Alice consulted papers on her desk. "We have exactly what you've described in our newest five-story building under construction. It has several advantages. Because it's in progress, you can choose how close you want those apartments and what floor you like for the view. You could also pick cabinet styles, tile, wall and carpet colors and consider various upgrades at this stage of construction."

Jennifer smiled. "We studied the floorplans in your online marketing. Would they be the same in this new building?" Alice nodded and Jennifer continued. "But we don't see any square footage on your plans and these ladies would like units 1,800 to 2,000 square feet."

"That's easy." Alice held up some papers. "Here's a packet of floorplans for each of you. I'll write the square footage on your copies if you'd like to step into the next room to see a short video about life here at Pebblebrook Manor. Then maybe you'd want to visit some model apartments with the floorplans you prefer?"

The three nodded as she filed them into the video-viewing room and started the film.

When Alice returned, she handed them the requested information. "Two apartment styles have the square footage you want," she explained. "But many of our apartments are so well laid out, you might find you like a smaller one after all."

Jennifer asked, "When could they move into this new building?"

"It's under construction now. We expect occupancy in 11 months."

Grammy's brow wrinkled, remembering her remaining two-month lease of the neighbor's house across the cul-de-sac from Jennifer. "That's way too long," she said. "I'm 87 and Veronika's 89. We want to move *very* soon."

Veronika nodded. "Do any apartments in your existing buildings meet our needs?"

Alice pursed her lips in doubt. They followed her back to her computer. "Let me see." Her fingers danced over the keys. "No, I'm afraid not. So sorry."

The three women in front of her desk sagged in disappointment. This was the only CCRC in the area with the apartment sizes they wanted.

Now what?

CHAPTER 14

Seeing their disappointment, Alice returned to her computer. "I could try one last thing—the *remote* chance an occupied unit became available today. "No, sorry, I...wait, something's just...yes. Here are two large apartments on the same floor. A Willow and a Wesleyan. The Wesleyan just became available this morning. It isn't cleaned up ready for viewing, but maybe we could peek in. You'll need to envision it completely refurbished for a new occupant." She handed them each a page. "Here are the floorplans. Would you like to see those apartments?"

Studying the floor sketch, the older women tried to imagine three-dimensional versions of this one-dimensional floor plan.

Jennifer encouraged them. "Both units meet your square footage desires. Want to look?"

When they nodded, Alice stood. "I'll get the keys to drive us over.

On the way, Grammy asked, "How close are these two apartments?"

"Right across the hall from each other."

The two women smiled conspiratorially, and Veronika spoke, "And on which floor?"

"Third. Do you have cars?"

Grammy answered, "No, we no longer drive."

Alice smiled. "Pebblebrook has a campus shuttle bus system for non-drivers to reach on-campus amenities like beauty shop, bank, medical center, pharmacy, library, fitness center, covered pool. And weekly bus shopping trips to groceries and malls. For meals, you can choose from three main dining rooms. We also have a café and a deli. Ah, here we are. I'll drive us into the underground garage, where it's easy to catch the elevator up to these units."

On the third floor, Alice said, "Let's look first at the Willow. This way, down the hall."

They followed Alice along the bright, attractive hallway to the unfurnished unit. "The Willow's a two-bedroom, 2½ bath with separate den and a laundry room." As they entered the apartment, she pointed out features. "Granite kitchen and bathroom countertops, new appliances and an open floorplan connecting kitchen, dining room, living room and den." Alice continued. "Here's the half-bath and your guest room with its own bathroom and tub/shower combination. Or some residents turn this room into a den or hobby room for arts or crafts. But Pebblebrook also has separate studios available elsewhere for those activities, plus a ceramic room with a kiln."

Jennifer trailed behind as wide-eyed Grammy and Veronika followed Alice. "How do you like this large master bedroom?" Alice opened double doors to reveal a spacious walk-in closet, eliciting appreciative gasps. "And this master bath has double sinks, a separate shower and a Jacuzzi bathtub." She waited while they ogled everything. "Shall we step out onto the screened porch?" They did. "What do you think?"

"Wow," Jennifer said. "Wish I could move in."

"It's beautiful," Veronika agreed.

"Ditto," voiced Grammy.

"And notice the view?" They gazed out across a pond, past woods and fields, to distant buildings. "Questions?"

After a silence, Jennifer turned to Alice. "No, but may we look at the other unit now?"

"Yes, but remember, it still has the previous tenant's lived-in look. Think past the furniture and knick-knacks because the new occupant will find it freshly painted, carpeted and new appliances." They crossed the hall. "This is the Wesleyan."

Alice and Jennifer watched the two women wander through the rooms. Grammy said, "These furnishings actually help me envision living here better than the empty one across the hall."

They stopped in front of the living room's large windows. "This view is completely different. A Pebblebrook Campus scene with street, sidewalks, grassy areas, landscaping, and more senior apartment buildings. Want to step out onto the balcony?" They did.

"Should we see any other units?" Jennifer asked.

Alice considered. "Yes, but only these two large units are currently available and close together, exactly what the ladies described would suit their needs."

When they finished and started down the hall toward the elevators, Alice said. "If you like those apartments, we can go back to my office to discuss them. I'll wait by the elevator if you'd like a private minute to talk."

"Thanks," Jennifer said, and when Alice left, she turned to the others. "What do you think?"

"I love the modern, airy apartments and the beautiful campus," Grammy said.

Veronika nodded. "Let's learn more from Alice about the amenities and costs. Then we can weigh all the facts."

They trouped to the elevator to join Alice for the business information phase. Would this seal the deal or break it?

Back in her office, Alice explained, "If you like Pebblebrook, we invite you to a seminar series to familiarize you with activities and dinners in our restaurants. When you're serious about moving in, you get on our priority wait list with a refundable $1,000 deposit. We even offer a 'Live the Life Staycation' where you stay a couple of nights to 'try on' life here. Once a prospective resident decides to move here, he reserves a specific apartment. Here's a list of our many clubs, card groups and mahjong. The average time from new lead to occupancy is four years, but some residents sign their contract the first day they visit."

Jennifer hid her concern. "Did you say priority wait list? Is it long?"

"When your name reaches the top of the wait list, we offer you units available then. If you're not ready to move or prefer to wait for a different unit, your name stays at the top so when you *are* ready, you get in quickly. Once a person decides it's time to move, he reserves a specific apartment."

Grammy frowned. "But we don't have time to wait."

Alice smiled. "Right now, our new construction creates an unusual situation. We have more units than wait-list people ready to move. If you picked the two apartments we saw today and passed the registration criteria, you could move in next week."

Alice saw three expressions of relief.

"Our two registration criteria are your ability to live independently when you arrive and your financial capability to cover the entry fee and future apartment monthly maintenance. The square footage of the apartment you choose dictates the one-time entry fee you pay. So, a 900-square foot apartment entry fee is this much," Alice turned the chart toward them, "and for the square footage you like, the fee is this much."

Jennifer whistled. "*Quite* a difference."

Alice hastened to add, "But 90 percent of this entry fee is refunded to your estate when you're no longer with us."

Jennifer eyed her wards. They obviously liked this place. She did, too. "Have you two the energy now to tour the facility, including the health care building?"

Seeing the two elders' doubtful expressions, Alice volunteered, "I could put a couple of wheelchairs in the sales van so when we get out at each destination, Jennifer and I could wheel you around there. You'd see everything without wearing out."

Grammy grinned. "Now that's what I call a clever plan."

CHAPTER 15

On the drive home from the senior residence, animated chatter filled the car. They all found Pebblebrook Manor impressive, knew they'd exhausted their area's other senior options and realized time to decide had narrowed.

Jennifer's fingers tapped the steering wheel as she drove. "Are you glad you put down your priority-list deposit?"

Veronika smiled. "Yes. Refundable if we change our minds, or our ticket in if we don't. And smart of us to put 48-hour holds on the two apartments we like—close and just the right size."

Grammy looked smug. "We passed the registration tests for finances and independent living."

Veronika added, "And once we're in, if our health changes to needing assisted living or memory care, those facilities are right on campus."

Grammy nodded. "And we signed up for the 'staycation' tomorrow."

Veronika nodded. "So far, I like the whole setup. It's a perfect confluence of events. A senior residence on a beautiful campus with two apartments the size we want, close together, with appealing upper-floor views and available in a week."

Grammy clapped her hands. "Serendipitous."

Keeping them on target, Jennifer said. "You've reserved the two apartments. How will you decide who takes which one?"

Discussion filled the back seat while Jennifer focused on the road, glancing back at them occasionally in her rearview mirror. Finally, she nudged, "With both apartments on the same floor and about the same size, isn't the main difference the view?"

Whispers behind Jennifer grew louder.

Veronika's said, "We have a plan."

Grammy agreed. "A good plan."

"Oh?" Jennifer encouraged.

Grammy explained. "Because we'll spend time in each other's apartments, we'll share one's rural nature view and the other's urban people view."

Veronika added, "Both different enough that we won't get bored with only one or the other."

Jennifer smiled. "Good. But how will you decide who gets which?"

Grammy cleared her throat. "We'll flip a coin."

"Great. Big progress. But we still have some homework to do," Jennifer reminded. "When I helped you move from Florida, I brought a copy of a Naples professional senior resident consultant's checklist. Let's review it to cover every angle in making this important decision."

Back home, Jason joined them. They updated him as Jennifer pulled out Bruce Rosenblatt's list.

"Let's see. '**Number 1** - start the process early (better five years too early than five minutes too late!)'"

Grammy laughed. "We sure missed out on that one."

Jennifer continued, "'**Number 2** - tour the health-care facility to understand its capabilities and limitations in providing quality care.'"

"We checked that out during our wheelchair tour today." Veronika folded her hands in satisfaction.

"'**Number 3** - review state inspection reports.'"

"I could do that for you," Jason offered.

"Great," Grammy said, and Veronika patted his arm.

"'**Number 4** - review policy and procedures to know rules and regulations of the places you consider before moving in, such as dress code, housekeeping, whether you can order wine with dinner, and so on. Also, who are their emergency responders and their qualifications.' Alice can answer those questions for you tomorrow." Jennifer returned to the list.

"'**Number 5** - sample activities and dining for a window on the community's lifestyle to see if it's a good fit for you.'"

Grammy and Veronika chorused, "Tomorrow." Then laughed at their duet.

"'**Number 6** - seek the advice of a senior-housing adviser professional to narrow choices and provide valuable insight about the places you consider."

Jason grabbed a piece of paper. "When we finish here, if you tell me your criteria, I'll investigate who else we might contact."

Veronika put an arm around Jennifer's shoulder. "Skip that one. This dear lady has already narrowed our search to Pebblebrook. Thank you anyway, Jason."

Jennifer read further. "'**Number 7** - get your family involved in the research process.'"

Grammy and Veronika laughed aloud until Grammy managed to say, "Thanks to you and Jay, we've covered that one."

"'**Number 8** - Don't be swayed by deals. Many places offer incentives or discounts to motivate you to buy. While it's great to get a bargain, you first need to make sure you want to live in that community.

"'**Number 9** - ask for the facility's financial statement to understand their solvency. If you're not sure what you're reading, ask your CPA or other professional to interpret it.'"

"Again, I could help you with that," Jason offered.

The two elder women accepted his offer.

"That's it." Jennifer put down the checklist.

"My driver can take us to Pebblebrook tomorrow."

Jennifer looked relieved. "Good, because I promised to babysit baby Z for three days."

Jason picked up his to-do list. "We should have answers to all these questions by your return from your overnights at Pebblebrook."

Tears of gratitude sparkled in Grammy's eyes as she turned to her daughter and son-in-law. "Have I told you both today how much I love you?"

"Me, too," Veronika chimed in.

They melted into a spontaneous group hug.

CHAPTER 16

S ummer days in Virginia often swelter, but this June afternoon's 73-degree temperature lured Becca onto the front porch. Garage-saling with her mother this morning, she'd missed her neighborhood walk. Feeling the comfortable temp and gentle breeze, she decided to peck away at her daily 10,000-step-goal by taking the neighborhood stroll she'd missed earlier.

As she approached the community's park, she noticed kids with drones on the field. Getting closer, she recognized Gerry and Arnie.

She waved to the boys, intending to walk past the field. But as she watched, the activity grabbed her interest. The group had erected twenty-plus hoops of various heights and diameters. As she watched, she realized each drone operator flew his drone as fast as he could through or around the series of obstacles, while others timed his flight. Each contestant's super-nimble fingers trilled between the drone-controller's left and right toggles.

As a megaphone reported each challenger's speed in successfully negotiating the course, the group responded with cheers or groans. A few drones hit obstacles, disqualifying them from the competition. At such impacts, some veered, crashed or fell inertly to the ground.

Becca walked over. "Hi Gerry...Arnie. Mind if I watch?"

Arnie shuffled shyly and said nothing, but Gerry said, "Sure."

Becca eyed the two boys. "Have you competed yet?"

"No, we're at the end."

Thinking this a way to better understand not only drones but also the two teens, she said, "Hey, I've never flown a drone before. Could you clue me in?"

To his surprise, Arnie stepped forward. He knew nothing about girls and little about socializing, except the basic manners his mother had taught him. But he knew drones. "Best to tell and teach you, like, at the same time. But with this competition today, we only have time to tell you."

Becca smiled. "Why not tell me today and maybe show me another time?"

Despite the bewildering closeness of this girl of his dreams, Arnie's usual shyness faded, replaced by confidence in his knowledge. "Our drone club uses quadcopters. Quad means four and," he held a drone toward her, "you can see these, like, four propellers, one on each corner. We also use line-of-sight. That means you must always be able to see your drone when it's, like, in the air. That way you know where it goes and what it does."

Listening, Becca wondered if this meant one of them was close enough to her home to watch his drone hover outside her window."

Gerry distracted her thoughts. "In our club we build them and tune them before we fly them. But anybody can, like, skip those first two steps by buying one ready-to-fly right out of the package."

"Does the package mean those cases I see over there?"

Gerry fielded this one. "No. Some purchases include a case, but if not, you can, like, buy one separately. These quadcopters are, like, sturdy and fragile at the same time. You don't want to bend or damage their little propellers. Cases make safe places to store them or, like, transport to competitions."

Becca extended a hand. "May I hold one?"

"Sure," Arnie said. "The propellers are off now so you can touch them, but when they spin, they could cut you if you, like, make a mistake and accidentally guide the drone into yourself or someone else."

"Okay, what else?"

Arnie took the quadcopter she held, handing her a controller. "The remote controller you're holding gives the drone directions. Remember those remote-control cars we had as kids? You only needed one toggle for them because they, like, stayed on the ground. Here you need two toggles because besides going left, right, forward and back the way the car did, they also go up and down."

Becca considered this. "Okay, say I buy a drone. How long would it take to learn to fly it?"

Arnie said, "First you'd practice take offs and soft landings. That's to develop smooth control over the fundamentals. Might take a week if you work at it, like, a few hours every day."

Gerry pointed to the correct toggle. "Then you'd practice hovering. It's not as easy as it looks and learning to do it could, like, take another week."

Becca looked surprised. "So...this isn't something you learn in an afternoon?"

Arnie and Gerry laughed. Gerry said, "Well, you wouldn't be very good at it that fast, and what we've talked about is just the beginning."

"Okay, tell me more."

Arnie picked up on this. "Next you'd practice maneuvering."

"Maneuvering?"

Arnie gestured with the controller. "Yeah, like, first you'd get the quad in the air, which, after the first week's practice, you'd know how to do. Then you'd practice using this toggle to direct it forward, backward, right and left."

"I'll bet that takes another week."

The boys laughed again, nodding.

"And that's it?"

The boys exchanged patient looks. Gerry shook his head. "Then you'd practice 360-degree circles and, like, how to yaw." At Becca's puzzled look he added, "Yaw is when you tilt it like this." He tipped his hand at a 45-degree angle.

Arnie volunteered, "After you've mastered that, you'd practice flying your quad in figure eights, and then, like, in a circle with the nose facing forward."

Becca shrugged. "For another week, I bet."

Gerry nodded. "And then you'd learn to fly it in a circle, reversing that direction, with the nose toward you."

Becca shaded her eyes, looking toward the club members. "So, if I have this right, by the time you compete like they are, you've been at this a good month or longer."

Both boys stood a little taller, grinning with pride in their skill.

"Anything else?"

Gerry held up his quad. "Yeah. The FAA calls anything designed for sustained flight an aircraft, so these drones are, like, aircraft, same as planes or helicopters."

Arnie gestured. "You 'fly' a plane but you 'operate' a drone. One drone advantage is it doesn't need a landing field like a chopper or light plane."

Gerry shrugged, "One drone disadvantage is when a plane motor fails, it becomes a glider, but when a drone motor fails, it becomes a rock."

"Well, thanks, Gerry...Arnie. I learned a lot today from you two." She started off on her walk but turned for one more question. "What do you do if you lose control of your drone and it's coming straight at you to cut you up?"

Gerry smiled. "To stop the propellers, you kill the juice. Then the drone falls straight to the ground like a dead bird."

Arnie added, "When that kind of danger happens, sometimes you barely have time to, like, think what to do, or, like, do it fast enough to stop the disaster. So we all memorize the solution until it's, like, part of us."

Becca arched an inquisitive eyebrow. "The solution?"

Arnie supplied, "When in doubt, throttle out.'"

CHAPTER 17

TUESDAY

Three mornings later, Jennifer put Zealand in his playpen to answer the ringing phone.

"Oh, hi, Mom."

"Jen, our Pebblebrook visit confirmed our decision. Remember they called our two-overnight visit 'Living the Life'—and did we ever. We tried all their restaurants, peeked in on various clubs and activities and even went to a jazz performance in their auditorium. And we met a lot of other residents. Thanks to Jason's research, we know the place is financially sound and well-managed. So...hold onto your hat. We signed, were accepted and paid our entrance fees."

"Mom, what terrific news. Congratulations." She hoped her relief wasn't audible over the phone. "We're all thrilled for you."

"And get this. They send someone to show me how my furniture fits into the new apartment's floorplan and someone else to help mastermind details of my move. They even help field things I haven't room to keep. Easier for me because you helped me downsize before I left Florida, but Veronika faces a large house full of valuable stuff. Fortunately, their staffer will help her, too."

"I'm so glad you're both pleased. Jay and I want you happy and safe. And congratulations, Mom. You made this *big* decision easily. Some seniors go kicking and screaming to senior residences, yet you and Veronika didn't hesitate about this huge step. Give yourselves big credit."

"Kind words. Thank you, dear. Guess what, Veronika wants to give a farewell party at her estate next Saturday for our whole family, even the grands. Short notice, but we move in less than two weeks, and she wants us to visit her home before she leaves it. This party is her thanks to our family for adopting her unofficially. She hopes everyone can come. I'll help her by phoning invitations once she picks the time of day."

"Let me know if I can help with that or any other way."

"Are you still babysitting Zealand?"

"Yes, but this is the second day. Hannah picks him up tomorrow."

"Was it as easy to take care of him as your own babies?"

Jennifer laughed. "Same routines as then, but I admit to less energy now. Sometimes I wonder how I lived to tell about raising my five."

"And it isn't over yet, dear. You'll feel the mothering responsibility right to the end."

"Your end or their end?"

"Whichever comes first. And speaking of 'the end,' there *is* one problem with Pebblebrook."

Jennifer winced. Just when the decision appeared settled. Was this a deal breaker?

"Lately I've noticed people my age seem much older than I am."

Jennifer laughed and Grammy joined in.

"Love you, Jen."

"You, too, Mom."

As Jennifer replaced the receiver, Becca wandered into the kitchen, groping for coffee. Brushing aside the proffered *Washington Post*, she mumbled. "Remember? My generation reads news online."

"While Zealand's in a happy mood, want to join me a few minutes?"

Her eyes still slits as she filled her coffee cup, Becca nodded.

Once her daughter settled in at the table, Jennifer asked. "Out with Nathan last night?" At Becca's mute nod, she added, "How is he?"

She took a deep coffee swig and sighed. "He's fine but getting serious, and I'm not ready to settle down with one person yet. He's a great guy—if I were ready—but I'm just not."

Jennifer looked thoughtful, remembering Jason told her months ago that Nathan asked permission to marry Becca, but his consent meant nothing without Becca's. "Yes, he's appealing, and from a big family, so ours doesn't scare him."

"If we're supposed to end up together, couldn't it still happen a few years from now?" Becca looked up, curious about her mother's reaction. But at Jennifer's non-committal expression, she added, "If he's still around then..."

"That's a risk, isn't it?"

"Yeah. I even thought we might live together, but basically that's the same drill as marriage, just easier to undo if it's a mistake."

"Do you think it would be a mistake?"

"No, that's the funny part. I think we'd be good together. But...just not yet."

"Someone else?"

"Well, other guy friends, sure, but they're more like brothers. No, Nathan hasn't any real competition in my life. It's just..."

"Want to talk about it?"

Becca downed the last of her coffee. "Not yet. I need to think it through first." She brightened. "But I do have some good news."

Jennifer's eyebrow lifted.

"No drone buzzed my window for three days—at least not when I was looking. Do you think the patrolman Adam said he'd send to talk with Gerry made a difference?"

"Something must have. By the way, Grammy and Veronika signed on at Pebblebrook. They move next week."

"Oh, Mom. Wonderful news. And a relief for you. Isn't that the place you liked for them?"

"Yes, but Grammy needed to make her own decision. Same as you do about Nathan."

Becca looked up. Uncomfortable, she shifted gears. "After our scary Florida experience, rescuing Grammy from that couple trying to kill her, at least Pebblebrook's a safe place."

"I certainly hope so."

"I'm heading up to get dressed. See you later, Mom."

When she left, Jennifer scanned more newspaper pages. She passed, but then hastily flipped back to a photo which riveted her attention. Her eyes widened. "No. Can't be..." Leaning closer, to verify, her jaw dropped open. "...but it *is*."

Jennifer stared at a photo of the woman at the garage sale in the Obit section!

The line beneath her photo read *Katherine Kalinsky (age 43)*.

Realizing she held her breath, Jennifer gulped air before reading further.

Died June 6 in McLean, VA. She attended McLean High School and Northern Virginia Community College. Survived by her aunt, Jean Abingdon, of McLean. Visitation at Trafalgar Funeral Home in Vienna, VA on June 13 from 1:00 - 4:00 p.m.

Jennifer ripped the page from the paper. With Vienna only a fifteen-minute drive, she could easily attend, perhaps discovering at last why the woman looked so familiar. She checked her calendar. No conflict for June 13. She penciled in the visitation details.

CHAPTER 18

FRIDAY

Three days later, Jennifer stepped onto the funeral parlor's carpeted hallway. Soft music wafted in the background. Hallway arrows pointed to viewings in different rooms. She followed the "Kalinsky" sign.

Entering the room, she paused at the guest-book podium. Only five visitor names listed. Her watch read 3:45 p.m. Light attendance for a 1:00 - 4:00 viewing? She wrote her name in the guest book and glanced into the room. Was she about to solve the mystery?

Fifteen chairs formed a two-row crescent facing the coffin. An older woman sat alone in the front row, head bowed.

Jennifer walked to the open casket on the raised bier. A modest spray of yellow roses lay on the closed bottom half of the coffin. Thanks to mortician skill, the woman from the garage sale appeared comfortably asleep, a peaceful expression replacing the sad one Jennifer remembered. Whoever this woman was, she wished her safe passage on her journey to the unknown.

As she turned toward the chairs, the older woman in the front row looked up, face pained with grief. She patted the seat beside her with one hand and beckoned Jennifer with the other. Given this clear invitation, Jennifer knew it would be rude not to sit next to her.

"Thank you for coming," the woman said.

"Are...are you okay?" Jennifer asked with concern.

The woman lifted a tissue to her eyes. "Not really...but we do what we must."

Jennifer patted the woman's hand.

They sat silently. Jennifer wondered how to explain her awkward reason for being there.

"Did you know Katie?"

"I felt as if I did. I...I saw her at several garage sales, thinking we were somehow acquainted. Have you ever been to one of those sales?"

"Oh, yes," the woman brightened somewhat at this new topic, "though not in recent years."

"I...she looked so familiar to me, I felt sure I knew her, although I couldn't place how or where. Seeing her picture in the newspaper was a surprise, but it was unmistakably her. Did you write the newspaper obituary?"

"Yes...there was no one else." The woman sniffled into her tissue. "I want... I need to do everything I can for her now since I didn't seem to do a good job helping her in life."

"Are you related?"

"Yes, I'm Jean Abingdon, Katie's aunt. Everybody calls me Aunt Jean. You can, too. With Katie gone, now I'm the last one alive in my family."

Jennifer groped for some positive spin to lighten the conversation.

"Well, then, you're the family matriarch."

Jean turned to Jennifer in surprise. "I hadn't thought of it that way, but...yes, you're right."

Jennifer continued carefully, "Compared to you and me, Katie seems young to leave this world..."

Jean didn't answer.

This seemed the only chance for insight into Katie's mysterious familiarity. Jennifer tried not to fidget.

"She had...," Jean took a deep breath, "a *dreadful* accident."

Jennifer's hands stilled. "Accident?"

"Her car has push-button ignition and quiet motor. You can hardly hear it running and even less when it idles. Hard to know it's turned off unless you make sure the ignition light's out."

Jennifer wondered where this story headed. "Oh?"

"She came home late, parked in the garage and lowered the door, just as she had thousands of times. She'd seemed... troubled lately; I think something related to her work. She started that job with such enthusiasm—couldn't wait to go to work. But recently that changed. She talked about quitting. The police think she committed suicide...deliberately left her car motor on until enough carbon monoxide filled the garage to...."

"Oh, Aunt Jean. I'm so sorry...."

Jean dried her eyes with the hankie. "Next morning, I thought she slept late or maybe felt sick. But when I saw the made-up empty bed in her room, I walked through the house, calling her name. Soon I felt a bit light-headed myself. When I got to the garage, there she was...slumped over the wheel. I hurried to open the garage door for fresh air, but it was too late." Jean began crying hard. Jennifer put a comforting arm around the woman's heaving shoulders.

Eventually regaining composure but still dabbing at her eyes, she looked straight at Jennifer. "Thank you for coming here today. I wasn't sure I could get through this. Katie has so few friends, except for work and that man. Only a few neighbors came by today, even though I've lived in the same house for fifty years. I guess they don't know what to say."

Jennifer patted her hand. They sat quietly a few minutes. She didn't recall a man's name in the guest book when she signed, so she broke the silence, "Did you say, '...except for that man'?"

"Katie's boss. For years they had...I guess you call it an *affair*. Katie loved him and thought he loved her. She had so little love in her life, except for me. I don't know, maybe she misunderstood and blew his attention out of proportion. But I never liked him, as a person or for his sleazy involvement with Katie." She looked into Jennifer's eyes for emphasis. "He's married, you know."

Jennifer absorbed this as they sat silently. Finally, she asked, "Had she worked for him long?"

"About four years, maybe five. She answered a newspaper ad for receptionist and salesclerk at a shop in Vienna. The easy commute from McLean thrilled her—unusual in this northern Virginia area."

"That *was* a dream commute." Jennifer thought of Jason's awful commute into D.C. before he moved his engineering firm across the Potomac River to Virginia. Though Arlington was closer to home, rush hour could still stretch his McLean/Arlington drive from thirty minutes to hours.

Jean spoke again. "And she liked the job. Said she learned a lot. Once the affair began, she *loved* the job because she *loved* the man. He didn't come by today, although he knows she died, because I called to tell him why she wouldn't come to work that day. He's a sorry excuse for a human being."

Trying to console her, Jennifer sneaked a glance at her watch: 4:05 p.m.

A male voice beside them said, "Mrs. Abingdon?"

Probably the funeral director ready to close the door on the viewing, Jennifer guessed. But when they both looked up and saw him, Aunt Jean flinched, and Jennifer's lips formed an O.

CHAPTER 19

They stared into the face of the surly mustached man who had confronted Jennifer at the garage sale last weekend.

"Mrs. Abingdon," he repeated. "Sorry to...ah, learn about Katie. She was, um...a competent employee. She said you raised her."

Jean nodded. "Yes, but Katie spent more waking time at work and with you than with anyone else. Come, would you like to take a last look at her."

"I...ah," the man seemed flummoxed, "I really can't stay...er, just wanted to...ah, pay my...er, our company's respects. And don't worry, we're making do at the shop without her."

Jennifer and Jean exchanged surprised looks at this comment. Jean tried to control her dislike of this man, for Katie's sake, but his crassness pushed her feelings to the surface. "Today isn't about you or your store. Today is about Katie's *death*."

Confronted, the man blurted in defense. "Well, I assumed you'd be concerned about the store since she isn't coming in anymore."

Angry now, Jean spoke through clenched teeth, "I know about your affair with Katie. You left her grief-stricken when you ended it. You broke her heart."

This clearly shocked the man. But his confidence soon returned. "Affair?" he blustered. "Preposterous. I...I don't know where you got *that* idea. Why, I'm a married man. My wife's my business partner. She...she's regularly in the shop." As if this defense were insufficient, he added pompously, "This invention sounds like another manifestation of Katie's disturbed imagination."

"You shameless reprobate!" Jean shouted. "You used this sweet girl with no regard for the heartache you caused her. And now you imply she made things up." She grabbed his arm with surprising strength and dragged him toward the coffin. "Look into her face and repeat those words."

Unable to shake Jean off, the man found himself against the bier, staring awkwardly at Katie's still body and fixed, final expression. He didn't speak. They waited.

"Haven't you even the heart to say goodbye to her?" Jean shouted, "Do you recognize how you hurt another person? Aren't you even man enough to take responsibility?"

The man stared uncomfortably at Katie.

"No? Then just get out of here. Get away from my Katie. She's free of your torment at last."

Not used to being challenged, let alone ordered about, the man blanched.

Hearing raised voices, the funeral director stopped at the door. "May I help?"

"Yes," Jean hissed. "Get this monster out of my sight."

"Sir," the director's soothing voice invited the man, "visiting hours have ended. May I help you find the parking lot?"

The two men left, the director's hand guiding the man's elbow.

Jean looked close to collapse. "Thanks for being here with me," she gasped. "I had no idea this would happen."

After the garage sale, Jennifer expected never to see the unpleasant man again. She cleared her throat. "Who...who was that, Aunt Jean?"

"Robert Radner." She spat out the name. "Owner of Radner Antiquities. Imagine, denying his relationship with Katie. A two-timer *and* a coward."

Jennifer struggled to weave this information together. Katie had worked for the very man who threatened her—the same man Veronika felt wary about. But seeing Jean's distress, she put a comforting arm around the woman's shoulder. "Have you someone to stay with you when you get home today?"

Jean looked confused. "No. I knew the funeral would be a strain but didn't dream I'd feel this shaken. If he hadn't come, I might have made it through, but now..." She lurched heavily, about to fall. Jennifer steadied her just in time. She guided Jean back to their seats.

"Change is hard for me. I'm a creature of habit, comfortable with the same predictable schedule every day. Katie's death and now this funeral... I feel overwhelmed. Before Katie joined me, I easily controlled simple routine in my spinster life. But children operate off-schedule, so I had to adjust. That's one reason raising Katie was tough for me. But when her parents died in that car crash and she was only twelve, there was nobody else to take her. Raising a child meant chucking my schedule, but although it started out as my obligation, I grew to love her, which helped. Then, once she became an adult, I gradually returned to my comfortable, predictable routines. But Katie's death, arranging the funeral, and now that awful man...I...I'm not sure I can cope."

"She's been with you since she was twelve?"

Jean nodded.

"And the paper said she is...was 43 now?"

"Yes."

Barely two years older than her own firstborn, Jennifer realized in surprise.

"I didn't marry and had no children, but my sister was her mother. With only a social services alternative for Katie when her parents died, raising Katie myself seemed right. I tried my best, despite starting with no experience. But I'd been a librarian for thirty years, so I knew where to find child-rearing books. They helped a lot."

The funeral director returned to the visitation-room door. His voice resonated calm. "Unless you're expecting someone else, may I close the door now? It's 4:25."

Jean nodded. "Let me take one last look at my Katie and then we'll go." She shuffled to the bier and touched the lifelike, albeit cold, hand of the woman in the coffin. "Goodbye, sweetheart. At last you're at peace." She dabbed again at her eyes and wiped her nose before turning. "Will you walk out with me?" she asked Jennifer. "I feel a little dizzy after all this."

"I'm glad to. Did you drive here?"

"Yes, but I ...would you mind following me home in your car to make sure I get there? I live just off Westmoreland, this side of Kirby Road. Do you know where that is?" At Jennifer's nod, she took the guest-book pen. "Will it take you far out of your way?" When Jennifer shook her head, Jean continued, "Here, I'll write down my address and phone number." Suddenly Jean smiled at Jennifer, "Why, I don't even know your name, dear..."

Jennifer told her and they exchanged information.

After following Jean home, Jennifer watched until she parked in her driveway and opened her front door. Lowering the car window, Jennifer called, "Feeling a little better now, Aunt Jean?"

"I...I think so. Thanks, Jennifer." Jean waved weakly.

"Want me to come in with you?"

The woman hesitated. Jennifer sensed she wanted to say yes, but instead she called back. "No... but thank you again."

Jennifer waited in her car until the woman fumbled her way inside the house and closed the front door. Then she drove away, her heart filled with compassion for this fellow human in such distress. But at the first stop-sign, she gave a small gasp of realization—she still had no idea why Katie's familiar-looking face haunted her.

CHAPTER 20

At the same moment in another part of McLean, Arnie sat in his parked car in the lot near McLean Hardware. Toby purred in his lap. Six days had passed since the drone discovered Mrs. Ogelby. Arnie felt nervous every time he thought about her, never mind the bad thing he did afterward inside her house.

His anxiety increased earlier today when Gerry said, "Another policeman came by our house again to, like, get my version of what happened—not the one who asked all the neighbors about seeing anything suspicious. He wants to talk to you too." At Arnie's wince, his friend continued, "which makes sense since you and I are, like, the ones who found her. Here, he told me to give you his cell number."

Arnie stared at the slip of paper. Why did they want to talk to him again? Did they figure out what he'd done? That scared him, because why else a second interview? Worse, the interview itself presented a major problem. Where could it happen without causing him more grief?

He told Toby, "Home is out. I can't risk Magda learning anything that could, like, make my dad mad at me. A cop talking to me at work could, like, end my job, and I need that job. There's Gerry's house, but his family are the only nice people in my life. I'd, like, blow that if they learn what I did at Mrs. Ogleby's. Depending on how this police interview turns out, Gerry's family could hate me, too." He rubbed his cat's ears. "If they do, there's nothing left in my pathetic life...but you." He sighed. "So before I call that cop, I need a plan."

His anguished but intelligent mind sifted possibilities. "What if the interview happened right at the McLean police station? That would, like, protect my home, my job and my friend. But Toby, whoa—I've never gone inside a police station." His face clouded, envisioning a TV-stoked institutional backdrop where cops peered at everyone with laser-eyed suspicion.

Vacillating over what to do and say, his stress level rose while anticipating this cop's inevitable reach for him. "Wait, Toby...maybe they'll overlook me. If all the neighbors' stories agree on nothing looking suspicious about Mrs. Ogelby's death, maybe they'll, like, close the case. Yeah, I should wait to see if they want me enough to find my cell number and call me. *Then* I'll suggest meeting at the police station."

He rubbed Toby's neck and frowned. "But we've seen TV cop shows where they try to interview witnesses at home to, like, size up stuff in the background that might throw new light on the case. What if the cop *insists* on meeting me at home?" Arnie shuddered. He had no idea how to deflect such a situation.

"Hey, new idea, Toby. What if I don't answer cell calls unless I recognize the caller number? That could work. If they can't reach me, wouldn't they, like, wrap the case? They already took my story once."

Arnie felt the twist in his stomach again. Why couldn't he get his life on some normal track? He popped an antacid pill. Instead of waiting for it to work, he figured food might quiet the grinding sounds from his middle. He moved Toby from his lap to the passenger seat, started the car and turned toward McDonald's.

As he drove, his hatred shifted again to Magda. With her in control, he had no chance with his dad. How to get her out of his life? He thought about the shooting range with Gerry and his father. Everybody commented about his good aim. The target proved this true. "Wait a minute, Toby. Dad has guns. And ammo, too. He used to keep them in his den. I bet they're still there. Magda's the problem. If I had a gun, I could solve that problem."

His eyes glazed as he imagined his indescribable pleasure watching Magda falling to the floor, riddled with bullets— the fairness and satisfaction of revenge would at last be his. His sudden maniacal laugh made Toby jerk away, but Arnie didn't notice this in his trance-like vision. What intoxicating satisfaction to see the shock and horror on Magda's face as he forever destroyed her power over him and his father.

Justice at last...

CHAPTER 21

"Becca, could we talk a minute?"

Becca shot her mother a quick look. "Sure, what's up?"

Jennifer hesitated. "I...I don't know where to start."

Surprised at her mother's serious expression, Becca nudged, "...at the beginning?"

"Right..." Jennifer collected her thoughts. "Okay, at a garage sale last weekend, I saw a 40-ish woman who looked unusually familiar, but who I still can't place. That's also where I snatched up the Chinese wine goblet seconds before a man with a moustache grabbed for it. He was furious and hissed at me that he's an antique dealer who needed it for a customer. He offered to pay me triple the garage-sale price. When I refused, he turned mean, saying I'd regret my decision."

"So...two unrelated events at the same sale."

"I thought so, too. But last week I saw that woman's picture in the *Washington Post* obit section, giving her name, Katherine Kalinsky. The obit said she grew up in McLean. Her death at age 43 seemed odd, making me suspect some unusual cause, like an accident."

"Accident?"

"I'll get to that. The obit listed the funeral home viewing time today in Vienna. On impulse, I went. A woman about my age sat there alone. I said hello. She needed to talk, and I wanted to listen. She's Katie's Aunt Jean, who raised the twelve-year-old girl after her parents died in a car accident. She said Katie worked for *and* had a secret affair for years with that same rude, *married* antique dealer I met at the garage sale."

"Ah...which connects them."

"But Aunt Jean said something ended that love relationship. Apparently despondent over it, Katie took her life in her closed garage with her car motor running."

"OMG, Mom. How awful...carbon monoxide poisoning?"

"Exactly. This antique dealer acted like such a narcissistic jerk at the sale and, according to Jean, treated Katie badly, so what if he *silenced her* so his wife wouldn't find out about their affair?"

"Mom, isn't that...well, reaching pretty far?"

"Aunt Jean says police are treating Katie's death as suicide, not homicide. But I wonder..."

"Why not tell Adam what you know? He's with Homicide now..."

"I did—today. But he needs facts, not guesses, and I don't have facts yet. So, yes, I'm reaching but it's not just *my* intuition. Veronika met this same man when he appraised her antiques. She says he's not only obnoxious and ill-mannered, but she noticed his dark aura."

"*Dark aura?*" Becca laughed. "Your vague intuition plus an 89-year-old part-time psychic's aura-vision?" She shook her head and turned away. "Mom, this is too much."

Jennifer sighed. "I understand your take. Maybe you're right. Maybe I'm carried away. But I can't shake this feeling Katie deserves help, and I'm somehow her path to justice." She paused. "So...I have an idea."

"Uh-oh! Haven't your past ideas drawn us all into ...ah, some serious problems? Even danger?" At her mother's crestfallen look, she softened. "Okay Mom, what's *this* idea?"

"Well...to get more information, we need an insider-look at Robert Radner. I can't myself because he knows me from the sale. But you've finished college and not yet found a job you like. This antique dealer likely needs to hire Katie's replacement. What if...what if you applied for that job?"

Becca's eyebrows rose and she guffawed. "Please! Tell me you're joking..."

Jennifer hurried on. "Temporary, of course. You could quit any time. Meanwhile, you might learn something important to help us figure this out."

"Bizarre, Mom...even for you. Look, I...even if I tried, what qualifications could I possibly invent for such a job?"

"Fair question. How about curiosity, enthusiasm, attraction to beautifully crafted old furniture, appreciation of exquisite silver, china and art from the past, college grad with business degree?"

Becca shook her head. "Totally far-fetched...I can't believe you're saying this."

"But what if we learn whether a despondent woman took her own life or was murdered instead?"

"Murdered? Mom, don't even you admit this scheme is *way* weird?"

Jennifer took a deep breath. "Maybe you're right. It's just... Katie looked so sad at that sale and now she's dead and if that awful man did it, we need facts for his arrest." She rubbed her hands together. "Look, if I thought this meant any danger for you, I'd never suggest it. But unlike Katie, you'd be a new hire, working daylight hours, and have no emotional connection with Radner. He couldn't know your real purpose, so you're no threat. You'd be completely safe."

They fell silent. The pause in conversation lengthened as each mulled the situation. Finally, Becca sighed. "Mom, sometimes I think I know you well and other times you...." She stared at her fingernails and shrugged, "But what the heck. I have nothing better to do right now and this experience might even prep me to follow in your mystery-solving footsteps."

Jennifer brightened. "Really?"

"Really. It's only fifteen minutes away. I'll try right now. *IF* he hires me, and Mom, that's a colossal if—*if* he hires me, there's no guarantee I'll learn anything useful. But out of school and without a job gets boring. Pathetic that my only excitement was those dratted drones at my window. At least now I'll have a purpose, *crazed* though it is."

"Thanks, honey, for thinking out-of-the-box."

"Thinking *and* acting, Mom. It's a 'two-fer,' as you would say."

"Ah...there's just one more thing."

Becca faced her mother, lips tight. "Uh-oh, now what?"

Jennifer cleared her throat. "Let's...let's not tell Dad about this. He'd just worry."

CHAPTER 22

A bell jingled as Becca opened the door below the "Radner Antiquities" sign.

She wandered among antiques positioned importantly around the front of the store—desks, dining tables, credenzas, china cabinets displaying Dresden, Meissen, and other Old-World figurines—to some collectibles artfully arrayed toward the back of the sales room.

"May I help you?" came an impatient voice from the mustached man at a desk near the back.

Per her mother's description, this must be Radner.

"Just browsing. I'm drawn to antiques by their history and craftmanship, and because of the long-ago time, and talent evident in their making. So different from the slick, cheap, crude manufactured stuff rolling off assembly lines today. Seeing your shop, I couldn't resist communing with your masterpieces."

"Oh? That's why you're in Vienna today?"

"Funny you ask. No, I just graduated from Virginia Tech with a business degree and I'm job-hunting today. I live in McLean, so Vienna's an ideal commute. Tysons Corner next door offers plenty of jobs, but the skyscrapers and hectic urban pace there turn me off. Vienna appeals to my 'village instinct.'"

Sarcasm tinged his voice. "Good luck." His attention returned to the papers on his desk.

How might she get his attention? Becca picked up a spray of jade grapes. "I saw one of these at a garage sale last week. The Seller didn't know what he had and priced it at $1.00. And although professional estate sales company staffs are knowledgeable and experienced, they're sometimes too busy to scrutinize each item carefully. For example, my sister bought an estate sale purse for $4 and found two $20 bills inside. And I've watched shoppers use loupes to examine gold jewelry to buy at bargain prices. I recently paid $2 each for a set of six Waterford crystal brandy snifters. Don't you love their pure ringtone when you tap them together during a toast?" She waited a beat. "Are you the proprietor? Mr. Radner?"

At this, he glanced up from his desk and with pride, answered, "Yes, I am."

"You have a remarkable shop here," she admired.

He sat taller with undisguised satisfaction. "Yes, I do."

"...and a fine reputation in McLean. Several neighbors recommended your shop."

"Who?"

Becca scrambled to invent an answer. "Oh, Veronika Verantsova, among others. They say trust is important when buying antiques and they trust your knowledge and ethics."

"Thank you." Radner basked in her compliments. "They've placed that trust well."

Becca improvised further. "I really longed for a job in an antique shop because of my appreciation for fine things, but I guess my business degree pushes me in a different direction. I don't suppose you need someone to help out in your shop, or maybe a picker."

He didn't answer, seeming to return his attention to the papers on his desk.

Her chatter running out, Becca groped to fulfill her objective.

"An honor to meet you, sir. When I'm ready to choose some quality pieces for my own home, I'll be back to see you. Will you remember me...Rebecca Shannon?"

"Uh, sure," he mumbled, glancing up as if really noticing her for the first time.

"Well, goodbye. I hate to leave your store to go back to the real world. Thanks for my antique-fix for the day."

She eased the door open, heard the bell jingle and stepped outside.

She paused a moment on the sidewalk, thinking of her mother's disappointment at learning their scheme hadn't worked. Bad news. Not only had she failed her mother, but she'd already begun thinking of her mole-role in this job caper as adventure. Sighing, she walked away.

She had walked ten steps when the shop bell jingled behind her and she heard Radner call, "Oh miss. Miss...ah, Shannon? May I speak with you?"

A smile crossed Becca's face before she composed her expression and hurried back to the shop.

CHAPTER 23

Returning home Friday evening at 6:00 p.m., Becca unlocked the front door and called, "Mom, got a minute?"

"Sure. Keep me company in the kitchen. I'm starting dinner."

Becca's Cheshire grin caught Jennifer's immediate attention. "Uh-oh. Something good on your mind."

"Several somethings. I got the job at Radner's antique shop."

"You *did*? Woo-hoo!" They locked arms and jumped up and down like little girls. "And..."

"And I not only met Robert Radner, but also Mrs. Radner *and* Bobby."

"Bobby?"

"He's Radner's son, about my age, and a fellow Virginia Tech alum, two classes ahead of mine."

"You little rascal. Congrats." She poured her daughter a glass of wine and raised her own glass to toast Becca's triumph.

"I'm a permanent/temporary employee there."

"Isn't that an oxymoron?"

"Permanent—meaning I stay as long as it's mutually advantageous. Temporary—meaning they understand I'm searching for a business degree-career job and when I find it, I'll quit their shop."

"So it fits your needs exactly. Meantime, you play detective."

"Mom, wait 'til you hear this. After my I-love-antiques spiel failed, I left the store. I hadn't gone far when Radner opened the door to call me back. He said, 'How would you like to work for a handsome man like me?' I pinched myself hard to keep from laughing. I mean, he's an ancient guy in his sixties or seventies. What an ego."

Sixty-one herself, Jennifer overlooked the "ancient" designation. "How did you answer him?"

I said, "I'd like to work with your handsome antiques."

"And..."

"And he said, 'Maybe I *am* a handsome antique.' And I said, 'Maybe you are but I'm engaged to be married.' That stopped him short."

"Well done. And Mrs. Radner...?"

"Maybe sixty. Hard to tell. Like her husband, well-dressed. Unlike her husband, lovely manners. Not beautiful but beautifully put together. Uses make-up well and clearly visits a beautician and manicurist weekly. Both parents dote on Bobby."

"You observant Sherlock. This Bobby, does he work in the shop, too?"

"Not sure, but I might tell you more soon."

"Oh?"

Becca looked smug. "He and I are having dinner tonight at Café Renaissance."

"You little imp. Amazing. Describe him for me."

"Tall, dark and handsome covers it pretty well. College grad. Smooth. Smart. Living well."

Jennifer frowned. "Might you slip Katie into your conversation tonight?"

"Let's see what unfolds. Remember, I'll eavesdrop daily at the shop. I may even have access to office files."

A door banged as Jason came home from the office. "What a commute. Rush hour plus an accident on the GW Parkway. Is that wine?"

Jennifer handed him a stemmed glass and Becca showed him the bottle's label, saying, "And this wine's even good for you." At her father's quizzical expression, she added, "Made with organic grapes, Dad. It's an Italian red blend I bought today for us to try."

He studied the label. "Nero D'Avola Sicilia, Terramore, 2018." They clinked goblets and savored the velvety scarlet liquid. As Jason settled into a chair beside them, Jennifer and Becca exchanged conspiratorial winks.

CHAPTER 24

That evening, Becca entered Café Renaissance, ogling the spectacular bouquet of fresh yellow gladiolas on the foyer credenza, the Old-World décor and artfully arranged tables.

"I'm joining Mr. Radner," she told the maître d', who led her to his table.

Bobby jumped to his feet and guided her chair as she sat down.

"Good evening, beautiful lady," he began. "Any trouble parking?"

"No, right across the street. Are you a regular here?"

"Our family eats out a lot, so we're pretty familiar with local restaurants."

Their waiter greeted them and presented menus. "What kind of water would you like?"

"Pellegrino, okay?" Bobby asked. Becca nodded. "He'll return next for our drink orders. A cocktail for you?"

"Perhaps a pinot noir?"

He studied the wine list. "Ah, you might like this one. Bel Glos is a favorite of mine." He turned to the waiter. "We'll take a bottle." Minutes later they savored the rich flavor of this ruby red wine on their tongues.

"Mmm. Smooth, with arresting berry flavors," Becca purred.

"Glad you like it."

"As a new hire at your parents' store, I have a few questions, if you don't mind. For instance, do you spend much time at the shop?" Becca asked.

"Yes and no. I'm their buyer, so I'm away a lot at antique auctions and following other leads. But when in town, I drop by."

"A buyer. Sounds like fun."

"Fun, yes. Easy, no. The antique market suffers huge competition these days. With the current trend toward modern decor, fewer customers appreciate antiques." He pointed to his wine glass. "Drinkware's an example. With valued antique goblets and decanters, you find thicker crystal with elaborate etched patterns designed to catch sparkle from surrounding light. They combined a glass's natural contour with the artisan's skilled cuts made by hand or on rotating machine wheels. The result was many distinctive patterns. Different size crystal glasses in the same pattern formed sets. In contrast, today's taste leans toward thin glass, plain styles and simple shapes, like Riedel wine glasses."

"I see. So what's the future for antique shops like your parents' store?"

"Antiques have always formed a small niche in the furnishings market, but it's shrinking. I've urged them to add more contemporary collectibles. They resist but I'm making headway, as you probably noticed looking around the shop."

"Are you also the buyer for those collectibles?"

"Some, but we also have other sources."

"Do your parents both work at the shop?"

"We hire a regular employee like you so someone's always on duty during regular store hours. In addition, one of our family members often spends part of the day there. Usually my dad. Sometimes my mom. Occasionally me."

Becca realized this meant Katie and the senior Radner would have had time alone together at the shop, reinforcing Jean's info about their affair. She leaned forward. "Then I'm not their first hire of this sort."

"No, we've always had someone on the floor. The last girl worked at our shop about five years."

"What was her name?"

"Does it matter?"

Becca thought fast. "No. I just thought if I knew her name, I'd understand when they mention her. After all, won't I try to fill her shoes?"

He gave a wry smile, as if at a private thought. "No, you'll put your own stamp on any job you undertake."

Becca smiled appreciation. "I'll drink to that." And they did.

He looked thoughtful. "Her name was Katie and I'm glad you mentioned her, because I want to warn you Dad can act the lecher, if given a chance."

Becca's eyebrow rose with interest.

"He's a long-time skirt-chaser, so you're forewarned."

"Does your mother know?"

"God, no."

"And Katie succumbed to his charms?"

He hesitated. "If I knew, why would I tell you?"

She grinned disarmingly, "To warn me because you like me and care what happens to me."

"Look, you're a smart chick who knows how to take care of herself. But you're right about one thing."

Becca waited...

"I do like you and care what happens to you."

She gazed into his eyes. "Thank you."

They ordered. Becca asked, "Do you use pickers to find collectibles at estate and garage sales?"

"Funny you ask. Katie did some of that for us. She got rather good at it, before she...ah, quit."

"Quit? Something her replacement should know?"

"I think she had...health issues."

Becca stiffened. Cold if he referred to Katie's death as a "health issue." Instead, she said, "Enough of that. Tell me about you."

"I'm named Robert, after my father. They called me Junior in my toddler years. Then my first-grade teacher introduced 'Bobby.' Later I could have shortened it to Bob, but Bobby has a comfortable, good-old-boy connotation. Made me sound friendly and non-threatening in school. Ditto in business. And especially effective in the south, although they'd probably prefer a double name like Bobby-Glen or Bobby-Joe. Otherwise, I grew up right here, attending local schools. Then a fine arts degree from Virginia Tech, after which I marched straight into the family business. How about you?"

"Also local. McLean elementary and middle schools. Langley High. Virginia Tech business degree. So we have things in common. My father owns a design/build engineering business in Arlington and my mother..." she tried to think how to describe her mother, "is a stay-at-home mom who explores garage and estate sales on weekends."

"Do you go with her to these sales?"

"Sometimes."

"Then you're already schooled for a picker role at your Radner Antiquities job—if you want to."

The waiter poured more wine. Over an excellent meal, they shared memories of familiar Tech college haunts, professors, and mutual friends.

When they folded their napkins on the table at the end of the evening, Bobby said, "I'll walk you to your car."

As he opened her door, his lips brushed her cheek before she slid into the driver's seat and rolled down the window.

"Thanks for a lovely evening, beautiful lady."

"Thanks for suggesting it, kind sir."

He gave her a promising real kiss. "See you tomorrow at work?"

Smiling, she nodded, started her car, and drove home. Dazzled.

CHAPTER 25

SATURDAY

Next morning Becca fumbled into the kitchen in her usual early blur.

"Good morning, honey." Jennifer spoke across her garage sale notes.

"Coffee...." Becca zombie-walked toward the machine. Pouring a cupful, she took a generous slurp, slid her coffee onto the table and flopped into a chair. Coming to life, she noticed her mother's expectant look.

"Curious about last night?" Becca grinned. "Café Renaissance. Continental menu. Wonderful experience. Our family should eat there soon. I had a terrific time."

"Good idea."

"And I have a report. Bobby admitted his father's a womanizer, but his mother has no idea. He didn't say if Katie was one of his father's conquests. He said she quit the store because of 'health issues.'" Eye-roll. "She was also a picker for their store, which probably explains why you saw her at garage sales. That's it for now, but Bobby's their store's buyer, so I'll doubtless see him again. And Mom, he's a charmer plus good-looking. What's not to like?"

"Are those stars in your eyes?"

Becca laughed. "That's too strong. I've known him less than a day. But I enjoy him."

Jennifer picked up her purse. "Well, see you later. I'm on my way."

Becca looked surprised. "Where?"

"It's Saturday." Jennifer cupped her ear. "Hear that garage sale siren song? Dad's playing golf. What about you? Going to work?"

"I don't work weekends but...," she sat up straight, "could I go with you? Maybe find something unusual to sell at the store."

"I'm walking out the door right now. How fast can you be ready?"

"Five minutes to throw on my clothes. I'll do shoes, hair and makeup in the car."

"Five minutes, that's all. I'm backing out now. Lock the front door when you leave."

"Got it, Mom."

Five minutes later, barefoot Becca lurched into the car clutching a bulging carryall tote.

Hands on the steering wheel, Jennifer glanced at the list in her lap. "First stop, a Chesterbrook area community sale. I brought bran muffins and bottled water for us. Fun to have you along, hon. Now that Hannah's distracted with little Zealand, she hasn't garage-saled with me for a while. And Kaela's too busy with her family and career."

Entering Chesterbrook's neighborhood, Jennifer curbed the car at the first participating house and jumped out. She looked through the sale's baby section, collecting a few toys for Zealand. Becca examined candlesticks, china and crystal. She spotted a ginger jar sitting on a matching-pattern tray. "Mom, what do you think of this?"

"I like it. The consignment shop I use says anything Oriental blue-and-white ceramic jumps off their shelves. But this looks unusual. You might find separate platters or ginger jars, but here's a matched set. See, you could use just one or the other or together. It's a two-fer. Any maker's mark on the bottom?"

Becca flipped the pieces over. Instead of "made in China" or Japan, they saw an Oriental symbol they couldn't decipher.

"Do you think this might sell as a collectible at the shop?"

"Not fair. I'm biased. Asian pieces always call my name. How much is it?"

Becca checked the tag. "$20 for the pair."

"Maybe less if you bargain? If you don't take it, I will. Or if your shop doesn't want it, I'll buy it from you. Win-win."

The next sale offered little of interest. Everything looked too worn out to entice them. Even the couple running the sale from front porch chairs looked as old and frayed as their merchandise. As she and Becca turned to leave, Jennifer recognized some dated toys. "I remember these from childhood visits to my grandmother. Look—original boxes. That ups the value. And how about this jack-in-the-box?" She removed the toy from the box and gently turned the crank. As the tinny melody played, Jennifer sang along. "All around the mulberry bush, the monkey chased the weasel. The monkey thought 'twas all in fun. POP goes the weasel." Out sprang a lolling clown head. "It works." Next, they examined a wind-up chimp who clanged cymbals as he moved to music.

"I don't know what sells at your store, but these are sure-fire e-Bay winners." She turned to the Sellers. "How much for these two toys?"

The old man wheezed, "How about $5.00 each? We're moving to a retirement home in three weeks and this is our last chance to get rid of things."

Jennifer looked doubtful. "Sir, have you thought of selling these on e-Bay?"

"Don't know how to do that."

"Could your children or grandchildren help you? I think you'd get a lot more money for them that way."

"Nope. Today we sell what we can. Do you want them or not?"

Becca answered fast. "We do."

At the next sale, a framed painting caught Jennifer's attention. The rural scene reminded her of Indiana, where she'd visited grandparents several memorable childhood summers. She couldn't quite make out the painter's signature. "How much?" she asked the Seller.

"$40. The frame alone is probably worth that."

Jennifer studied the oil-painting: a weathered barn on the left with a ring of summer-leafed trees behind it, a field of unidentifiable crop in the center and a plow in the right foreground. She vacillated, then made an impulse decision. "How about $20?"

"Sold."

"Do you know this picture's history?" she asked, tucking it under her arm to fish for money.

The old Seller scratched her chin. "I think my folks brought it from Indiana when they moved here 50 years ago." Jennifer grinned as she paid.

She started toward the car but skidded to a halt. Looking across the garage sale she froze—her face pale, eyes wide, mouth agape. One hand clutched at her chest.

Frightened, Becca had never seen her mother like this. "Mom...what is it? A heart attack?"

Jennifer couldn't move and seemed unable to talk.

Becca grabbed her arm. "Mom, snap out of this or I'm calling 911."

Jennifer gulped, staring.

Becca felt her mother's cold hand grab her arm in a clammy grip. Pulling her daughter close, Jennifer whispered, "It's impossible."

"What's impossible?"

"There...."

Becca followed her mother's line of sight but saw nothing unusual.

"Where?"

"It's...it's Katie Kalinsky."

"The dead girl?"

"Yes."

CHAPTER 26

Anxiety etched Becca's face at her mother's semi-coherent behavior. Jennifer stumbled and Becca steadied her. "Please sit down, Mom, while we figure out what's happening."

"No, Becca... quick. That woman. I...I must talk to her before she leaves." Pulling away from her daughter, she started toward the woman with blond hair pulled into a ponytail.

Becca caught up, held her mother's elbow and walked with her to the woman.

But as Jennifer closed the distance, she floundered at what to say. Certainly not, "You look like a dead person I saw in her coffin last week." Thinking fast, she improvised, "Hello there. Sorry to bother you, but I couldn't help noticing you from across the sale. You look remarkably familiar to me. Do we know each other?"

"I don't think so."

Jennifer continued quickly, "I'm Jennifer Shannon and this is my daughter Becca. This community sale in such a nice neighborhood caught our attention and," she indicated the painting under her arm, "we've had good luck today. How about you?" Had she introduced enough common ground not to spook this stranger by coming on too strong?

The woman smiled. "Aren't these sales fun? And you're right, lots of quality stuff here today. My name's Aubrey Bishop. And, no... I don't think we've met, but perhaps I have a common face."

"Oh?"

"Friends sometimes say they've seen me at the library or a restaurant where I knew I hadn't been at that time."

Jennifer knew this was her only chance to link this woman's ghostly resemblance to Katie. In all her years in McLean, she'd never seen this woman before and might never again. She winged it. "Maybe a McLean connection. We live here. Do you?"

"Yes. Near Langley."

"Do you attend garage sales often?"

"I'd love to, but my job keeps me busy most weekends, so today's a luxury for me."

"That's unusual. Most people work weekdays, with weekends off. What do you do?"

"Residential real estate, and you've described exactly why my weekends are busy. It's the only time many working clients can house-hunt."

Jennifer thought fast. She couldn't let this woman disappear without exploring her uncanny resemblance to Katie. "Do you sell estates in Great Falls?"

Aubrey laughed. "That's a specialty."

"Then I may have a client for you—an elderly friend about to move to a senior residence."

"Wonderful. I'd like to know more." Aubrey fished in her purse. "Here's my business card."

Jennifer felt a flush of relief.

"And how might I reach *you*?" Aubrey asked.

Jennifer shared her info. "My friend's giving a small party next Saturday. I'll phone you with the address, time and directions. Her name is Veronika Verontsova. Think you might come?"

"I'll make a point to attend. See you there. And thanks for the real-estate lead, Jennifer."

When Aubrey left, Jennifer felt elated over this improbable meeting. If Aubrey in fact appeared at Veronika's picnic, maybe she'd solve this mystery at last.

Becca stared at her mother before shaking her head. "Why aren't our garage sale experiences like everyone else's?"

When they finished numerous stops in this community sale, Jennifer drove them to another neighborhood and then to an estate sale.

They returned home about 3:00 p.m., ecstatic with their purchases and ravenous for their missed lunch. Jennifer made sandwiches. As they ate, Becca wondered aloud, "Mom, I've known you my whole twenty-one years of life, but days like this, I'm not sure who you are."

Jennifer's eyes twinkled. "Honey, sometimes it's not that people change but that you finally see them for who they are. On the other hand, sometimes we even surprise ourselves by what we do, so maybe who we are keeps blossoming."

Becca grappled with this thought as the phone rang.

CHAPTER 27

Jennifer answered the phone. "Hello."

"It's your mother," Grammy's voice announced.

Jennifer tapped a phone button. "Hi, Mom. You're on speaker. Becca's here, too. Is all well?"

"Yes, readying for the move. Have you told the family who own this rental house that I'll be out so soon?"

"Gee, no. Thanks for reminding me."

"I'm calling now with details about Veronika's party. Next Saturday, arrive at noon for lunch at 1:00 p.m., plus outdoor games. She needs a headcount. Will you three come?"

"Jason and I, for sure." She slid the phone to her daughter.

Becca's eyes sparkled. "Hi, Grammy. I'm coming and besides Nathan, would Veronika mind if I also bring a new friend? He's in the antique business and may have input about her treasures."

"I'll put you down for three then. I'm sure it's fine, Becca. Veronika expects a crowd," Grammy laughed, "but crowds are what we get whenever your big family gathers."

"True enough." Jennifer didn't want her mother overwhelmed by the transition to Pebblebrook Manor. "Your move's happening fast. Need any help?"

"Maybe later. Pebblebrook has already sent their moving consultant. I feel confident about everything. But thanks for your loving concern, dear."

They said goodbye. Jen clicked off the phone and arched an eyebrow at her daughter. "Assuming your party invitation involves Bobby, and if I factor in the things you picked today for the antique shop, seems you're trying to impress someone...."

Becca grinned. "Why not? Shouldn't the new girl on the job try to make a good impression?"

The phone rang again. Jennifer answered and as she listened, her face sobered. "They did? You what? Yes, of course, I will. Please give me your address again." Jennifer scribbled the info. "When? Okay, thirty minutes." She disconnected and told Becca. "Katie's Aunt Jean. She wants me to see new information she just discovered."

"Why'd she pick you, a stranger?"

"Maybe she thinks I'm a foxhole buddy for surviving that interlude with Robert Radner at the funeral home with her."

"Should I come along?"

Jennifer considered. "She sounds anxious. For some reason she's comfortable with me. I think I should go alone this time, but I'll share with you what I learn. Aunt Jean doesn't know you're the frontline investigator into her niece's death. Besides, I'm not sure how long this may take, and don't you have plans for this evening?"

"Yeah, a date with Nathan."

"You don't sound too enthused."

"We always enjoy each other. It's just...I hope he doesn't push me about our future when I'm not ready. But you know guys. He's focused and does everything he can think of to bring the outcome he wants."

"Don't we all?"

Becca shrugged. "I guess you're right"

Jennifer hugged her daughter. "Have fun."

Thirty minutes later Jennifer approached Jean's bungalow on a street of similar modest older houses. When she rang the doorbell, Jean opened the front door, wringing her hands.

"Oh, Jennifer, thank you for coming. So much has happened, I...I've lost perspective. Maybe you can help me understand it all. Here, let's sit down in the living room."

Jennifer took in the 1950s-style furnishings—a postcard from the past. She compared the low ceilings, weakly-lighted interior and dark furniture with her own home's high ceilings, bright interior, and light-colored furnishings. She'd feel morose in this house. Thank goodness, styles had changed.

Expression serious, Jean sighed. "Four things have happened. First, Robert Radner's son came here yesterday. He said his father wanted him to tell me their family felt deeply sorry about Katie's death. Bobby, that's his name, seems like a nice young man, the opposite of his nasty father. He apologized for his dad's poor manners, explaining it was just the man's unfortunate personality, which Bobby didn't like either. He said they all enjoyed Katie's part in their business, and they wanted to contribute to her funeral expenses. He put an envelope on the table. When I opened it after he left, I found $5,000 cash inside."

Jennifer's neutral expression hid her reaction as Jean continued. "This gave me a much better impression of the Radner family, although I still think the father's a rat for his affair with Katie."

Jen nodded.

"The second thing is something I found in my sister's papers. With Katie gone, and my sister dead over thirty years, I finally started the overdue task of weeding through her old papers. In one of her files, I found an envelope with "Katherine" written on the front. Katie can't open it now, so I opened it for her. Inside I was amazed to find this. She handed papers to Jen.

Jennifer squinted in the dim light. "Mind if I turn on this table lamp to read?"

Holding the papers under the light, Jennifer frowned at the heading: "Tri-State Adoption Agency" dated May 28, 1977, and under that "Certificate of Adoption." She scanned further. "Adoptive parents: Bernard and Diane Kalinsky. Child: Katherine Jean Kalinsky. Birth Date: May 28, 1977."

This cover page described amending the original birth certificate to show the adopting Kalinskys as her legal parents. But nothing about that original certificate or any mention of Katie's biological parents. Nor was the newly generated birth certificate there.

"Was this a total surprise, Aunt Jean?"

"Oh my, yes. My sister told me nothing about an adoption. They lived in Pennsylvania awhile, when we saw each other maybe once a year. Diane hadn't mentioned expecting a baby, but when next we met, Katie was an infant and I accepted them as a family of three. I just assumed Katie was their own child. Then came that awful car accident. Katie moving in with me meant a triple shock for the poor child—losing her parents, leaving her familiar surroundings and friends, and starting her new life with me, practically a stranger. To her credit, she survived those difficult adjustments, but I think they took a terrible emotional toll on her. I even wondered if she thought of Robert Radner as the father figure she'd lost. I've read about women seeking their father's love in the form of a willing older man."

"This is a lot to absorb," Jennifer agreed.

"Why do you think the birth certificate's missing?"

Jennifer thought about her own kid's certificates. "Maybe used for school registration? This amended birth certificate legally shows Katie as the Kalinskys' child, with no mention of adoption. Maybe you'll find this new certificate with Katie's school records or other Kalinsky legal papers."

"Follow me and I'll show you the challenge." Jean led the way to a storeroom, where about fifteen boxes and a footlocker stood in a corner. "That's the stuff I hadn't the inclination to look at all these years. But now I'm the only one left. I know I need to start downsizing, but in the process, I'm learning things about my family I really didn't want to know."

Jennifer put an arm around Jean's shoulder. "Look, there are a finite number of boxes so it's a project you *can* complete. You might decide to go through a box a week or a box a month. Once you decide, you can do this yourself, but if you want help getting started, I could..."

"Would you? I mean, just until I get the swing of it?"

"When I get home, I'll e-mail you some possible dates. Pick one and we'll work out a plan for you to deal with this."

"Oh, thank you, Jennifer."

"If you have a computer printer, could you make a copy of these adoption papers for me? I know someone affiliated with Tri-State Adoption. Maybe I can learn more."

"Yes. Upstairs. I'll make the copy on your way out."

Jennifer picked up her purse. "Well, I'll be on my way now."

Jean raised a warning hand. "Wait, there are four things. The third thing...." Her attention seemed to drift. "You may wonder why I'm telling you all this. As an insider, I'm too close to put this all together, but as an outsider, you're objective. You were interested enough in Katie to come to her viewing and befriend me. You're smart and organized, and for some reason, I trust you."

"Why thank you, Aunt Jean." She hesitated. "What's the third thing you think I should know."

"The Medical Examiner's report arrived this morning. The tox screen blood samples show Katie was heavily sedated when she died that night. Do you suppose she just fell asleep in the running car? Wouldn't that mean her death was accidental, not suicide?"

"Maybe...let me think about that. And the fourth thing?"

Aunt Jean dabbed a hankie at her eyes, fighting a sob. "I...I wasn't sure I should even mention this, but maybe it's another clue to understanding what happened to Katie."

"Okay..."

"The report also said Katie was pregnant."

CHAPTER 28

Jennifer's mind whirred as she drove home from visiting Jean. The Radner hush money, the drugs in Katie's system and her pregnancy ratcheted up suspicions about motive.

She hurried into the house to find Jason busy with tools in his garage workshop and Becca upstairs readying for her date.

Becca's curiosity showed when she answered her mother's knock on her bedroom. "Mom, what happened with Katie's aunt?"

Jennifer sat on the edge of the bed and studied her hands. "Honey, I thought about this all the way home. Before I tell you, I think you should decide if you want to continue with this project."

Becca frowned. "What *are* you talking about?"

"Remember your reason for the antique-store job—searching for info relating to Katie's death? You're like a covert agent on a special assignment. That role looked easy with strangers but maybe not now, if you're developing a personal relationship with someone there."

"Bobby?"

"Yes. If so, it changes things. Think now whether you can be honest and dishonest at the same time. And even if you can, are you willing to? Continuing means drawing a hard line between your spontaneous honest self and your secret spy self."

Caught off guard, Becca stared at her mother.

"Honesty's natural to your nature and spontaneity's a part of your bubbly personality. Before I share what I learned today, you should decide if you're willing to go forward playing these two roles at the same time."

"I...I hadn't thought of it that way. Just figured I could do both. But if it's a conflict..."

"Then you must choose. One way is to continue without knowing what I learned today. You can still explore your relationship with Bobby—that is, short of telling him you're there to gather information. You might still discover clues related to Katie's death or implicating Radner senior."

"Or..."

"Or if I tell you what I learned, you'll dive deeper into this mystery, with no turning back." Jennifer stared at her hands. "It's my fault for suggesting this crazy scheme in the first place, but I wanted to help Katie, and I didn't know Bobby existed, never mind that you'd be drawn to him."

Becca considered the situation. "I think I can do both."

"You *think* you can?"

"I can."

"You're sure?"

"Yes."

"Even if you can, do you want to?"

"I...yes, I do."

"Last of all, what I tell you stays between us. Okay?" Becca nodded. "All right, here goes." Jennifer described the adoption, the hush money, Katie's drugged condition and her pregnancy.

They both startled at a knock on the door. Jason's voice said, "Hey, anybody ready for dinner?"

Jennifer put a finger to her lips in a let's-not-bother-Dad-with-this message.

"Hi, Dad. Come in," Becca said.

"How are my two favorite girls this evening?"

Jennifer smiled. "Well, this favorite girl's about to transform into your favorite cook and Becca's almost out-the-door with Nathan tonight. Good golfing day?"

"Not bad. I got two birdies."

"Good going, hon." Jennifer gave him a light kiss and took his hand. "Off to the galley. Talk to you later, Becca."

The doorbell rang as Becca followed them down the stairs. They greeted Nathan. After goodbyes, Jennifer locked the front door behind them.

Finding themselves alone downstairs, Jason asked, "Everything okay with Becca?"

"Nathan's pushing marriage before she's ready, making it awkward."

"I was afraid of that." He poured them each a glass of wine. "How did we avoid that block back in our dating days?"

She thought about this. "Maybe we both felt ready for the marriage plunge at the same time. I went steady with several boys in high school and college, but you had something none of them did."

He nuzzled her cheek, "What was that?"

"You're impossible to resist."

He chuckled appreciatively.

"And what about you, Jay?"

"Oh...that's really going back. Let's see, I dated a girl through high school, but it ended when we went to different colleges. And at college, I met you. After that, I had no doubt about who to spend my life with." He wrapped his arms around her. "And here we still are, 41 years later."

"Remarkable. And they said it wouldn't last..."

He nuzzled her neck. "Who said it wouldn't?"

She melted against him. "Certainly not our five children..."

CHAPTER 29

SATURDAY, A WEEK LATER

At seven-thirty Saturday morning, Jennifer rapped on Becca's door. "If you still want to go to garage sales this morning, better get coffee now."

Sleepy mumbling preceded a weary, "Okay...I'll ...be right down."

After assembling food on the kitchen island, Jennifer tapped on her laptop, adding *Washington Post* classified section sale addresses to the Craigslist her printer upstairs would spit out.

Ten minutes later, Becca shuffled in."

"Great, you're dressed and ready."

"Grab and go?"

"Over there—bagels, cream cheese, smoked salmon, fruit." They each foraged a take-along-breakfast and climbed into the car.

"Becca, would you navigate?"

"Sure. Where first?"

"Langley Oaks. In the list of sales to visit today, Langley's number one, with a circle around it. Just put that address in your mobile's GPS. I know the way to the neighborhood, just not all the streets once we're there."

"Got it. On the way, could we talk about what you learned last night from Katie's aunt?"

"Good idea."

Becca pulled out a notebook and pencil. "You mentioned four new facts: Katie's adoption, Radner's money gift, the drugs in her system and her pregnancy. Right?"

"Right."

"Let's scratch her adoption. She didn't know about it, so it doesn't likely factor into her death."

"Good point."

"The funeral-expense money's either Radner's generous gesture *or* calculated to discourage Aunt Jean from causing a scandal where his wife could learn about his infidelity. And maybe also affect their shop's reputation. You said when Aunt Jean revealed at the funeral home that she knew about his affair with Katie, this surprised him. So he realized this was no longer his secret. If Radner felt sorry for what he'd done to Katie, giving that money helped absolve him. And if he worried his wife might find out, the money also discouraged Aunt Jean from going public with a scandal. Therefore, we could read that $5,000 as sincere—or insincere."

Driving, Jennifer nodded. "He knew from the funeral home that Aunt Jean despised him, so he couldn't deliver the money himself, and he shielded his wife...which left his charming son."

"It worked just as Radner hoped. Aunt Jean felt kindlier toward the Radners because of that gift."

Jennifer picked up on this. "We can also read Katie's pregnancy two ways. Another reason for an already depressed girl to think suicide solved *all* her problems, or a motive for Radner to quiet her for good and simultaneously dispose of the baby."

Jennifer considered this. "What if he suggested she get rid of the baby, but she refused? Or what if she threatened to tell his wife?"

"We can guess about motives, but having drugs in her system is a fact. Did she take them herself to ease mental pain, or did someone drug her on the sly? Or even force her to take them?"

Jennifer considered. "Another double read. If only she'd left some clues. But where? Maybe in her bedroom? Aunt Jean hasn't touched Katie's room since she died. Perhaps I could look there when I help sort through the sister's boxes."

"Good idea, Mom. Otherwise, we have circumstantial clues." Becca put away her notebook. "Wow, look at the branches and leaves on the ground after last night's big storm."

"Yes. The morning news showed fallen trees and lots of area damage. We were lucky. By the way, remember Veronika's party at noon today, which shortens our garage sale time. I hope the storm didn't affect her plans. With a thirty-minute drive to her house plus time to change clothes beforehand, we should get home no later than 11:00."

Becca tapped her watch. "It's 8:00 now so three hours to go."

"Want to drive there with Dad, Grammy and me?"

"No thanks, I'm going with Nathan, but I painted myself into a corner."

"How?"

"When Veronika first mentioned the party, I invited Nathan because in the two years we've dated, he's at our house so often he's almost part of the family. He knows everybody and was a logical choice. But then I met Bobby and invited him for the antique angle. With both there, who do I spend time with? Do I want Bobby to know I have a longtime boyfriend, even though Nathan and I aren't exclusive? Do I want Nathan to think I'm putting off getting engaged because I have a new interest? It's awkward."

"Mm," came Jennifer's non-committal response.

"If I hang around you and Dad to avoid them both at the party, you'll understand?"

"We will." Jennifer smiled as they approached the first garage sale.

CHAPTER 30

"**D**estination ahead on the left," announced the GPS voice as they approached the garage sale. "Look at all the cars, Mom."

"Can we find a parking spot?"

"This space is way too small," Becca warned as Jennifer paused at an opening between two cars.

"Let's test my parallel-parking skills." Jennifer pulled parallel to the car in front of the space and with four tight gee-haws, executed a perfect park.

"Wow, I could never squeak into that spot."

"Off we go." Jennifer tucked her car keypad into her fanny pack and zipped it shut as they walked up the driveway. "Has the shop asked you to find collectibles for them again today?"

Becca grinned. "Yes."

"What interests them?"

"Seeing what I brought last week, even grumpy old Mr. Radner called them 'interesting.' High praise from him. And Bobby thinks I have an instinct for marketable stuff, but you and I know I depend on your seasoned experience."

Jennifer laughed. "Then let's hope we get lucky again today."

"Bobby also wants to look at Veronika's antiques and maybe make offers. I e-mailed her about him to be sure I had her permission to invite him. She hesitated about the name until I explained Bobby was the Radner son, not the father."

"She also okayed Aubrey Bishop when I called, and welcomes her real-estate input."

They passed a table of toys—Legos, board games, Star Wars figures, TY beanie babies and dolls—the usual. Jennifer passed them to pick up a large puppet.

"What's that?"

"Why, I think it's Charlie McCarthy, an Edgar Bergen dummy."

"Who's Edgar Bergen?"

"A ventriloquist."

"Like Sesame Street?"

"More like Jeff Dunham. One man voicing one puppet."

"How do you know about this one?"

"From when I was a young girl." Jennifer examined the puppet. "He's in good shape. Looks vintage to me. What about this for your antique shop? How much are they asking?" She handed it to her daughter.

Becca frowned at the homely puppet. "Well... if you say so. You're sure?" Jennifer nodded. "Okay, I'll check the price." She wandered off to do so, returning soon to announce, "$20."

"I think it's worth the buy. He might retail in an antique shop for $60 to $100. And look, I think this is a flow-blue china plate."

"Mom, the pattern's all blurry. It looks like a factory-second discard."

"Believe it or not, these are collectible. And the price is only $5. The Sellers don't know what they have. Shall we finish up here to check out more places in our restricted time?"

Becca agreed. They bought their finds and chatted in the car en route to the next sale.

"Are you looking forward to Veronika's party today?"

"Definitely."

"How many of our family plan to come?"

"Grammy and Veronika gave me a copy of their list. Everyone. About thirty plus a few guests like ours. And some of the grands may bring little friends. Veronika hired a caterer. This is the last big splash at her estate before she moves to Pebblebrook, so a nostalgic time for her."

"Funny how we welcomed her into our family. Must have been your idea, Mom."

"Hard to explain. Impulse, I guess. But it seemed so very right at the time. And don't you think she's a fun addition?"

Becca thought about this. "Yes. She's educated, personable, upbeat, loyal, positive...never mind her occasional, weird psychic visions. What do you think about them?"

Jennifer stared into the distance. "Visions like hers defy current logic, but scientists learn more all the time about how our brains work. Maybe there is an explanation we don't yet understand. And remember, one of her visions alerted you to take action that saved my life from those terrorists. It even helped spoil their sinister plot. So she has my attention, because without her vision..."

Becca squeezed her mother's hand. "...you might not be here today."

CHAPTER 31

At the same time Saturday morning, the manager of the upscale grocery where Arnie worked received an urgent phone call.

"Hello, Armand. It's Ginny at Classical Catering. We had a double disaster during last night's thunderstorm. A tree fell on our building, seriously damaging two of our three vans, and a squirrel sizzled our transformer. With our refrigerators off all night, the food's ruined for two big catering jobs today. We're cleaning up the colossal mess now. Anyway, I'm desperate. Could you put together a bunch of platters for me: cheese, cold cuts, shrimp, chicken, finger sandwiches, fruit, desserts? If you can do it, I'll e-mail my list to you ASAP. I warn you, it's an exceptionally large order."

Armand chuckled. "So... even squirrels know to get out of the rain. Sorry about your problem, Ginny. Of course, I'll help. You and I have worked together many years. Just let me know what you need."

"Armand, *thank you*. But still another problem. Our one operable van needs to go to the big Maryland gig. I'll drive it and pick up their food from you to deliver myself. But that's our only transportation today. Any chance you might deliver the rest to Great Falls? It's not that far."

"I think we can find somebody to deliver. Give me that address when you e-mail the list. How many people at your events today?"

"Two hundred guests in Maryland. Only forty-five in Great Falls. I have your brochure about how many each platter serves; I'll factor quantities into my e-mail order. Oh, and I need cut flowers for the buffet tables, too. Shall I add those to my list?"

"No problem. And the time of the Great Falls event?"

"By noon to prep for a one o'clock lunch."

"I'll get right on it."

"Armand, a thousand thanks."

"My pleasure, Ginny."

"Oh, one last thing. My bartender for the Great Falls job arrives there at 11:30. Could your driver stay on a couple of hours to pass appetizer trays among the guests? Besides everything else, we're short-staffed today. Rolf knows the ropes and can tell your worker what to do. If I survive this, I may quit the catering business."

"Don't. You're a legend. Nobody can anticipate acts of God like last night's storm." He thought a minute. "Don't your crew wear special outfits?"

"Black trousers, white shirts. If you tell me the person's approximate size, I'll drop off a shirt. We ask them to provide their own trousers. If not black, any dark color works. And black shoes."

"I'll give you the shirt size once I decide who I can spare."

"Thank you, Armand. I owe you a cocktail for this."

He laughed appreciatively. "I'll collect it one day soon."

Armand strolled from his office onto the floor. The grocery buzzed with patrons. He strolled past endcaps of several aisles, glancing down each to assess activity. In the third aisle he spotted a stock boy loading shelves and strolled in his direction. "Are you wearing black slacks?"

"Yes, sir."

"And black shoes?"

"Yes, sir."

"Do you have a valid driver's license?"

"Yes, sir."

"Do you have a cell phone and know how to use GPS to find an address?"

"Yes, sir."

"Then I have a job for you. Say, aren't you're the new hire?"

"Yes, sir."

"Isn't your name," he frowned, "...Arnie?"

"Yes, sir. Arnie Anderson."

CHAPTER 32

"**D**estination ahead on your right." Arnie glanced at his cell phone. Relieved at driving the store's van here without mishap, he double-checked the street number on the iron gate's stone column before turning into the property. The gate stood open. He followed a sign pointing: "Deliveries in the Back."

Arnie circled around the house, passed the rear patio and parked. Uncertain what to do next, he jumped when his cell rang.

"Hi. I'm Rolf, the caterer's bartender. Arnie, is it?"

"Yeah."

"Thanks for helping us out today. Let's unload your truck. Once the stuff's refrigerated inside, I'll show you where to park and explain what to do while you're here. Drive right up to the back entrance. See a door marked 'deliveries'?"

Arnie scanned the house. "Yeah."

"Park in front of that sign. I'll meet you there."

Arnie followed instructions, but as he stepped from the van and walked purposefully to the house, he stopped short when a female voice he recognized said, "Arnie, is that you?"

Glancing up quickly, Arnie couldn't keep his mouth from falling open. "Becca?" He stared dumbstruck at her and at the man with his arm around her.

"Arnie?" she answered.

Barely able to respond, he managed a strangled reply. "Yes."

"What brings you here today?"

He gulped, praying his voice didn't crack. "Caterer."

"Great. Nathan, this is Arnie. He's our neighbor Gerry's friend. They're both in the high school drone club. Arnie, this is my boyfriend, Nathan."

Boyfriend? *What*? Arnie tried to process this shocking information without looking as if he'd been bashed by a brick.

Nathan extended a hand. "I'm with the fire department. We use drones. Want to talk more about them later today?"

Hesitant, Arnie nodded as Nathan shook his hand.

Disarmed by Becca's heart-melting beauty and grateful she'd singled him out for recognition, Arnie tried not to gape hungrily at her. Instead he gave an awkward laugh and hurried toward the delivery door.

When he was out of earshot, Nathan asked, "Is he the guy droning your window?"

Becca nodded. "Or one of two suspects. Both have the voyeur MMO."

"MMO?"

"Motive, method, opportunity."

"Right. Want me to set him straight this afternoon?"

"Would you? But maybe as a gentle big brother instead of a fearsome firefighter? That way he'll stop window-peeking but save face. He's a nice kid, but at that awkward age—and painfully shy."

"I've already faced similar stuff with my younger brothers, so that's easy." Nathan sighed, remembering. "Teen years are tough for guys. Hormones rampant while struggling to learn to deal with powerful urges in civilized ways."

Becca giggled. "And you're an example of this civilized restraint?"

He linked his arm in hers. "Well, at least some of the time."

*****

Arriving fifteen minutes early, Jason drove Jennifer and Grammy through Veronika's open iron gate. Their car circled the impressive three-tiered fountain in the driveway's center. The two women got out, removing an overnight suitcase for Grammy. Veronika welcomed them at the front door, dressed in a flowing batik-print kaftan, her silvery hair pulled back into a long braid.

"We came a few minutes early to help, if needed," Jennifer explained.

Veronika smiled. "The caterer arrived on time. The ponies were delivered to the stable this morning, plus a few horses for adults. I think all is under control."

Jennifer hugged her. "Veronika, you've planned an exciting party. Thanks for doing this."

"My father entertained often and lavishly. I was young and shy then, hovering on each party's fringes. My husband and I entertained a bit during those few years of marriage, but no parties during my later years alone here. So, you might say, celebrating my move is timely *and* overdue. Meantime, please wander around. I'll stay by the front door awhile to greet those arriving."

As they strolled into the mansion, Jennifer touched Jason's arm. "Isn't this a remarkable place? Plus a bonus: we'll see all five children today *and* the many grands. What fun. Why don't we try catering for our next family event?"

"Great idea." Jason took her elbow as they walked through the main floor to the back patio. "Look, there's Dylan now."

Their oldest son and wife hustled over to them, flanked by their kiddies: Asa, Christopher, Ethan and Gabe. After hugs all around, they chattered about recent happenings in their lives.

Dylan looked toward the patio. "Here come Kaela and Owain."

Dylan's son, gregarious seven-year-old Asa, piped up. "And my cousins! Hi, Christine. Hello, Alicia." He high-fived young Milo. Then, tugging at his father's sleeve, he wiggled with excitement. "Can we see the ponies now, Dad? Can we? *Please...*"

Dylan rumpled his boy's hair. "Sure, let's start toward the barn. And on the way we'll add your three little girl cousins, too, because I see Uncle Mike and Aunt Bethany's car parking now."

Beaming, Jennifer touched Jason's hand. "Thank you, my love, for our five. We didn't imagine in those early days how our family could mushroom this way."

Jason put his arm around her. "It amazes me." He looked down at her. "And so do you, my Jen."

She looked up into his eyes. Would he still say this if he knew the eerie web she'd allowed the woman at the garage sale to spin into their private world?

CHAPTER 33

B y twelve-thirty, guests' cars filled all spaces around the house and patio. Children of various ages skipped about, herded by their parents. Others played *bocce* in the yard. Some sat near Jennifer and Jason on the patio, enjoying the gentle June afternoon.

At one o'clock, Veronika strolled through the rooms, ringing a brass handbell and announcing, "Lunch is served in the solarium."

As they descended the stairs from the second floor, Becca relaxed in Nathan's easy company. She checked her watch. "Bobby's an hour late to ogle Veronika's antiques."

As if thinking of Bobby triggered his arrival, the doorbell rang and there he stood, handsome and dapper. As Becca stepped toward him, he hugged her warmly and pressed a lingering kiss against her cheek.

Nathan knew of her temporary job at the antique store and how Bobby fit that scenario, but he wasn't prepared for the man's greeting. Wasn't this a business relationship? He adored Becca, longed to marry her, and would protect that outcome any way necessary.

Becca introduced Bobby to Nathan, and they headed for the buffet. As the two men followed her into the solarium, each felt a tingle of awareness at the unspoken tension over their female prize.

The caterer's colorful display of food and flowers spread across a long, linen-covered buffet table. The elegant result showed no hint of this lavish feast's rocky start that morning.

Following Rolf's instructions, Arnie filled buffet platters and passed appetizer trays among arriving guests. To his amazement and relief, he discovered he could deal with complete strangers just by being attentive and polite. The catering unfolded smoothly.

Guests settled at several tables in the solarium and others scattered around the outdoor patio. Conversation buzzed. When all were served and seated, Veronika rang her bell again. Once attention turned to her, she began. "Thank you for coming today to this double celebration: to show appreciation to the Shannons for adopting me into their warm family circle *and* to celebrate moving from this home of seventy-nine years to my new home at Pebblebrook Manor."

She paused at the outbreak of clapping, cheering and whistles. "For after-lunch entertainment, at the stable you'll find ponies and horses to ride. Also, badminton and *bocce* ball set up in the yard and tennis equipment in the shed beside the court. Feel free to look around my home and wander the property. Eat, drink, play and enjoy."

Grammy rose. "A toast to Veronika, author of today's feast and celebrations."

The guests stood, raised full or empty glasses and cheered appreciation for their hostess.

After a grand lunch, some guests settled back to talk. Others scattered for barn or yard activities. Many explored Veronika's home, where a few hired security personnel on each floor watched to protect her valuable antiques.

Finding the tension between Nathan and Bobby palpable when she was with them, Becca slipped away from her two beaus to explore Veronika's beautifully furnished Old-World upstairs rooms. With her new awareness of antiques, she hoped to see and learn more.

In the Oriental room, she passed elegant hand-painted and carved wooden screens hanging on three of the four walls, original scroll paintings of mountains, oceans and tigers, Cloisonné vases on intricate, carved-wood stands and larger ones on pedestal pillars.

As she lingered at an Asian curio cabinet displaying bronze objects, her eyes widened at the Shang Dynasty bronze ritual wine goblet—this must be the one Veronika described, so much like her mother's recent garage sale find. She slipped it from the shelf to examine. On impulse, she whisked a red sharpie from her purse, turned the goblet upside down and in the small cleft where the three legs met, made a tiny but discernable dot. The red ink melting into the verdigris patina became a nearly invisible tiny black dot.

Only someone who knew to look there would find her mark. Shouldn't affect the relic's value, she reasoned, but she could distinguish it from her mother's, were the two ever together. As the security guard moved toward her, she quickly replaced it on the shelf, smiled at him and moved on to the English room. There she admired Chippendale furniture, oil paintings in gilded frames, artfully crafted silver, and several sets of china and tea sets displayed in glass-fronted cabinets.

"What catches your eye?" asked a familiar voice.

"Grammy, you're wandering this museum also?"

"Veronika's given me the tour many times. She knows stories about most pieces. For instance, she said the oldest porcelain manufacturer in England makes this Royal Crown Derby china. This pattern is called Imari, but the company created many others." They stared at the brilliant Chinese-red and navy-blue colors vivid against white backgrounds and twined with gold accents. Grammy described several other items until a male voice intruded.

"Ah, there you are."

Becca looked up with a smile. "Nathan. Want to continue the tour with us?"

"Wish I could, but I must leave now...a fireman buddy just called me. I promised months ago to sub for him at the station when he takes his wife to the hospital to have their baby. And today's the day. Could you spare a few minutes together before I go?"

At this, Grammy turned toward the door. "You stay here. I'm heading downstairs for dessert."

When she left, Nathan reached for Becca's hand and pulled her into his arms. Hugging her close he said, "How long are you keeping that antique-shop job?"

"Probably until I find the career job I want. Why?"

"Just wondering. Gotta go now, sweet. Love you very much."

"Love you, too."

He kissed her passionately. She returned the kiss in kind. Looking into her eyes, he touched a finger to her lips, turned and hurried out the door.

CHAPTER 34

Hustling to his car, Nathan saw Arnie. Per his promise to Becca, he approached the teen, "Got a minute to talk?"

Arnie felt nervous. He fidgeted. This guy wanted to *marry* Becca. Shaken and defensive, the teen mumbled. "Uh, not really. Gotta help clean up."

"Okay, I'll make this fast. Two things. First thing: please remind your drone club members that looking in people's windows is illegal. No reason for any of them starting life with an arrest on their record. Second thing: how about coming by my fire station next Saturday? I'd like to show you around and talk to you about drones."

Arnie gulped. "Uh, okay."

Nathan scribbled on a piece of paper. "Here's the station's address. See you there Saturday, about 10:00 a.m.?"

"Yeah," Arnie heard himself say. He shoved the paper into his pocket.

*****

Becca found Veronika sitting in a patio chair, her feet elevated on a stool. "Beautiful party. Thanks for sharing your magnificent estate with us. Are you okay?"

Veronika looked up. "Oh yes. Just enjoying a reflective moment."

"I saw the Chinese bronze wine goblet upstairs, the one like my mom's. If you're not taking it to Pebblebrook, might I buy it from you as a Christmas present for my mother? She's so excited about the one she found at the garage sale. I think having a pair would delight her."

Veronika leaned forward, smiling. "You've given me a different idea. Why don't I give it to Jennifer as my personal thanks for her many kindnesses to me?"

"Oh, Veronika, she'd love it."

"Then, consider it done. It will be our secret."

"Won't you miss all these beautiful things after your move to Pebblebrook?"

"I've enjoyed them all, but they were never mine to keep. People come and go; belongings outlast their owners." Veronika pointed to Becca. "You work in an antique store where what you sell was owned before by someone...maybe many someones. Take the ritual wine goblet—how many human hands touched it those thousands of years since the Shang Dynasty? They are gone, but it's still here. We enjoy possessions while we can, and hope others will again, after us."

"The estate sales Mom attends usually sell things belonging to someone who recently died."

"Exactly. Here's another way to look at one's treasures. If you can't bring yourself to part with something, do you own it, or does it own you?"

Becca shivered. "Eerie thought."

"Here's another. Owners tell stories about their possessions, but do things communicate about their owners? Archaeology says ancient items can tell stories about their owners. And here's still another dimension: are objects energized by their owners? Did the Shang goblet receive positive or negative energy from the rituals involving it? Can objects be cursed or charmed?"

Becca shook her head. "Objects are inanimate."

Veronika's eyes twinkled. "Imbuing inanimate objects with mysterious energy is an ancient, yet persistently modern, idea. Consider a lucky charm, a talisman or the Greek 'eye of protection.'"

"Nobody believes that stuff now. It's superstition."

Veronika shrugged. "Then how do we explain Harry Potter's popularity?"

Becca shrugged. "No matter how much magic entertains us, we know it's illusion...not real."

Veronika sat straighter in her chair. She began to stare at Becca long enough that the girl felt uncomfortable. Was the woman having a small stroke?

Veronika's lips compressed. An odd expression clouded her face. "Do...do you smell lilacs?"

Becca sniffed the air in front of her, then left and right. She shook her head.

Veronika couldn't seem to break her stare. "You...I must..." She stopped speaking, blinked, and started over. "May I give you something? Well, not a gift exactly. More like a loan." She pulled her kaftan to her knee, revealing an ankle bracelet, but one such as Becca had never seen. Unfastening the bracelet, she put it in Becca's hand. "As a favor to me, will you please wear this awhile to...ah, to let me thank you for being my friend." She touched Becca's arm. "Will you?"

"Well, sure... I guess. But what is it?" Becca studied the leather connecting tiny stones, seeds, claws, animal teeth, textile beads and wood slivers, all fastened with an etched wooden bead which fit into a leather loop on one end.

"My amulet, but you...but I ask you to wear it until...it's time to return it to me. Soon. I'll tell you when." She smiled disarmingly. "Okay?"

Weird, Becca thought, but in a world where you can be anything, why not be kind. She'd humor this well-meaning old woman, however medieval her views. "Okay..." Becca fastened it on her own ankle. "Thanks, Veronika, for sharing it with me."

Dead serious now, Veronika pointed her finger at Becca. "Remember, don't take it off until I tell you."

"Even in the shower?"

Veronika's voice lowered to a whisper. "*Don't* take it off until I tell you."

The woman's intensity scared Becca. Puzzled, but knowing she'd do what she promised, Becca said, "Okay...not until you tell."

CHAPTER 35

At that moment, elsewhere in Veronika's house, Jennifer spotted Sally and Greg Bromley. "Hello. How are you newlyweds a year later?"

Greg hugged Jennifer. "Better than ever, thanks to your introducing us after your surprising detective work."

Sally added her hug. "You were the only person who recognized our unlikely link to the same wonderful boy...well, he's a man now, our Adam."

Jennifer grinned. "Exciting, wasn't it?"

Greg grinned. "We're both so proud of Adam...and Hannah. And now they're parents, too."

Jennifer pointed at them. "Which makes you..."

"*Grandparents*," they chorused happily.

Jennifer winked. "Fun, isn't it?"

They nodded enthusiastically.

"Greg, if you have a minute this afternoon, may I ask you more about that adoption agency—the same one we discussed regarding Adam's adoption?"

"Why not now?"

As Sally excused herself to mingle elsewhere, Jennifer stepped closer, speaking confidentially to the respected McLean attorney. "A friend who raised a child she thought was her dead sister's biological daughter recently discovered adoption papers for the girl. Meantime, the girl, by this time a 43-year-old adult, died under circumstances I think mysterious. The agency you once worked with, Tri-State Adoption, is named on her documents, but shows only the adoptive parents, not the biological parents. Can we find out who they are?"

"Tough. You may remember the company went out of business about ten years ago. I'm not sure I can get my hands on their archived records now. But I'll look into it."

"The name, 'Tri-State Adoption Agency' operated in which three states?"

"Virginia, Maryland and Pennsylvania. How are you involved in this?"

"I saw the girl, Katherine Kalinsky, at a couple of garage sales, thinking maybe I knew her. But before I could talk with her, I read her obit in the *Post*. On a whim, I attended the viewing and met the aunt who raised her. Katie died of carbon monoxide poisoning in her car in a closed garage—apparently accident or suicide. But I'm doubtful, especially in view of the ME's report that she was pregnant. If there's foul play, police need proof. For that reason, I'm trying to put a larger picture together. The adoption's a puzzle piece."

"Was she married?"

"No."

"She wouldn't be the first desperate unwed mother to become suicidal over her situation."

"You're right, but I'm not ready yet to rule out other possible explanations."

"I'll let you know what I learn. How soon do you need this?"

"ASAP. Sorry."

"I hear ASAP a lot." He sipped his drink. "By the way, Jennifer, since my son is married to your daughter, I want you and Jason to know I'll follow through today with a salary offer on my earlier invitation for him to join my law firm as chief investigator. He's a fine policeman, well-connected and now has additional exposure at Homicide. Since he's a father now, I'll remind him investigating for me pays better than his current job."

"And is safer." Jennifer sighed. "Police wives hope their husbands live to come home each night."

Greg nodded. "I know he's loyal to the Fairfax County P.D., and God knows we want high caliber officers like him there, but now he'll have a choice. Just want you to know what's going on."

"Thanks, Greg."

"You might guess I have an ulterior motive in this."

Jennifer smiled. "You'd like more time with your son, and working together provides it."

"You got it."

"Adam's decisions affect my Hannah and baby Zealand, and we love Adam like a son." She smiled. "So I have three horses in your race."

A woman walked up to them. "Hello, Jennifer."

"Hello, Aubrey. May I introduce attorney Greg Bromley. Greg, meet Aubrey Bishop, a real-estate agent I met at..."

He guessed, "...a garage sale?"

Jennifer giggled. "You know me too well."

Aubrey smiled "In fact, I already know Greg. He's handled some of my real-estate closings."

"Small world."

"This property's fabulous." Aubrey gestured toward the window, beyond which lay the garage, stable and wooded acres. "All local agents know about this place, but this is my first time here. Thanks for inviting me to see it and talk with Veronika about a potential sale."

"Maybe you can help her solve one of her two biggest problems: selling this property for a good price in a way that, hopefully, preserves its natural setting."

Greg cocked an eyebrow. "What's the other big problem?"

"Finding honest dealers to buy her valuable antiques and furnishings for the best price."

CHAPTER 36

A few minutes later, Aubrey Bishop prowled Veronika's mansion, familiarizing herself with real-estate details needed for her proposal. She snapped cell-phone pictures and jotted notes, before heading outside into the June sunshine to check the stable. As she counted the stalls, a good-looking man galloped up beside her and dismounted.

"Hello, pretty lady," he said. Looking closer he showed a flash of recognition, followed by confusion. "Katie?"

She shook her head. "Aubrey Bishop, real-estate agent."

"You...you look just like someone—someone I worked with." Recovering from this distraction, he hurried to add, "How do you fit into the Shannon family?"

"A family friend."

"What a coincidence; so am I. Bobby Radner from Radner Antiquities."

Aubrey introduced herself and they exchanged business cards.

"Do you ride?"

"I have, but not recently."

"Want to go for a gallop?"

"Okay, but more like a trot. *And* an easy way for me to scope the property. Lucky I met you here today."

"The luck's all mine." He called to the hired stable groom. "Got a gentle mount for this lovely lady?"

"Yes, sir. Saddled and ready to go."

*****

On the patio under the shade of a large maple, Adam cuddled Zealand in his arms. "Is he asleep?" he asked Hannah.

"Yes. Shall we put him in his baby seat?"

He nodded and managed the transfer without waking the child. "While I'm here, I want to look at security on Veronika's property—inside her house and also around the land's perimeter. Want to come along?"

"Sure. I'll find a grandparent to watch Z while we're gone." She returned in a few minutes, trailed by Sally and Greg. "Make that two grandparents."

Adam laughed. "How lucky can a little boy get?"

Hannah pointed to a chair. "There's a bottle in the diaper bag if he fusses, or I'm only a cell-phone call away."

Sally shooed them. "Have a nice walk together and don't worry."

*****

Arnie sat in a shady spot outside the servant entrance, eating from the buffet plate Rolf told him to fill. "What craziness," he marveled to himself. Plucked from his boring job at the store to spend the day in a mansion on an estate...wow! And this quality meal sure beat fast-food. He got along well with Rolf, who obviously knew catering well. But the day's thrill: seeing his secret love, Becca. He hadn't figured how all these guests fit together until she explained it, chatting with *him* when he served her his appetizer tray.

"Veronika's my mother's friend," she'd told him. "When we learned she had no family left of her own, my family asked her to join ours. Then she and my grandmother met and became instant friends. They're both in their late 80s and both are moving to the same senior residence. Veronika's about to sell her fabulous estate that's been her home since she came here from Russia at age ten. With such deep roots in this place, she's brave to leave."

Arnie prayed he didn't appear the goggle-eyed idiot he felt like when in her presence. He tried to nod at the right junctures as she talked, but his fascination with her every movement made his heart thump and his hands clammy. Each time she looked directly at him he feared he might pass out.

"How long have you worked with catering?"

"What? Ah... today. Started today."

"Well, you learned fast. How do you like the job?"

"Ah...good."

"Thanks, Arnie, for telling Gerry to stop droning my windows."

His mouth opened. Was this a trick? Did she know he did it alone?

He gulped. "Okay." Then, in a burst of bravery that appalled him, he heard himself say, "Nathan...Nathan is your...

"My boyfriend. We've dated about two years now. He wants to get married but..."

His voice came out in a strangled cry. "*Married*?"

"...but I'm not ready yet. I may try a career first."

"*Career*?" he parroted, his voice cracking.

"Not sure which yet. Well, there's Nathan. See you later."

As she walked away, Arnie trembled from warring emotions coursing through him. Adoration for Becca. Jealousy for rival Nathan, who offered her so much more than he ever could, who held her hand, who put his arm around her, who wanted to *marry* her. He cringed at facing reality, admitting the horror that she moved in a whole different circle than he could. What had he to offer her when this successful firefighter wanted to claim her?

His despair increased as he stared awestruck at this mansion and the unattainable lifestyle it represented. He hungered to be part of a warm, congenial family like the Shannons, who adopted strangers like Veronika. Despair grew over his own situation, followed by frustration at his inability to change his pathetic life. And finally, rage seethed toward Magda, and even his dad, for creating this nightmare for him.

Though he sat in shade, sweat glistened on his face and trickled from his armpits. He choked back the desire to vomit, which he dared not do here to disgust people he wanted to like him. He grudgingly admitted that Becca operated in an unattainable league worlds apart from his. He had no chance with her. The four-year gap in their ages made too huge a difference now. Dejected, he knew he had to pull himself together to finish today's job. Five minutes later he straggled into the solarium. "You need me anymore, Rolf?"

"Help me gather the leftovers on these disposable trays. Then refrigerate them for the customer's future use. The flowers stay on tables. A few things to wash up and we head for home."

Thirty minutes later, Arnie walked toward the grocery van parked behind the stable. He ducked into the stable's shade and, curious, wandered into an empty horse stall. Hearing hoofbeats closing in, he shrank against the wall.

As Bobby and Aubrey returned from their ride and dismounted, the stable groom took their horses.

"May I see you again very soon?" Bobby asked his riding companion.

Attracted to his suave, confident manner and good looks, Aubrey said, "Perhaps...."

"How about dinner tomorrow?"

"Maybe..."

"May I pick you up?"

"No thanks. I'll be out on real-estate business anyway. Easier to meet you."

"Not all restaurants are open Sunday nights. I'll find just the right place and phone. Your number is on your business card?"

"Of course. By the way, what does a dealer like you think about this mansion's antiques?"

"Lots of valuable pieces. Got plenty of photos. I hope to buy a number of them."

"Well, got to go. Pleasant meeting you today, Bobby."

"Goodbye for now, beautiful lady."

On impulse, he kissed her.

Caught off guard, Aubrey had seconds to react. Pull away? Tell him off? Say nothing? Offer a flirtatious farewell?

To her surprise, she responded to his kiss. Her arms circled around him. When they finally eased apart, she smiled to show she enjoyed it, and walked away, conscious of the feminine sway of her hips. She chuckled as she got into her car, glanced at her reflection in the rearview mirror and said aloud to nobody, "Did you really just do that? What were you thinking? You're twice his age. Let him down easy when he calls about dinner tomorrow night."

When she drove away, Bobby waved to her from the stable. Then, seeing nobody else around, he dialed his cell phone and spoke in a low voice. "Hi. Yeah, I'm there now. Exterior security minimal. Great grabs inside. Like a museum. Where's your guy now? Okay. I'll text what I want. When will you have it for me? Okay. Meet you same place as before. Yeah, I leave here within the hour."

Bobby pocketed his phone and strolled away to find Veronika and discuss antiques purchasing.

The stable fell silent behind him, except for an occasional whinny. A few minutes later Arnie crept out of the stall where he had hidden. He'd witnessed Aubrey and Bobby's exchange through a hole in the stall's wall. As he walked the few steps to the van, he mentally replayed the eavesdropped phone conversation. Had he heard what he thought he did? Did it mean what it seemed to mean? If so, who should he tell? Veronika? The police?

As Arnie climbed into the van for the drive back to the grocery store, an answer came to him. For one final chance: he'd tell Becca.

CHAPTER 37

Gesturing toward the door of her wood-paneled den, Veronika touched Jennifer's elbow. "Would you come into my office for a minute?"

"Of course. This gives me a quiet moment to thank you again for this remarkable party."

"You are most welcome. But now something new, Jennifer. Last night I smelled lilacs, which, you may remember, signals a vision coming...and one did. In the vision, I saw that dreadful antique dealer, Robert Radner, coming to harm you. In fact, I felt the force of his family threatening your family. This seemed vague at first, so I almost didn't tell you. But, Jennifer, my awareness is much stronger today. I feel this dark energy growing toward terrible confrontation with you and yours... coming very soon. You need to know the Radners pose danger for you and your loved ones."

"Then we'll take extra care. I don't understand your visions, but I respect them. Thank you for the warning."

Veronika bit her lip. "Jennifer, there's more. Before I move, I need to...I want to give you something. I won't need it anymore, but you...you could need it soon."

"This party's the best gift I could imagine."

"No, this is different. Do you remember when my Russian half-sister, Anna, lived with me and was murdered..." she looked around, "in this very room. The week before, she surprised me with an unusual present. At that time, I feared she wished me dead so she could sue to inherit this property, but her gift preserved my life instead. Thus, her gift was strategic to my being here today. It came into my possession just when I needed it. Now the need is yours."

Puzzled but intrigued, Jennifer wondered what this meant.

From her oversized hand-carved wooden desk, Veronika removed a box and placed it in Jennifer's hands. "The Russian word on top in Cyrillic script translates to 'candy,' camouflaging the true contents. This box is called a custom presentation case. Open it, please."

Jennifer lifted the lid. Her jaw dropped. She frowned, shaking her head in confusion.

"My sister gave me this unusual antique pistol. You'll find ammunition in the box's closed compartment. Press that little button. See, the drawer pops open. Notice the ornately engraved surface, elaborate etched design and the lustrous mother-of-pearl handle. It's a remarkable artistic achievement but also a fully functional pistol. My sister was told this weapon belonged to the Romanoff family. I believe it, because only someone fabulously wealthy could have commissioned such an exquisite lady's weapon. The small size allows concealment in a pocket or a small purse."

Jennifer marveled at the box. "Look at these compartments: a special niche for the gun, another for cartridges, but also these small brushes, rods and the patches of cloth."

"Cleaning tools. Yes, the box alone is clearly old and designed to house this specific weapon. Imagine the craftsmanship for a pistol that still works perfectly today."

"Who do you suppose fired it last?"

"I did, Jennifer. I...I killed my sister's murderer when he turned his gun on me. The police called it clear self-defense and filed no charges against me. Because of Anna's Russian involvement with those Middle Eastern terrorists, Homeland Security further hushed up the incident."

Jennifer's eyes widened at this revelation.

"I assure you, the pistol fires true, but of course success depends upon the user's skill. I practiced shooting it on my own estate, but you might need a firing range. I had these modern cartridges especially made for shooting practice, but you should load the gun with the original ones to ensure it works best."

Jennifer locked eyes with Veronika. "You're serious about this, aren't you?"

"Deadly serious. Here, I'll show you how this Derringer works. You load it like this." She showed how to open it. "It's called an over-and-under gun because one cartridge goes here on top and the other below. Then you close the pistol and cock the hammer, like this, each time you shoot. But there's one problem."

Jennifer thought a gun in her possession was problem enough. "Oh?"

"This little gun fires only two shots before you must reload. So choose your targets well."

"I'll lock the gun in my car right now and go to a shooting range tomorrow."

As she walked the box to her vehicle, Jennifer replayed their conversation. Veronika spoke of clear, imminent danger from Radner's family. She remembered Robert Radner's believable threat at the garage sale when he snarled: "You'll regret this." Yet that seemed remote until now.

A gun to protect from sudden danger must stay handy and loaded. Did that mean in her purse when she left her house? Wouldn't she need a carry permit? But Veronika indicated the threat also affected her family. Was that limited to Jason and

Becca, living in the same house with her, or did the net cast a shadow over her other children?

Her children, the grands—they all visited frequently and had the run of the house. How could she safely keep a loaded pistol near her fingertips there?

CHAPTER 38

At the party's end, Jennifer and Jason hugged their hostess, thanking her again for the party.

"First to arrive and last to leave," Jennifer observed. "Easy to see we had a terrific time. You thought of *everything*." For Veronika to see but not Jason, her finger mimed a pistol barrel and her thumb the hammer. "Fabulous food, exciting entertainment, and a museum-quality tour of your home. We'll all talk about this day for many years."

Veronika covered her sly nod with a smile. "And thank *you* for bringing the real-estate agent and the antiques buyer. They plan homework tonight to give me feedback tomorrow."

Grammy joined them on the front porch. "You remember I'm overnighting here, so I won't ride back with you now."

Jason shifted a sack from one hand to the other. "Thanks again for these leftovers. Are you both ready for the move to Pebblebrook?"

Veronika clasped her hands. "Yes. Pebblebrook maintenance people even hang pictures and mirrors for us. And if a lightbulb burns out, they change it. How convenient is that?"

Jason laughed. "Too bad we can't move in, too."

They started down the driveway toward their car, but as they opened its doors, a car rocketed into the driveway and pulled to a stop next to Jason.

Out jumped Hannah. "Sorry, we forgot Z's bottles in your refrigerator. May I dash to get them?"

"Of course," Veronika laughed.

Jason climbed into their car, but instead, Jennifer walked over to tap on Adam's driver-side window. When he lowered it, she said quietly, "How can I get a look at the ME's DNA results for Katie Kalinsky's fetus?"

His head sank forward. "You still worrying about that case?"

"Look, you need facts. I need some tools to get those facts."

"You know that's confidential information."

"What if Katie's aunt requests it?"

"Yeah, I guess so, but what will it prove?"

"Another link to help us see where the chain leads."

Resigned, he sighed. "Okay, if her aunt requests it, I'll help it along if I can." He looked at her defensively. "You're not the typical mother-in-law."

Jennifer chuckled. "And I'm happy to say you're not the typical son-in-law..."

"But" he added grudgingly, "you do have a good nose for case-solving."

She brightened. "Why, Adam, thank you."

"Though often in wild ways that risk your safety... and sometimes the family's...." His voice trailed off.

Jennifer deliberately changed the subject. "What did you learn about Veronika's security."

"Not good. Her land's wide open to trespassing and the house is poorly protected. They're way out here where police can't respond immediately in case of trouble. I'll put my notes together for her. Then she can decide what to do. You know she's leaving in a few days. Maybe she won't think security is important when she and her staff vacate."

Jennifer tapped a finger on the car window's ledge. "Won't your notes remind her it's quite necessary?"

"I hope so. She's hired a security house-sitter when she leaves, but one person isn't enough to protect her house and its contents—even if she had an elaborate camera system, which she doesn't."

Hannah appeared at the front door and skipped down the steps holding baby bottles.

"All set," she called, climbing into the car. "Thanks again, Veronika. We had a terrific time. Bye to all."

Adam revved his motor and they sped away.

Veronika and Grammy waved from the porch until the driveway emptied, and then went inside.

As Jason drove through the iron gate, he turned to Jennifer. "Are you...are you fishing for trouble again?"

"Of course not. Only regular fishing, like always."

She smiled at the windshield.

CHAPTER 39

SUNDAY

T he next morning, Arnie crept down the back stairs of his Great Falls house with Toby tucked under his arm. After breakfast at McDonald's, he'd stop by a park for an hour so as not to reach Gerry's house too early on a Sunday. Then routine friend-and-drone stuff most of the day, except for one special thing—not routine at all. Something daring and scary he'd make himself do. Knocking on Becca's front door to tell her what he'd heard at the stable.

Just a few more steps would take him out his back door, across the driveway and into his car. Inches from success, he eased open the back door of his house. Then it happened: the sharp pinch of fingers on a hand clamped on his shoulder...and Magda's dreaded whine.

"Good morning, Arnie. We haven't seen much of you lately. Since you hardly use your room anymore, we plan to clean out your garbage and decorate it as a nice guest room for the house. So here's notice in case you want to keep anything before it's tossed. This is Sunday. You have until Wednesday to get your stuff out."

Flickers of the friendly Shannon and Wilberforce families flashed through his mind. They weren't like this. It didn't have to be like this. The outrage of injustice suddenly pumped him with such courage that, to his horror, he spun around and shouted. "You can't do this. Even you know this isn't right. I'm just a kid. Why do you treat me like this?"

To his amazement, Magda stood speechless, her eyes blinked with incredulity. Had he called her bluff? Was this all it took? Then why hadn't he stood up for himself sooner? But as he watched, her face reddened. Her brows knitted over laser-like eyes. She bristled with a frightening *new* malevolence never before displayed, a lethal force he felt even before her cruel words shot out like a machine-gun barrage.

"*Talk back to me, will you*? Well, there's a *penalty* for that. Now you must get your stuff out by Monday. That's tomorrow. Or I promise you'll see none of it ever again."

He rushed out the door, lurched into his car and sped away. His brain whirred in confusion. How could he tell his dad about this to get help? His father never answered Arnie's calls to his mobile phone. That was hopeless. With his father's office closed on Sunday, phoning him there today to bypass Magda was out. She didn't say what time she'd ditch his stuff on Monday. Just like her to do it at 8:00 a.m. or earlier. He needed to move his things out tonight. He'd get empty cardboard boxes at the grocery, but how many would he need and, once packed, would they fit in his car along with Toby's cat litter, food bowls and pet bed?

Fear of Magda dashed any hope of wandering through the house to find his dad if he was even at home. His unpredictable business travel included frequent weekends as well as weekdays. Magda alone had his father's ear and knew his schedule. God knows what she'd told him about Arnie. Maybe she said turning his space into a guest room was *his* idea? He put nothing past her.

Where could a kid his age live without a family? Go to a homeless shelter? Ask to live in a friend's basement? Enlist in the military? Hit the streets? He grimaced. He almost lived at Gerry's house now.

Twenty minutes later, he guessed he looked like any other teenager in line at McDonald's. Sitting in his car with his breakfast purchase near the park's entrance, he looked like any other young McLean high school student on summer break. But Arnie knew his miserable life distinguished him from McLean look-alikes. They might as well live on different planets.

Driving at last to Gerry's neighborhood, he parked down the road, as usual. Then, he and Toby walked to Gerry's house.

A car he didn't recognize parked in front. Should he go inside if the family had unexpected company? Even if they did, he guessed Gerry would want to extricate himself ASAP. He knocked on the door, which Gerry opened.

"Hey, man. You're just in time." He reached down to pet Toby.

"In time for what?"

Gerry clapped his friend on the shoulder. "You'll see."

They stepped into the living room, where Gerry's parents sat on either side of a uniformed policeman on the couch.

Arnie froze.

"Hello. You must be Arnie Anderson. I'm Detective Adam Iverson. Could we talk a few minutes?"

Arnie glanced around at the Wilberforce family, trying not to show the panic he felt. "Sure," he heard himself say.

Adam turned to Gerry's parents. "Have you somewhere Arnie and I can converse privately?"

Matt Wilberforce stood. "How about the den? You can close the door. Here, I'll show you."

Once seated there, Adam took out his notebook and turned to Arnie. "Thanks for talking with me. Mind if we start with the routine stuff: name, age, address, phone?"

Arnie recited the information.

"You know about the situation next door with Mrs. Ogleby?"

Arnie gave a small nod.

"Gerry said you helped him use the drone that discovered her. Right?"

Arnie nodded again.

"What was your reaction?"

"I guess...ah, surprise?"

"So...had you ever met Mrs. Ogleby?"

Arnie shifted position. He'd struggled to shape a plan for this very confrontation, but without success.

"Yeah."

A seasoned detective, Adam knew the boy's nervous body-language weighed into whatever he said. "How *did* you meet her?"

Arnie gulped a thready breath and began....

CHAPTER 40

"Toby and I were walking down the street from where I parked my car."

"Toby?"

"My cat."

Adam nodded.

"When we passed Mrs. Ogleby's house, she called to me from her front porch to, like, help her move some boxes. I said okay. She walked me to her garage at the end of the driveway. Inside, I moved four boxes, and, like, they weighed a lot. She warned me books were heavy as bricks. Man, was she right."

Adam. "And then..."

"She...she wanted to pay me. Told me to wait on the back porch while she got the money. She gave me $10.00, said it was two dollars each box and a two-dollar tip. And then..."

The policeman looked at Arnie. "And then..."

The boy drew a ragged breath. "And then...I...I left."

Iverson studied the boy. Was his nervousness a tell, or just a kid scared of the uniform and what it represents? "Would you say she acted normal?"

Arnie shrugged. "Like, who knows what's normal for her? I mean, she hoards. Is that normal?"

Adam stifled a smile and jotted a note on his pad. "Anything else that might help us?"

Arnie shrugged again, his hands palms up.

"Okay, Arnie. This tracks with a neighbor who saw you walking with her down Mrs. Ogleby's driveway to the garage, earlier on the day your drones found her." He noticed Arnie's relief. Remembering sister-in-law Becca's request, Adam tapped his pen on his notepad. "And that brings up something else. Not even police are legally allowed to conduct drone surveillance without official probable cause; certainly not civilians like you. We understand Mrs. Ogelby's case was unusual. Even so, looking in people's windows without their permission is invasion of privacy and illegal. So if you find yourself in another such situation with genuine concern about a neighbor's problem, work with police, not on your own. Do you understand?"

Arnie nodded sheepishly.

"Do you understand?" he repeated.

"Yes, sir."

"Now let's talk about drones. You already know they're remarkable tools. You'll find lots of takers for your drone expertise. You might even shape a career around drone operations. Police can use them for tactical support—like searching for missing children, event documentation, surveillance of barricaded individuals and bomb threats, documenting traffic accidents, to mention a few. Police departments not using them yet are investigating how to do so because they're extremely useful. Just learn and heed the legal restrictions so you don't break the law as spelled out on the *FAA Drone Regulations* website, or, for our local take, *FAA Dronezone*."

Adam tore a page from his notepad. "Here, I've written those down for you. Good luck, son. Thanks for talking with me, Arnie." He stood and opened the den door.

Matt Wilberforce accompanied the policeman to the front door and shook his hand. "Thanks for keeping an eye on our community, Detective."

"You're welcome. Goodbye."

Gerry hustled over to Arnie. "All good?"

Arnie shrugged. "Yeah."

Connie looked at her husband. "Do you think this ends the Ogleby investigation?"

Matt shrugged. "Looks like it. Good thing you dug up her relative's name and phone number."

"She gave it to me years ago. I thought I'd lost it but finally remembered the file."

Matt tucked the morning newspaper under his arm. "Suppose her relative will sell the house or move in next door?"

Gerry grabbed two apples from a fruit bowl and tossed one to Arnie. "First they'll have to, like, ditch all her *stuff*."

His father shook his head. "You're right. What a job."

Gerry's mother looked thoughtful. "Maybe her Will's in there somewhere."

Gerry laughed, "Or they'll destroy it if it says they don't inherit her house."

Arnie nudged Gerry. "Now *you're* talking like a detective."

"Hah, that'd make me The Drone Detective."

Arnie smiled. "What color cape and goggles? What symbol across your chest?" The two boys guffawed at this awesome vision.

Then, in the teen version of short attention span, Gerry jumped to his feet. "So, Arnie. Before we take the drones to the field, wanna go up to my room and do some YouTube?"

As they thumped up the stairs, Connie closed the door and sat closer to her husband. "Matt, what do you make of Arnie these days?"

"Quiet, but that's how he is."

"I wonder if his cat problem is a symptom of something more—maybe trouble at home."

"What do you mean?"

"Well, if our Gerry had a brother with a German shepherd, would we allow it to terrorize Gerry's cat so much that he had to find a different home for his pet or make it live in his car?"

Matt shrugged. "Uh, put that way, you're right. It *is* odd. Should we ask Arnie about it?"

"And risk him withdrawing further? Maybe not. Most kids his age want to fit in, not stand out because of their problems. Why don't we try to give him some attention and encouragement? If I'm right, and if he learns to trust us, maybe he'll volunteer what's going on."

"Don't we already treat all Gerry's friends almost like they're our own kids?"

"Maybe, but I think this might be different. You know, Gerry's an only child and, for now at least, Arnie's his best friend. Do you think we could open our hearts to this boy the way we've opened our doors?"

Matt looked uncomfortable. "Why didn't I notice all this?"

"You notice things I don't. Maybe just another example of how we complement each other."

He studied Connie then took her hand and pulled her to her feet. "Have I told you today how much I like you?"

Her eyebrows rose and she tucked in her chin. "*Like* me?"

"Yeah. It makes loving you even easier."

CHAPTER 41

J ennifer studied the Sunday morning garage sales on her list. After their preparation and advertising, many sellers listed two-day sales for a second chance to display any unsold merchandise. She noticed all today's ops were indeed yesterday-spillovers. No need to repeat. This decision opened her day for other activities.

Usually the first person awake in her house, she sipped coffee while lingering over Sunday's *Washington Post*. Then she added her kitchen desk calendar to the table and started a to-do list.

Help Grammy with Upcoming Move? She paused. Her mother had spent last night at Veronika's after the party. Who knew how quickly she'd return to the rental house across the street? Would Veronika's driver bring her home, or would she call Jen for a ride? After her original notation, she wrote: *Call first.*

Call Aunt Jean re: Katie baby DNA request. How to approach the woman? Did closure appeal to Jean now more than intrigue? Had Jean the energy to focus on justice for Katie, wherever that led? Jennifer's pencil point tapped the paper.

This outcome was too important for a phone call; she should drop by Jean's house to talk.

Phone Hannah re: settling into new house

Carry permit?

Shooting range

In case Jason or Becca saw her list, she shortened "carry permit" to *carry* and "shooting range" to *range*. She understood, but they wouldn't.

Last night, driving home in the car, Jen had told Jason about Veronika's vision.

He'd said, "Always smart to lock outside house doors and keep the garage door closed. You know, I don't like any threat of danger for you or our family, Jen. It's my job to protect you all. You make that harder for me to do when your actions put us at risk." He looked over at her, his face dead serious, "...and you know that's already happened several times."

She wanted to tell him about the antique pistol Veronika thought she might need, but when she saw how the vision-news upset him, she didn't. Why worry him further...especially if he knew she wanted to figure how to keep it armed and instantly available until this situation resolved?

Back at home, they'd parked in the garage and gone inside the house together. After he walked upstairs, she'd retrieved the boxed weapon from the car and hidden it temporarily in the laundry room.

But that was last night. Too early to make phone calls on a Sunday morning, so she padded barefoot across the sunporch and onto the patio. Descending the brick steps, she inched her feet into the backyard's cool grass. How she loved the way nature strummed her senses. She quieted the impulse to pull weeds or pinch spent blossoms she passed. Instead, she reveled in the rich colors and textures her gardening efforts created.

Wandering down the path to the gazebo, Jen stepped inside, eased onto a cushioned chair, and propped her feet on the coffee table. Closing her eyes, she savored a quiet count-your-blessings moment. With Jason operating as the level-headed, practical half of their relationship, she could unspool her curiosity and adventurous inclinations. A picture floated into her mind of Jason standing strong on a hillside, firmly holding onto one of her ankles as a gas-filled balloon lifted her toward the sky. He was her anchor. She was his sail.

"Jen? You okay?"

She looked toward the voice. Jason stood at the patio door. She waved. "Just vegging. Be right in."

He shuffled back inside.

She lay back again, eyes closed, breathing deeply. Bird songs from nearby trees in her yard and the parkland beyond sounded clear. She sniffed the breeze-wafted fragrance from blossoms somewhere close.

In the distractions and urgencies of busy daily life, she missed these gentle moments, even though she need only wander to her own back yard to indulge in them.

With tasks arranged on her to-do list, she felt her mind clear of distractions and open for creativity.

A few minutes later, her eyes snapped open. She knew exactly how to safely keep Veronika's small loaded pistol instantly accessible day and night.

CHAPTER 42

Sunday afternoon, Jennifer cleared away lunch dishes and picked up the phone.

"Hello, Aunt Jean. Have you time this afternoon for me to help you start emptying those stored boxes? Okay, in about 45 minutes? Right. See you then."

She grabbed her purse and headed toward the garage, where Jason toiled in his workshop. "Why aren't you relaxing on this lovely June Sunday afternoon?"

Clamping glued boards into a vice, he looked up. "I'm working here, Jen. Need something?"

"What's your project?"

"You mean which project? Shelves for the basement storeroom here. Materials to repair the broken kitchen drawer there. And way over there," he pointed, "is a bow repair...."

"*Bow* repair?"

"As in bow-and-arrow. For one of the grands. Then there's..."

"I get the picture. You plan a productive afternoon."

He sighed. "Somebody's got to do this stuff and, truth is, I kinda enjoy using my engineering knowledge in practical ways around the house. Working weekdays, I have only weekends to...."

"Got it. Would this Happy Builder Boy like a snack or a drink before I dash out on a few errands?"

"I already have bottled water by that upside-down glass...to keep sawdust out. Thanks anyway, hon. When will you come back?"

"Latest, in time to cook dinner. Probably sooner. I invited Grammy to eat with us tonight. Want to grill?"

"Sure."

"What?"

"How about wild-caught salmon if they have it? Have we any Allegro Hickory-smoke Marinade left?

"I'll buy extra just in case. Bye, Jay. Love you."

He put down his pliers and leaned close for a kiss. "I love you, too. Hurry back to me."

Jennifer climbed into her car and headed toward Jean Abingdon's house. Jean greeted her, in apparent good spirits, and together they headed to the basement.

"Have you opened all the boxes?"

"Just the one."

"Once we look inside, we'll understand the job better."

Jean nodded, grateful for someone to guide her.

"Shall we take along some tools?" At Jean's blank look, Jen suggested, "A knife to open boxes, scotch tape, a sharpie, paper and pencils for notes or labels and some large plastic bags?"

"The fall leaf-gathering kind?"

"Yes. We'll need a few."

They carried these to the basement. "Probably easiest to sit here on the floor by the boxes."

Jean nodded. They sat cross-legged as Jennifer sliced open all the cartons and folded back the flaps to expose the contents. "Before we take anything out, how about four categories? Keep. Donate. Toss. Defer. The Toss pile goes directly into a leaf bag.

Would you make a sign for each pile, so we remember? Good. So, how did you get these boxes?"

"When Katie's parents died in that accident, I drove to their house in Maryland to arrange a funeral and to bury them. I took a month's leave from the library to help Katie through the ordeal, to find a Realtor to sell their house and to bring her home with me. She was grieving, confused and miserable. What twelve-year-old girl could handle all that without an adult around to lean on? With her parents gone, her home, her friends and her school were all she had left of her life there, but I had to take her away from all of those to bring her here."

Jennifer touched her arm. "What a difficult time for you both."

Jean nodded. "We packed up her things and selected some framed photos from the rooms plus anything special she wanted to keep. She chose a few things, not much. During that month I also went through all the closets and drawers to take along whatever looked important, and finally brought these unopened boxes and the footlocker because I hadn't the stamina or the will to unpack them at the time. After storing them here in the basement, I forgot about them in my efforts to give Katie attention. I still worked at the library then, you know. Now, these are all I have left of any of my family, and when I finally go, whatever's here will be lost for good. That's why I need to sort through it now."

Jennifer opened the footlocker's hasps and lifted the lid. "Looks like winter clothes. Shall I take them out for you? Perhaps you'll find something you can use. If not, maybe donate?"

Jean nodded while Jennifer handed her pieces of clothing to evaluate. "I'll keep this wool scarf with matching gloves." She put most remaining items into Donation and threw damaged items into the Toss bag.

Jennifer studied the footlocker's empty interior space, then eyed the outside. "Look, this may have a false bottom." She compared the outside vertical dimension with the inside: a three-inch difference. "Do you have a tape-measure, a hammer and screwdriver or crowbar?"

Jean left briefly, returning with the tools. Jennifer attempted to loosen the interior bottom, but it wouldn't budge. Neither did her determination. She gouged a hole through the base on one corner by hammering on the vertical screwdriver. She pried at that hole with the crowbar until the bottom splintered enough for her to pry the rest up with the hammer's claw.

They gasped.

CHAPTER 43

Staring at the footlocker's original floor, their eyes met in a "do-you-see-what-I-see?" exchange. Five- and ten-dollar bills littered the space. At one end lay two drawstring pouches.

"Oh, my." Jean's hand covered her mouth.

"Inherited or second-hand items passed through other hands before yours. Wonder if your sister bought this footlocker new or got it used with these things already hidden."

Jean gathered the money into a stack. "Maybe we'll find a clue in the pouches. I'll count this if you'll pour them out."

As a garage saler, Jennifer recognized the blue-and-gold pouches as Crown Royal Whiskey bags—at one time gratis with every purchase. She poured contents from the first bag onto the floor near Jean. Old coins tumbled out. She shook the bag empty before picking up a silver coin, squinting at the date. "This one's 1928."

"Is that good?"

"Aunt Jean, I know nothing about coins, but isn't that about 90 years old? You'll need a coin appraiser." She picked up the other bag. "Ready for this one?"

At Jean's nod she emptied the bag next to the coins. Antique-style pins, brooches, bracelets, and hair combs tumbled out, along with a pocket watch on a tasseled fob. Jean separated the watch and combs from the rest. "This looks like a cover for the O. Henry book, 'The Gift of the Magi.' Remember that story?"

"Yes," Jennifer marveled. "What made you think of that?"

"Remember, I am a librarian." They laughed.

Jennifer examined some of the other jewelry. "Do these look familiar? Your sister's or your mother's?"

Jean looked through them. "I...I don't think so."

"A jeweler would know if they're valuable today. Some old pieces were costume jewelry then, inexpensive like ours today. Or these might be real gems in tarnished silver or gold settings."

Jean smiled. "This is like opening Christmas packages."

"Before we open the next box, may I ask if you'd mind letting me look at the Medical Examiner's report you told me about?"

"Why sure, when we go back upstairs."

"And is Katie's room the same as she left it?"

"I couldn't bring myself to touch anything there yet. The police looked around, but that's it."

"Did she have her own bathroom or share one?"

"Her own. I haven't changed anything there, either."

"May I look there, too, before I go?

"Of course, Jennifer. Looking for something in particular?"

"No. Just trying to better understand the last days of her life."

"You don't think she killed herself, do you?"

Jennifer drew a deep breath. "It's one possibility, but perhaps not the only one. To rule out others, don't we need to understand as much about her as possible?"

"I guess you're right, although it's tempting to stop scratching the healing wound."

"But wouldn't you like to know the truth about what happened to Katie?"

"Does it really matter now? She's gone. Knowing more won't bring her back."

Jennifer changed the subject. "Here, let's open another box while you think about it."

She pulled a carton over to Jean, who poked inside, pulled out various-sized papers and glanced at a few. "These look like old receipts and statements. I guess I'll have to go through each one to decide if it's worth keeping. "

Jennifer handed her the sharpie marker. "Then how about writing 'Defer' on the box? When you work on this later, just decide what's Keep or Toss in there. Here's the next box."

Jean probed. "These look like files. These would take too long for now, so Defer, but when I look later, Keep or Toss, right?"

"Yes. Next box?"

Jean looked. "Photographs." She pulled some out. "Oh, here are my parents and the house where I grew up."

"You'll need time going through this box," Jennifer predicted and looked at her watch. "Why not write Defer on it for now?" She handed Jean the sharpie. "You're in the swing of this now and, unfortunately, I must leave soon. May I look at Katie's room before I go?"

"Of course. I'll make a copy of the report you asked for while you look at her room. And Jennifer, I couldn't have attempted this without you. A thousand thanks for guiding me."

Jean led the way upstairs. "Her bathroom door is there, on the other side of the room."

Jennifer headed for the bathroom. The mirrored medicine cabinet revealed a predictable array of over-the-counter pain killers, dental products, antacid, cough medicine, allergy pills and Band-aids. The under-sink cupboard held cleaning products, toilet paper, tissues, and towels. She rummaged behind them but found nothing. She pulled open the shower curtain—only hair wash products, soap, and wash cloth on the wire shelf suction-cupped to the tiles. She checked the wastebasket: used tissues, cotton swabs, a candy bar wrapper—nothing unusual.

In the bedroom she lifted the foot of the mattress high, then the other end. Nothing hidden beneath. She started through the dresser drawers. Underwear—some scanty, which fit the affair. Chaste pajamas for at-home nights. A sock drawer, another for sweaters. A vanity table with one drawer full of cosmetics, and in front of it an upholstered, tufted cylindrical vanity stool. She inverted the stool. Nothing.

On top of the dresser—a few family photos, a stuffed toy, her high school and college graduation mortarboards. A sectioned antique dish with bobby pins and other miscellany. A wooden jewelry box with various simple pieces inside. None appeared valuable. She removed pictures from the wall, looking on the back for tampering, suggesting something secreted inside, but found nothing suspicious.

Jean reappeared. "Find anything helpful?"

"Not yet." Jennifer turned to Katie's desk, flipping through notebooks, pausing over papers, and stirring a finger into boxes of paper clips and rubber bands. She emptied pencils and scissors from a holder and peered inside. Nothing.

"Aunt Jean, can you think of a place where Katie might have hidden a diary or a calendar? Something that might help us piece together her last days of life?"

"Well, she knew I wasn't nosy and only the two of us lived here. She had no reason to hide anything since I never snooped. She cleaned her own room and kept it tidy, as you see."

Jennifer pulled the dresser, then the desk and vanity, away from the wall but found nothing taped behind. She upended the desk chair. "I don't see a bookcase. Did she like to read?"

"Oh, yes, but I'm a librarian so the McLean Library was like her second home. She didn't really need to own books, with the whole library system at her fingertips."

"Could you find out for me what interested her at the library this last month or so? Her book withdrawal list? Just in case there's a clue."

"Yes, I could get that. Would...would you like to borrow her computer for a few days to see if it has any answers? I can't bring myself to look, so I'd be a terrible detective. But you're trying to help me learn the truth about Katie's death and I'm grateful if you can." Jean fought tears.

Jennifer patted her hand. "Aunt Jean, I can't explain it, but I feel Katie wants me to learn what happened. She wants justice. Why else these crazy coincidences? That I was drawn to how familiar she looked, that I went to her viewing, that we met there, that you needed my help and I could offer it, that so many open-ended questions arise from her untimely death for me to understand how they fit together. I feel as if she picked me to help her." Jennifer considered what she'd said and shook her head. "Doesn't sound logical, does it?"

Jean looked doubtful. "If you do find light for Katie at the end of this tunnel, I just hope it isn't the front of an oncoming train...."

CHAPTER 44

When he left Gerry's house late Sunday afternoon, Arnie walked Toby down the street to his car parked near Becca's house. "I hope I can do this, Toby," he said, gently tucking his cat into the car. Screwing up his courage, he breathed deeply, shuffled up the sidewalk and made himself ring her doorbell.

If her parents answered the bell, he'd ask for her. That was easy. But *she* opened the door. "Arnie, how nice to see you. Would you like to come inside?"

He promised himself not to stammer in her presence. "Uh... no, that's all right. At the party yesterday, when I worked for the caterer, I...I overheard something I think someone should know. I thought you could help me figure out who to tell."

Aware of Arnie's shyness, she encouraged him. "Let's sit here on the porch chairs while you tell me about it."

"Ah, okay."

A moment passed as Becca gave him time to gather his thoughts.

"Yesterday, after you saw me at the party, when it ended, I went back to the grocery store's van, the one I drove there to help the caterer. I parked behind the stable so guests could, like, park close to the house. Since I'd never seen a stable before, I, like, looked inside. That antique-shop-guy called Bobby and the real-estate woman returned from a horseback ride. I knew who they were because I heard them talking about it while I passed out those snacks."

"...the appetizers? They were delicious. And you did a great job as a waiter."

Arnie gave an embarrassed smile and, to his horror, blushed. "Thanks."

Becca waited while he struggled to regain composure and return to his story.

"When she left, he didn't see me there in the stable, so I guess he thought he was alone. He called somebody on his cell phone and, like, talked about robbing the house."

Becca maintained a fixed expression, but her mind raced. Had Arnie made up this story as an excuse to talk to her? His crush on her made him her likely drone culprit. Teens often acted on impulse instead of thinking things through, wishing afterward they'd used better sense. She remembered those days.

"What did you hear him say on the phone?"

"I...I went over it a bunch of times and finally wrote it down to get it right." He pulled a paper out of his pants pocket, unfolded it, and read aloud. "He said he was there now. I figured 'there' meant the place where the party happened. He said there wasn't much 'security,' that's what he called it, so they wouldn't have trouble getting inside the house. He said the place was like a museum with a lot to steal and he'd text them a list of what he wanted. He said he needed them very soon and would meet this phone person at their usual place. That's it."

Surprised, Becca extended her hand for the paper and read it again. This sounded believable. "You're certain this is what you heard?"

"Yes."

"This sounds serious, Arnie. I think the police need to know about this right away. My brother-in-law is a policeman. We could tell him. They'll want to talk to you, to hear the story from its source. That means they'll need your address and cell phone number. You have a cell, don't you?"

Arnie froze. What had he done? He couldn't tell her or the police he must move all his stuff out of his house tonight to live full-time in his car. What a fool he'd been. Too late. He needed to think, but he couldn't concentrate in front of this woman who still melted his heart and mind.

"...don't you?"

"Don't I...sorry, I...I didn't hear what you said."

"Don't you have a cell phone?"

"Ah...yeah, I do."

"Okay if I give them that phone number?"

"Well...I." He couldn't weasel out of this terrible trap he'd set. With only himself to blame for this idiotic situation, he cursed the fool he was. She was the last person in the world he wanted to look stupid in front of. What now?

"Maybe you could just write it at the bottom of this note you made." She fished in a pocket for a pencil. "Okay?"

He gulped, desperate to make this go away but with no idea how.

"Uh...okay, I guess," he managed.

She handed him the pencil and paper. Cornered, he bit his lip, wrote the number, and dutifully handed it back to her. Suddenly a lightbulb blinked in his mind. "Ah, today is Sunday. Could you tell him tomorrow? I've got a lot of stuff to do tonight and it wouldn't be...ah, convenient until tomorrow."

She searched his face. This could be crucial information, but in a similar situation, how would she want to be treated? She hesitated. "O-k-a-y. I'll wait to tell Adam tomorrow morning. How's 7:00 a.m.?" She studied the boy, thinking he looked exhausted. "Is everything else all right, Arnie?"

He stifled his emotions so she couldn't read his anguish. "Yeah, just...a busy night ahead."

"Want to tell me about it?"

He looked up quickly. If only he could tell her the truth, but shame prevented it. How could she ever love him when his own father didn't? And he lived that miserable truth every day.

Becca changed the subject. "Did you say Bobby and the real-estate lady went riding together?"

Grateful to direct the spotlight from himself, Arnie mustered a little enthusiasm. "Yeah, they really like each other."

Becca looked up. "Oh..."

"Yeah, he called her 'beautiful lady' and they kissed a long time, just like in the movies." Arnie stood. "Look, I gotta go. Thanks, Becca." There, he'd said her name. "And thanks for helping me figure out who should know about this. Bye." He leapt off the porch, sprinted across the yard and climbed into his car.

Back on the porch, it was Becca's turn to stare like a deer in the headlights.

CHAPTER 45

S unday night, Arnie parked in the driveway of his home. He hated parking his car there to alert Magda he'd returned. But he had no choice while carting empty cardboard boxes up to his room and loading the packed ones into his vehicle.

He sighed with relief when his key opened the kitchen door. If she'd changed the locks, which she could easily do, he'd be lost. First, he took Toby to his room, then brought in the flattened grocery store boxes in three more trips. In his room, he reassembled the boxes with tape, moving fast. The closet held his winter coats and most of his clothes. He stuffed hard to compress them into four boxes and taped the tops closed. His shoes and winter boots filled another box. He emptied his dresser drawers onto the bed, sorted the contents and filled another few boxes. His desk stuff, laptop, books, pictures, and papers filled three more. He shook his head at his coveted posters. No way, unless...He pulled them down and rolled them into tubes held with rubber bands. Stripping his bed, he crammed sheets and blanket into another two boxes, tossing his pillows on top of the stack. Under the bed he found a shoe and tossed it into the last box. Time to load the car.

Struggling to carry several heavy boxes at a time down the servant stairs, he loaded each batch into his car. Finished and tired, he carried Toby to his car and backed out of the driveway, parking around the corner, out of sight from the house.

Returning with stealth, he sidled up the driveway along the bushes and entered the house for his second mission. Creeping through the dark kitchen, dining room and foyer, he stopped every few steps to listen for any sound of Magda. Finally, he reached the door of his father's den.

A shimmer of ambient light from the porch lamps leaked through the den's windows. He hadn't been in this room for months and realized, with anxiety, a rearrangement of furniture. His father's desk and chair now backed to a wall, facing the windows across the room. He eased back the desk chair to crouch on his knees behind his father's desk, in case anyone entered. Then he raised his head, periscope-like, to scan the dark walls for his father's gun cabinet. Gone. Was the pistol still in a desk drawer for a quick self-defense-grab if needed? He eased open the lower drawers, groping in their black interiors for the metal feel and distinctive shape of a gun.

Suddenly the room exploded with light. He shrank into the desk's deep kneehole. Who? If his father, he could leap out for one more attempt to get his attention. If Magda, how could he explain being in this room? He cringed under the desk, fighting to quiet his breathing, stanch his trembling and become invisible.

Magda's voice. "Otto, this is his office. The safe is behind that painting. Want to see it?"

Arnie heard a grunt, then feet moving across the Oriental carpet. One person's shoes squeaked with each step. He remembered the painting covering the safe opened like a medicine cabinet door. Hearing a snap, he knew they looked behind it at the wall safe.

"He keeps money and guns here," Magda confided.

To his horror, Arnie felt a sneeze coming on. He put a finger hard against his upper lip beneath his nostrils and pressed so hard, tears came to his eyes. A fatal sneeze meant the terrifying specter of instant discovery.

"I don't have the combination yet, but soon," Magda purred. Arnie heard another grunt in response. "After tonight, I'm rid of the boy and take control of the house. Now, I only need to persuade my husband to add me to his bank account and Will before we 'remove' him."

Arnie's threatened sneeze wouldn't stop. He used his other hand to double the force as he pressed the finger on his upper lip against the bone. This delayed the sneeze. He heard low mingled male and female laughter and the squeaking shoes retreating. The overhead light flicked off. His kneehole hiding place plunged again into darkness. The den door clicked shut.

The sudden relief of surviving catastrophic discovery caused him to choke as the stifled sneeze erupted in an odd chirp rather than the normal sound. He rubbed his arms to quell the goosebumps. Did he really hear what he thought he did?

He must warn his father! But would his dad even believe this bizarre story? Arnie hardly believed it himself. Yet, this new knowledge, superimposed over the past year's events, suddenly fit a larger, sinister pattern. Only he knew Magda's duplicity. If she or that man had found him tonight, would they have killed him, just as they planned to "remove" his father?

The gun he came to this room to find was not protection enough. He must escape. But he wanted the gun, too. He'd already checked the desk's lower drawers; now he risked leaving his safe kneehole hiding place to probe the upper drawers. Ever so gently, he slid open the left top drawer and felt around inside. No. Next, he eased open the wide kneehole-spanning center drawer, willing his fingers to identify what he touched yet couldn't see: a stapler, scotch tape, paper clips, scissors, pens, magnifying glass. He guided his fingers all the way to the back. No.

He slipped open the last upper drawer, put his hand inside and felt around. Small boxes, envelopes, post-it pads, magic markers. Pushing his hand to the back, his fingers touched something different. His eyes narrowed in triumph as he carefully withdrew his father's pistol. Probably loaded. He checked—safety on. Slowly, he slid it into his pants pocket. Now he reached to the back of the drawer a second time. A box. Extricating it, he lifted the top. Ammo.

Mission accomplished, but with Magda and the man in the house, how to escape? Was the way in the way out, or maybe a window instead? He eased the den door ajar. Darkness obscured the main floor. Using memory, he threaded his way toward the kitchen, pausing every few steps to listen. Hearing nothing, he inched his way along the once-familiar rooms, praying he wouldn't knock over an unanticipated plant or figurine in Magda's new decorating scheme.

At last, he reached the back door. He fought to slow his ragged breathing as his hand touched the door. On the other side lay escape. He gritted his teeth in concentration, slowly rotated the knob and eased the door open.

Then the unthinkable happened.

CHAPTER 46

A menacing growl caused Arnie's neck hairs to rise. He maneuvered one eye to the open crack in the door. From inches away came the hoarse breathing of something large and hairy. The neighbor's rogue dog loose again? Or a coyote? There'd been several verified sightings in their neighborhood. If that animal—whatever it was—barked or howled wildly, the sound would awaken the neighborhood, never mind Magda in Arnie's house.

"Hercules, is that you?" Arnie whispered in desperation through the crack, "Good dog." He peeked through the crack. An animal stood rigid, emitting a louder growl and retracting his lips to expose glinting fangs. "Hercules, is that you? It's... it's just me, Arnie. You've seen me before. We don't really know each other, but why not be friends now?"

This time the animal snarled, revealing more fang. Arnie had no choice. He tried again. "Shhhh. Good dog. I'm not going to hurt you. I'm just the kid down the street. Shhhh." To look less threatening, he crouched down to the creature's eye level. The animal growled again. Arnie cracked the door a bit wider to see his foe better and also for it to see him, while continuing to whisper in a soothing voice.

Then Arnie took a terrible chance, extending his hand through the door. "See, here's my scent. It's just me." If the animal's teeth clamped onto his hand, he prayed his scream wouldn't attract Magda's attention.

Suddenly the creature's posture relaxed. It lowered its head and a cold, wet nose sniffed Arnie's hand. Arnie watched the dog's tail whisk a tentative wag. Thank God, it was only unpredictable Hercules as opposed to something vicious from the wild.

The boy exhaled and slowly stood as he whispered. "Come on, let's go for a little walk." Outside in the driveway now, the boy patted the dog's head. Thrilled at any attention, the dog hugged the boy's leg so closely he hardly avoided tripping over the animal.

They moved along the sidewalk toward Arnie's car. The boy's mind raced. What would happen if the dog saw or smelled Toby? Nobody could control Hercules' barking then.

Desperate for what to do, as they passed the next house, Arnie reached through the iron fence rungs above a retaining wall. He groped for anything useful under those bushes— maybe a rock? Instead, his fingers touched part of a fallen tree branch. He eased the ungainly stick out through the fence bars. When their walk reached Arnie's car, he waved the stick near the dog's muzzle to excite the animal before hurling the branch as far as he could. When the dog dashed to retrieve it, Arnie jumped into his car, started the motor and drove away before the dog returned with his prize.

But where to go on a dark Sunday night in a car with boxes crammed to the ceiling? Security patrols investigated commercial and government office buildings for unrecognized vehicles in their lots. Ditto schools, libraries and restaurants. The same nighttime protection even took place in church parking lots. Police patrolled residential neighborhoods, looking for suspicious people or activity, in addition to Neighborhood Watch.

He bought two drive-through fast-food dinners and ate parked in their lot. A delighted Toby eagerly downed pinched-off chunks of Arnie's second hamburger. The boxes of belongings stuffed into the car made the cat litter harder for Toby to access, and his water dish sat atop the dashboard.

Suddenly, Arnie sat up straight as an idea blossomed in his mind. Why not park in Mrs. Ogleby's driveway, around back on the asphalt apron between the house and the garage? Nobody lived there now, and police had removed the yellow crime-scene tape. With the car invisible from the street and a thick row of Leland cypress trees shielding the view from either side of the property, who would know...or care?

Nothing drew attention in the dark like a light. Tearing off some tape from the roll used on his boxes, he opened his driver door and taped flat the automatic door light button, repeating this inside the passenger door. Now no interior car light illuminated when the doors opened. This way, if he had to pee in the night, darkness would shelter that activity.

As he entered Gerry's housing development, few lamps shone in windows as inhabitants slept. Most porch lights were off. No other cars moved on those residential roads as he drove slowly by to case Mrs. Ogelby's house. All looked quiet in surrounding homes. At the community swimming pool, he U-turned, doubled back, pulled into her driveway and parked, unseen, behind her house.

He rolled down his four windows an inch for ventilation. Exhausted from the day's physical and emotional challenges, he fell into a deep sleep.

*****

At the same hour in the Shannon house down the street, Becca stared at the ceiling from bed. Why did Arnie's story about Bobby and Aubrey niggle at her? Her logical mind confirmed that after one date with Bobby, they had hardly embarked on an exclusive relationship, nor would she have agreed if he'd suggested it. He had every right to date or kiss whomever he wished, as did she. Was Arnie's version even dependable? He had seen her with Nathan, whom she identified as her boyfriend, not Bobby. And Arnie hadn't volunteered the kissing info. She'd asked. Arnie's spontaneous description seemed innocent.

She winced. Why did she waste time even thinking about this? Because her illogical side felt a powerful attraction to Bobby. If he were a slick crook, she wanted no part of him. Tomorrow she'd tell Adam the situation and perhaps discover soon at the shop if Bobby had a criminal side. Howsoever the theft story unfolded, she'd doubtless see Bobby more at the antique shop to calculate whether he still interested her.

*****

At Gerry's house, Connie settled into bed as Matt set the alarm, explaining, "I want to get up an hour early tomorrow to get in a run before work." He slid under the covers, propping his head on a pillow to watch TV.

He looked up, surprised, when she muted the TV remote. "Mind if we talk a minute?"

"Ah, sure. What's on your mind?"

"What would you think about inviting Arnie to move into the guest room next to Gerry?"

Matt shot her a quick look. "Isn't that a big step? What does Gerry think about it?"

"He thinks it's a nice idea for a while—not permanent, just for a few weeks. I feel like Arnie needs a safe place right now where he can trust people. If I'm right... You know kids—this phase will pass. But for now, our extra attention and the cost of his food could be an investment in a boy's future, whatever that is."

"Seems you've given this some thought. And, you say Gerry agrees. Okay, let's try it. He turned to her. "You're pretty unusual, Connie."

She flashed him a doubtful look. "*Unusual?*"

"Yeah. Most wives gripe about too much to do—cooking, shopping, chauffeuring, laundry, cleaning—you know the drill. But here you're willing to add somebody else's kid to what's already on your list because you feel sorry for him. That's unusual."

Understanding now, she relaxed. "Look at it this way. If Gerry were in Arnie's shoes—whatever those shoes are—wouldn't you hope a family was kind to him?"

"When you put it that way, yeah, I sure would."

"Whatever's troubling that boy, I hope it's superficial. Meantime, maybe all he needs is a friendly hand."

"Then, we'll give him one," Matt concluded, as if this had been his own idea.

"Thanks for humoring me about this." She planted a kiss on his stubbled cheek.

"Okay. Now, how about some TV?"

Connie suppressed a little smile as she passed him the remote.

*****

At the same moment in her bedroom, Jennifer studied the ME report about Katie. "Says here she had a large amount of benzodiazepine in her system."

Jason put down the TV Guide. "What's benzo-whatever-you-said?"

"Google says it's a neurotransmitter chemical reducing activity of nerves in the brain. Used to treat anxiety and insomnia."

"So... a powerful sedative?" At Jennifer's nod, he continued. "Did she hedge her suicide certainty by combining drugs *plus* carbon monoxide?"

Jennifer considered this. "Or did someone else drug her, drive her home, park her car in the garage, leave the motor on, close the garage door, move her to the driver seat and escape out the garage side door to the yard? That's what I'll propose to Adam tomorrow."

At Jason's disapproving look, she added, "Don't you want to find the truth about this?"

"Well, I...sure, I guess. You *do* have an uncanny knack for sniffing out clues."

"What if my thing is being naturally inquisitive? Don't you want me to be happy?"

Jason gave a nervous laugh. "If Momma ain't happy, ain't nobody happy."

She giggled, turning off her bedside lamp. "And what makes Poppa happy?"

He reached for her hand, "You do, Jen." But in the darkened bedroom, his face sobered as he silently thought, but not the danger you manage to draw like a magnet.

CHAPTER 47

MONDAY

Puffing hard, Matt Wilberforce slowed the end of his early morning run to a cool-down walk for the last block approaching his house. His watch confirmed ample time to shower and dress before heading to work.

Unlike runners who follow a fixed course, Matt often varied his route for no reason—running into a cul-de-sac, sidewalk or new path not tried before. Today, he detoured up Mrs. Ogleby's driveway.

The sight of a car at the uninhabited house next door to his own riveted his attention. He circled the car in the early morning's thin light, wary for potential danger.

The cardboard boxes filling the car's interior looked like a homeless person's refuge. He eased his cell phone from his pocket and dialed 91, holding the remaining 1 to tap only if danger required.

Cautiously, he approached the driver-side window to peer inside. "My god," he uttered at the sight of the sleeping driver. Cancelling the 911 call, he tapped on the car window.

Wakened from sleep, Arnie squinted at the face outside his car window and, with difficulty, fumbled to life. His cramped sleeping position made his limbs respond awkwardly, never mind disorientation from waking for the first time in a car. Matt smiled so as not to scare the boy. He circled his finger, signaling Arnie to lower the window.

"Hey, Arnie. Good luck seeing you this morning, because our family decided yesterday, we'd like to invite you to stay with us for a while. You could use the bedroom next to Gerry's. If you like the idea, why not come on in now for breakfast? Mornings when I jog, I'm the first one up at our house."

Arnie couldn't speak as the problem-solving enormity and unimaginable generosity of this offer swept over him. "Thank you," he croaked, as a tear he couldn't control trickled down his cheek.

Overcome by the boy's reaction, Matt said, "Want to move your car over to our driveway now?" At the sound of a loud meow, he added, "Hey, Toby, welcome back."

Arnie nodded mutely and drove his car to the Wilberforce driveway.

Once there, Matt put his arm around the boy's shoulders and guided him inside. Toby followed.

At 6:00, the house was quiet when they entered. "Here," Matt said, "want to start with waffles?" When Arnie nodded, he pulled a box from the freezer. "You know how to put these in the toaster, right? And here's butter and syrup. I need to get ready for work now, so I'm going upstairs, but Connie's coming down soon. Later, you can settle into your room. Okay?"

Overwhelmed, Arnie nodded again.

Matt reached into a cupboard. "Here's some cat food you left us for Toby's breakfast."

When Matt left, Arnie sat at the kitchen table and put his head on his arms. How could his life swing in such volatile directions? So much so fast. He felt overwhelmed.

The syrup-drenched waffle helped. By the time Connie appeared, he felt better prepared to cope.

"Hi, Arnie. Glad you're here. How was breakfast?"

"Great."

"Gerry should be along soon."

As if on cue, a sleepy Gerry strolled in. "Hey, Dad says you're staying awhile. Awesome. I'll grab some waffles, too. Then want to take your stuff upstairs?"

"Thanks, but it's Monday and I'm due at the grocery at 8:00, so not sure I have time right now."

"Well, let's at least get the boxes out of your car and into the garage. Then we can hike them up when you get back this afternoon."

"That's great. Thanks, man." Arnie touched his chin. "Could I also sneak in a shave before work?"

"Of course, you have your own bathroom now."

When they emptied the car, Gerry said, "BTW, have you heard the news?" Arnie looked blank. "Some relative of Mrs. Ogleby is, like, moving into her house."

As Arnie drove to work, he remembered the pistol in his car. He no longer needed his father's gun, but his dad might. What if Magda cornered her husband in the den and he reached into the drawer for the pistol's protection...?

Arnie winced as he drove, mind racing. Should he risk going home to replace the gun? Should he phone his father at work to tell him Magda's plan and confess he'd stolen the gun? Would his father even believe him? Or might he laugh about it when he later told Magda the improbable story, unintentionally alerting her that she and Otto might need to locate and muzzle Arnie too?

When the vehicle in front of him stopped suddenly, the boy stabbed his foot on the brake, his car swerving hard. What if he'd hit this car and the investigating cop found the gun in the glove compartment? How could he ever explain it? Would they arrest him? And then ask pointed questions about Mrs. Ogleby?

Arnie pounded a fist on the steering wheel and cried out, "Will this insanity never end?"

CHAPTER 48

L ike all mornings, coffee brought Becca to life. "Mom," she said, still hoarse from sleep, "I need to tell you something that happened yesterday."

Jennifer frowned. She'd already confided to Becca about finding nothing helpful in Katie's room. Maybe her daughter wanted to talk about Nathan. "Okay, shoot."

"You may want to sit down."

Jennifer looked up quickly, thinking uh-oh, not good. Instead she said, "Okay, I'm sitting."

"Yesterday, Arnie stopped by to tell me something he overheard at Veronika's party and ask my advice about what to do about it." She described the stable scene and Bobby's cell-phone call. Jennifer read Arnie's note. "He and I agreed I'd tell Adam today. But I want you to know first."

"Don't you think we should tell Veronika so she can tighten security at her house? This might take days to arrange."

"Or would it just scare her? She's really old and busy planning for the big move."

"I don't think she scares easily. The sooner she knows, the sooner she can prepare. Wouldn't you want to know if the situation were reversed? When you finish calling Adam, would you pass me the phone? I have something else to ask him."

When Becca finished talking with Adam, she handed the phone to her mother. "Good morning," Jennifer said. "Has our favorite homicide detective another minute to talk?"

"A minute's just about it."

"In Katie's garage, did you dust for prints on the garage's side door that opens to the garden?"

"Uh...not sure."

"If someone drugged her and left her in the closed garage with the car motor running, wouldn't he escape through that side door? Katie's aunt never uses that door, so anything deposited there the night Katie died should remain untouched."

"You still worrying about that Kalinsky case?"

"What if that door has an overlooked clue?"

Silence.

"Adam?"

"If you weren't my mother-in-law, would we be having this conversation?"

"Because I'm a Fairfax County citizen, wouldn't any police officer I chose to share this with hear me out?"

He sighed. "You are correct, of course."

"Would you please at least check about dusting that door? If not, what's to lose by eliminating that evidence? Katie's aunt says they never use that door, so anything there's still pristine."

Adam sighed. "Anything else?"

"I appreciate your being an intelligent policeman and patient son-in-law."

He laughed. "Goodbye."

Jennifer smiled as she disconnected.

"Becca, since you actually talked with Arnie, would you mind telling Veronika what he overheard? Afterward, may I talk with her?"

"Sure, Mom." Becca did, handed the phone to her mother and left to get ready for work.

"Hi, Veronika. Sorry about this news, but knowing this, you can plan security. Since Becca told Adam, the police already know; you'll probably hear from them. Are you okay with all this?"

"Yes. I'll arrange more security here, although I may want to spend a few nights with Frances or you. But this wakeup call reminds me I've overlooked improving security and will need more than a house-sitter when I move out. Thanks to Adam's notes and now this, I realize the vulnerability of my house and everything in it."

"You amaze me with your independence, impressive at any age, even more so at 89. Stay in touch and let us know how we might help. Bye for now."

The minute Jennifer ended the call, the phone rang. "Hello."

"Hi, Jennifer. It's Aunt Jean. Thanks to you, the downsizing's going well. I decided to follow your suggestion to ask the medical examiner for DNA information about Katie's, ah, predicament. Their office says it takes a few days to get back to me. Shall I let you know what I learn?"

"Aunt Jean, you made a brave decision. Yes, please let me know right away."

"Of course. And thanks again for guiding me through this latest rough patch."

"Aunt Jean, we all help each other. Soon you may lend someone else a hand."

"Maybe, but you stepped up when nobody else in my world did. I won't forget it."

"You're welcome. I'll wait to hear from you."

CHAPTER 49

All business on Monday morning, Armand walked down the grocery store aisle and handed a cell phone to one of his employees. "Phone call for you, Arnie."

"For *me*?" Nervous, he hoped his hand didn't shake as he took the phone. Was this the dreaded police call about Mrs. Ogleby or the pistol in his car? Or worse: had Magda harmed his father?

Armand called over his shoulder as he walked away. "Bring the phone straight back to my office the minute you finish."

"Hello."

"Arnie this is Ginny Renaldi, owner of Classical Catering. Rolf tells me you did a good job for us at the party last Saturday and thinks you have potential in this business. I wonder if you'd like to work for us some more. For salary, we'd start you at the same hourly wage we paid you then and you could work your way up after that."

"I...I..."

Sensing his uncertainty, Ginny continued, "Your grocery job fits your summer schedule, but you won't be able to work those daytime hours once school starts in the fall. However, you could work our evening and weekend events. Meantime, we'd offer you opportunities during the summer that don't interfere with your current job. Does this interest you?"

"Yeah."

"Okay, I'll put you on our list. We have a job in Vienna this Friday evening 6:00 to 10:00. It's short notice, but would you like to work that job?"

"I would. Yeah."

"You'd come to our catering office Friday at 5:30 to go with Rolf in our van. Do you have a plain, white, long-sleeved, button-down-the-front shirt?"

"Uh, not really."

"Okay, wear black trousers and black shoes, just like last time, and we'll provide the shirt. You're a medium, right?"

"Think so."

"Meantime, could you drop by our office later today to fill out a job application? Armand can give you our business card with the address. All I need right now is to verify your cell-phone number."

*****

At 9:00 the same morning, Becca arrived at the antique shop, pulling a collapsible crate-on-wheels behind her.

Eyeing her, Robert Radner checked his watch and spoke gruffly. "Right on time." For a man exceedingly sparse with praise, this doubled as a compliment.

"Good morning, Mr. Radner. You invited me to do some picking this weekend. Might you consider these for sale at your store? Shall I put them on the edge of your desk for you to inspect at your convenience?"

He didn't smile or thank her. In his usual condescending voice, he allowed, "Yes, you may."

She placed the Chinese blue-and-white ceramic combo, the puppet, the weasel music box, and the cymbal-playing monkey on the table.

Radner looked at them a moment and then, expressionless, examined each, one by one. "Charlie McCarthy and the wind-up-monkey—I remember them from...from a long time ago. They're not antiques," he noted dismissively, followed by silence, "...but we'll group them with the collectibles and see what happens."

Becca exhaled. She watched him look for maker marks on both ceramic pieces. He grunted. "This, too. How much did you pay for these things?" She told him. He nodded and returned to papers on his desk. "We'll reimburse your outlay plus a percentage of the sale price. What's this painting?"

"Something my mother bought. I wonder if you might tell me whether it's kitsch or not."

Radner studied the painting, using a magnifying glass on the bottom right corner signature. "We usually charge for appraisals." He turned to his computer and tapped some keys. "Maybe from Indiana's Brown County Art Colony era? The signature's hard to read but maybe an early Edward K. Williams." He clicked his computer keys. "See, here's some of his other work."

Becca studied the on-screen paintings of rural farm and woodland scenes. "What's it worth?"

"Let's see." He punched more keys. "If this artist painted it and we compare it to others sold of comparable size...I'd guess about $5,000. But it would sell better at art auctions rather than my shop. I know about Brown County artists from my early days in that part of the country. Does your mother want to sell it?"

"No idea. What would you offer if she did?"

"$1,000."

"But..."

"In retail, we strive to buy low, sell high. Besides something's value, we include overhead: employee salaries, shop rent, utilities, insurance and so on."

Just then, Mrs. Radner entered the store and smiled warmly. "Good morning, Becca. Nice day outside, isn't it?"

At least this woman seemed human, Becca thought—unlike her husband, "Robot" Radner.

"Anything special for me to do today?"

Mrs. Radner smiled at her. "A new shipment of crystal needs pricing. I'll bring you the list and tags. When they're ready, I'll show you where to display them in the window."

"Good," Becca agreed, collapsing her mobile crate and putting it in the storeroom.

Was Bobby expected at the store today? Best not to ask.

*****

Jennifer strolled down the sidewalk, accompanied by Grammy pushing her three-wheeled Rollator.

"Thanks for taking a walk with me this morning, Mom." She pointed to the walker. "How do you like your new gadget?"

"It gives me confidence, Jen. Good to have something to lean on."

"Will you use it in those long hallways at Pebblebrook when you go to meals?"

"Oh, yes. They encourage us to stay active, and walking is good exercise. So it's a two-fer. I like their programs." She smiled. "I just didn't know getting old would take this long."

Jennifer laughed. "Good one, Mom."

Her mother paused. "Say, what's that up ahead?" She looked down the street at a truck with people around it.

Jennifer shaded her eyes. "Looks like the Ogelby house."

"The hoarder who died?"

"Yes." Jennifer slowed her step to better match her mother's.

"...from natural causes?"

"Not sure, but Adam might know. Ready for your move in five days?"

Grammy stopped a moment. "Yes. The movers come on Friday. Almost everything I brought north will fit in my new apartment. Veronika faces a whole different predicament."

Jennifer kicked a branch off the sidewalk to clear her mother's progress. "We'll all try to help her through it. Once she settles in her new apartment, I think she'll feel grounded again."

"Yes, these days she lives in only a few main-floor rooms at the mansion. Weeks go by when she doesn't go upstairs at all. Now, of course, she's all over her house, deciding what to take."

Jennifer mused, "True, but she has an advantage you didn't."

"Oh?"

"She doesn't have to empty out her house to sell it quickly, as you did. Once she moves to Pebblebrook, she can go back and forth until she's brought everything she really wants."

"But she also has disadvantages." At Jennifer's puzzled look, Grammy continued, "She must protect all her antiques until she sells them. What about vandals or someone torching the place?"

Jennifer agreed. "It's a problem. Hope she solves it fast so it doesn't become an on-going worry."

They reached the truck.

"Oh, my," Grammy exclaimed.

CHAPTER 50

The two women watched two uniformed workmen wheel stacks of newspapers and magazines on flat-bed dollies from the Ogleby house to a truck. A third casually-dressed man watched.

"Hello." Jennifer introduced herself and Grammy to the man watching. "We're neighbors from down the street. Looks like some excitement here today." Jennifer peered into the truck.

As the two workmen returned to the house for another load, the third said, "I'm Hugh Hamilton. Glad to meet you."

They nodded.

"My family will be your new neighbors soon," Hugh explained. "Matilda Ogleby was my cousin. She left this house to us at the very time we were looking for a place to live in McLean. I'm trying to remove all this *stuff* in three days and get the house thoroughly cleaned on Thursday so we can move in on Friday when our moving van arrives. We had no idea, no warning, about what we found here. She must have hoarded for years."

Jennifer shrugged. "She became a recluse. None of us really knew her well."

He shrugged. "Well, we *are* sorry to learn her final years were troubled. We didn't even know she put us in her Will. But she did and we're grateful. Moving in June is good timing so our girls will be comfortable in the house and the neighborhood before school starts mid-August."

"Your girls?"

"Yes, we have four daughters, ages 9, 13, 17 and 21."

Jennifer grinned. "I have a 21-year-old, too. Let's introduce them after you move in. In fact, once you're settled, may we host a little welcoming party for you to meet the neighbors on our street?"

"That sounds wonderful." A workman tapped Hugh's arm. "Uh, excuse me a minute, ladies."

The workman blew his nose loudly into a bandana handkerchief and stuffed it into his pants pocket. "We'll need another two laborers to get this stuff out in three days. Want me to call them?"

"Okay, whatever makes this happen."

Jennifer shaded her eyes. "Have you looked through the house to decide what's trash and what isn't?"

Hugh laughed. "We're definitely in the trash phase now—paper, bottles, cans, jars, clothes—everywhere. Dirty dishes and garbage in the kitchen. It's such a mess we can't even see most of the furniture."

"Have you someone to clean on Thursday before your family arrives?"

"No. I plan to hire a commercial team, unless you have another idea."

"I know someone terrific. She's worked for me for years and now runs her own cleaning business. I recommend her."

"Great. Would you give me her number?"

"Sure, and I'll let her know she may hear from you very soon. Once you've emptied out the hoarding stuff, if you find usable furniture underneath, consider donating it instead of junking it. I can e-mail you places to call who will pick it up."

"That would be great."

"Or, if you have a place to store resalable things, maybe in the garage, might you even consider a moving-in sale once you're settled?"

"We'll have garage space once we're rid of my cousin's car. A dealer's looking at her vehicle this morning, and if he doesn't make an offer, I'll donate it." He laughed. "My wife's a garage saler. She'd like giving one here."

Jennifer's smile blossomed. "Then she and I are kindred spirits."

Hugh handed her a page from his notebook. "Here's my e-mail address for your house cleaner. I'm staying at a nearby McLean hotel to get here early and leave late during these hectic clean-up days before the moving van arrives early Friday."

"I'll add my phone number in the e-mail in case you have other questions. The Wilberforce family right next door are nice neighbors. Have you met them yet?"

He laughed. "No, but it's barely 9:00 a.m."

"Sorry about your cousin's untimely passing, but welcome to our neighborhood."

Hugh sobered, "Thank you. Her death came as a surprise, as did this crazy hoarding. We've heard about this kind of behavior but have never seen anything like it with our own eyes."

Grammy chimed in. "Ever watched 'Hoarders' on TV? It documents real hoarders and their family's efforts to help them ditch the stuff, chuck the habit and resume normal lives."

"Really? After this experience, will I be brave enough to watch it?"

Grammy patted his arm. "If you do, you'll better understand your late cousin's problem."

Motioning Hugh to step closer so she and her mother could speak to him without workmen hearing, Jennifer said.

"Confused people like old folks and hoarders often hide valuables where they think nobody will find them. Sometimes hidden so well they themselves forget."

"Uh-oh..."

Grammy leaned on her Rollator. "My husband of sixty years, who I thought I knew well, hid paper money between the pages of most of the books in his den. When we gathered those books to donate them, one book fell, and the money fluttered out. Then we knew to check all his books. Sure enough, cash hidden in nearly every volume."

Jennifer added, "Mom also taped jewelry box and file cabinet keys under vases. Remember, Mom? In other words, once the superficial clutter is removed, take time yourself to investigate unusual, as well as obvious, places in rooms and in the furniture before they haul it away."

"I hadn't thought about this at all. Thanks for the advice. My wife's garage sale savvy, so she'd probably know. But she won't arrive with the girls until the place is move-in ready on Friday."

"Would you like me to come by later to suggest places to look for valuables?"

"Yes, I would. Thanks, Jennifer."

Saying good-bye, Jennifer and her mother continued their walk. Grammy said, "Pleasant young man, isn't he?"

Jennifer nodded. "Seems to be. You always hope so with new neighbors."

Grammy chuckled. "You know what Harry Truman said?" At Jennifer's blank look, she continued. "'To have good neighbors, we must be good neighbors.' And Jennifer, you *are* a good neighbor. Also, a good daughter."

Surprised, Jennifer reached for her mother's hand. "And you're the best mother I ever had."

She chided, "I'm the *only* mother you ever had."

Their laughter drifted behind them as they continued down the sidewalk, that happy sound blending with the hum of summer insects and melodies of birds into a gentle morning serenade.

CHAPTER 51

Half an hour later, after returning Grammy to the rental house across the street, Jennifer phoned her cleaner friend. "Hi, Celeste. How are you? Good. Interested in a possible job this Thursday? Someone on my street needs a one-day cleaning team for an empty house, *but* nobody's cleaned the place for a long time, so it's grimy. The new family wants to move in the next day."

Celeste consulted her calendar. "We could do it. I could send five people. Is price a problem?"

"Talk that over with Hugh Hamilton, the man moving in. I'll tell him how to contact you and here's his e-mail. You may want to see the job before committing. Hope you work out something. Anyway, see you this Friday at my house, as usual? Good. We'll talk more then."

Jennifer no sooner hung up than the phone rang. She heard Jean Abingdon's voice.

"Why hello, Aunt Jean. How are you today?"

"I've been better. The ME report about Katie's...they call it the 'fetal report'...came this morning. It says the father is Robert Radner."

"Isn't that pretty much what you expected?"

"I guess so, but now that it's on paper, it's real instead of vague. I...I know he's the logical person, given their relationship. But knowing feels harder than imagining."

"Thanks for letting me know, Aunt Jean. I'll add this to the other facts to see how it fits. This was important. Thank you." She artfully changed the subject. "How's your box-sorting?"

Jean's voice brightened. "I've made progress, thanks to you. The jewelry wasn't valuable, which fits with the small denomination bills also in the footlocker. Personal treasures for someone to save, but not for the big world. I haven't learned more about the coins or gone through my sister's file boxes or photos...slow but steady, as you advised."

"Good job, Aunt Jean. Progress at a comfortable pace."

"I don't know who sent you into my life at this particular time, Jennifer, but you've made such a positive difference."

"Before you know it, you'll pass the good deed along."

When they finished their call, Jen's phone rang again.

"Good morning, Jennifer. It's Greg Bromley. You asked me to investigate Katie's adoption. I located Tri-State's old files in a storage facility, got permission to investigate and I found something. Could you come by my office today to talk about it?"

"Thanks for checking this out for me. Would it be easier just to tell me on the phone?"

"No, it's more like show-and-tell information. What time's convenient for you?"

"How about in an hour, at 10 o'clock?"

"Good. See you then."

She hung up and dashed upstairs to change clothes. As she passed Becca's room, she thought about the other empty bedrooms on this floor, rooms once vibrating with energy from her now grown/flown children. When Becca found a career job soon, she'd doubtless want her own apartment. For the first time, Jennifer considered the coming empty nest.

An hour later, when she entered Greg Bromley's office, they shared small talk, including their delight in their mutual grandbaby, Zealand. Then Greg cleared his throat. "Someone at Tri-State Adoption overrode their stringent rules by tucking unauthorized notes into some adopted children's files, notes linking certain adoptees. For example, you already know the Kalinsky family adopted an infant girl they named Katherine. But this handwritten note in her file says she had an identical twin."

"*What?*"

Greg nodded. "It describes another family adopting her infant sister." Jennifer leaned forward in her chair. "A family named Hanson," he consulted papers he held, "naming her Aubrey."

"I knew it! Coincidence alone couldn't explain their striking resemblance. What remarkable detective work, Greg. You remember Aubrey Bishop at Veronika's party, the real-estate agent you've worked with and also the agent Veronika has hired to sell her estate? I'd like to tell Aubrey about this, if you don't object."

"How do you think she'll handle the news?"

Jennifer hesitated. "If it were me, I'd want to know. The truth is the truth, however people let it affect them. But I understand your point and will approach her with care. Thank you, Greg." She grinned and stood to leave.

"Wait, Jen. There's more."

Uneasy, she sat again, this time on the edge of her chair. "More?"

"I..." He hesitated. "I wondered about telling you this, but as you say, truth is truth, however people let it affect them. Is that what you really think?"

"Absolutely."

"You're sure?"

"Yes, Greg. Just spit it out."

"This adoption information also names the twins' biological parents. Their mother is Abigail Pomeranz. Their father is... Jason Shannon."

CHAPTER 52

J ennifer stiffened. "*What*? Would you...would you repeat that?"

He did.

She sagged in her chair. "Is this some weird joke?"

He shook his head.

"May I see this in writing?"

Greg passed the paper across his desk.

She read it twice, then marveled. "What a...blockbuster. Greg, you're brave to tell me this."

"Jen, there's no perfect way to handle such information. I considered telling Jason first. I considered telling you both at the same time. In the end, I decided to tell you, because I know you're strong, intelligent and level-headed. And, with your crime-solving experience, you're accustomed to dealing with sudden, unexpected jolts. This time, it's acutely personal, but I decided to tell you alone because I trust you and your judgment."

"This is staggering. You can imagine. May I take copies of these pages and the notes connecting them? I want to show them to Jason." She gave a thin laugh. "Seeing is believing."

"If you don't mind my asking, how *do* you plan to use this?"

"You already know I feel Aubrey should know the truth. Not sure yet how to absorb this startling new fact about Jason. It's a stunning surprise, Greg. I need to process it myself, and then think how best to tell him. But you were right to share this."

Greg came around the desk. "I'm relieved you feel that way. Here, I'll get those copies for you. And Jen, once you decide how to go forward, let me know the outcome?"

"Of course, Greg. Thank you for being a good detective yourself." She hesitated before turning the doorknob. "Speaking of detectives, has Adam decided what to do with your offer?"

"No. He and Hannah are still thinking it over."

"It's their decision, of course, but I hope he chooses you, Greg."

"Me, too. But I'll fully accept and support whatever he decides."

*****

That night, Jennifer felt preoccupied during dinner. She didn't whoop with typical excitement when Becca revealed Radner's evaluation of the E.K. Williams painting. It was Becca who reminded her she'd paid only $20 for it and what a *coup* that was.

After the meal, when Jason brought dishes to rinse at the sink, she asked, "What was the name of the girlfriend you dated back in high school?"

He'd long ago accepted her mind worked in ways his didn't, explaining her frequent out-of-the-blue questions. "Give me a minute to think... Abby. Abby Pomeranz. What brought that up?"

"Just wondering."

That night when they finally settled into bed, he said gently, "You seemed quiet this evening. Aren't you feeling well, hon? Or something on your mind?"

"I guess both, Jay."

"Want to talk about it?"

She sighed. "Yes, but not sure how."

He laughed. "How about your own advice: start at the beginning."

She sat cross-legged on the bed, facing him. "Remember how I thought Katie Kalinsky looked familiar and later that Aubrey Bishop looked just like her? When Jean Abingdon told me Katie was adopted, I asked Greg Bromley to look at the old Tri-State Adoption Agency records. He called me to his office today, to share what he'd learned. Turns out Katie and Aubrey are identical twins, separated at birth and each adopted by a different McLean family. So, although they are twin sisters, they had no knowledge of each other. Nor did their families."

Jason's face registered surprise. "That's amazing. Isn't Aubrey the real-estate agent from Veronika's party?" At Jennifer's nod, he added, "Are you going to tell her?"

"I think so. If I were Aubrey, I'd want to know. Wouldn't you?"

"Gee, it's hard to imagine, but I guess I would. After all, what's true is true. So that's settled. You have a plan?"

"Yes, but Jay, there's more."

"More?"

"Hold onto your hat." She passed him the report copy Greg gave her.

He put on his reading glasses and tipped the bed table lamp to illuminate the paper. As he neared the end of the page, his jaw dropped. Then his eyes rushed back to the top and he read it all again. Finally, he turned to gaze at his wife over the top of his glasses.

"Oh, my god." He read the page again and shook his head, unable to believe the words. "Is this a sick joke?"

Jennifer shook her head.

"Oh, my god," he repeated, covering his face with his hands. He leaned back against the headboard, eyes closed, trying to process this electrifying revelation.

She'd thought about it most of the day. She waited for him to catch up.

At last he looked at her. "I can't believe this, Jen. It can't be true. Abby could have written anyone's name as the father. This could be a cruel mistake."

Jennifer said nothing.

"I guess there's one way to prove it wrong. You think Aubrey would agree to a DNA test?"

Jennifer shrugged.

Deep in thought, Jason folded his arms over his chest. "On the other hand, if it *is* true... Abby went through that whole experience alone. I had no idea. Why didn't she tell me? She knew how to reach me at college and could have found me easily, any time, through my parents. She visited my home many times during those years we dated in high school."

Jennifer waited.

He shook his head, bewildered. "This is too much...too much to take in."

She looked at her hands.

"Jen, if it knocks me to my knees, what about you?"

She sighed. "At first I wondered if this happened after we met. That was its own gut-wrenching fright. But the adoption dates were before we met. So this in no way affects our trust or our love."

"Oh, Jen. My Jen. Come over here so I can hold you." She crawled beside him and melted into his arms. "How could I ever have found someone as wonderful as you?"

"Ditto," she whispered. Then she touched his chest with one finger. "Now I understand why Katie looked familiar. I saw *you* in her face. In Aubrey's, too."

He let silence fall around them for a while. "What do we make of this craziness, Jen?"

"Well, look at the bright side. Depending on DNA results, we may have a new daughter."

CHAPTER 54

Jennifer walked home, wondering what Hugh might find hidden in his new home. She unlocked her front door to a ringing phone and hustled to answer it.

"Jen, it's Veronika. I think...I think someone broke in and took some things last night."

"What? Could Bobby Radner's plan that Arnie overheard happen so fast? Does your added security provide any clues?"

"Yes, well, maybe it happened last night before we had security in place. I don't visit those rooms often, since I live now on the ground floor."

"Were the rooms as you remembered them for Saturday's party?"

"Yes. I visited each room that morning, to be sure the house looked tidy for my guests."

"Then this possible theft happened between the party and today, or in the last three days."

"Yes. This morning I went upstairs to make sure I hadn't overlooked anything I wanted packed for the move to Pebblebrook. That's when I noticed something amiss."

"Can you compare these rooms now with past inventory photos you've taken of these rooms?"

"Yes, but not now. My files are boxed and sealed for the imminent move, but several upstairs rooms seemed different. Since I'm not certain without the photos for proof, the police might dismiss my complaint as the senile ravings of an old woman."

Jennifer laughed. "You're not senile and the police will take very seriously whatever you tell them. But it would help if you could list some of the missing objects."

"With the move filling my mind, I can't recall specific missing pieces. My increased security starts today, and, because of the boy's tip, the police said they'll have someone here also. Or maybe this thief isn't Bobby but another criminal."

"Veronika, did you see any evidence of a break-in the last three days, like jimmied doors or broken windowpanes? Or more things you recognize are out of place, which a thief might have examined but returned to the wrong spot? And have you talked with your staff about whether they saw or heard anything the last few days or nights?"

"No, but I will do all those things right now. Thank you, Jennifer, for these sensible ideas."

"Do you have hidden cameras filming these rooms?"

"Some, but they require light—daylight or electric lights. They couldn't record someone in the dark."

"Veronika, if you or your staff find any evidence of a theft, contact the police right away. Meantime, why not take photos of the rooms as they are now to compare later with your packed-up photographs? Then you'll quickly see if those photos are the same."

"Excellent idea. You are quite the detective, my dear. Thank you, dear Jennifer."

They disconnected and Jennifer glanced at her watch: 10:00. She found Aubrey Bishop's business card and dialed her number. "Hi, it's Jennifer Shannon. Are you with a client or is this a good time to talk?"

"Jen, it's always a good time to talk to you. What's up?"

"Would you like to have lunch with me today? I have something to share."

"Lunch works well today, especially if you could make it in downtown McLean, where I have a 1:30 appointment."

"Okay, what about Café Tatti at 11:30? That should allow you time for both."

"It's a date."

"I'll make the reservation. See you there."

She went upstairs to change clothes and check texts and e-mails. Veronika hadn't called back, and she knew she'd be gone several hours with the lunch and local errands afterward. Just before she left, she dialed Veronika. "Hi, it's Jennifer. Any news?"

"No. It's a big house and takes a while to check all the main-floor doors and windows. But none of my staff remembers anything unusual last night. I'm still going through rooms, taking photos."

"I should be back by four o'clock. Call me then if you have anything to report."

"Yes, dear. Thank you, again."

CHAPTER 55

As Jennifer entered quaint Old-World Café Tatti, Aubrey awaited her at a table. After exchanging greetings, they ordered and talked while awaiting their meals.

As the waiter left, Aubrey smiled. "Thank you so much for referring me to Veronika. She's delightful. And what a unique property. She hired me and I already have several interested buyers. Just as she predicted, three developers want to divide the property into mini-estates, and one prospective buyer wants to live there and maintain it as the handsome estate it is. She'll make the final decision, of course. But I think she'll go for the offer from the one who won't sub-divide it. It's a big opportunity for me and you're responsible."

"If she selected you, she thinks you're the best person to further her interests. She's elderly but intelligent, *and* she has uncanny instincts about people. Looks like you made her 'A-list.'"

"I'll work hard to earn that honor."

"Didn't she plan a delightful party? The wonderful food, the backdrop of her estate. Even ponies and horses..."

"Yes, and also my chance to meet your family, friends and relatives."

Which reminded Jennifer of the reason for today's meeting. How to introduce the adoption topic? Such a bombshell could wreak emotional havoc for someone thinking adoptive and biological parents were the same. "Have you and your family always lived in McLean?"

"My parents moved here from Ohio a few years before they picked me, but this was always my home, except for college."

"Before they 'picked you'?"

"Yes. I'm adopted. They told me so from the start. They said I might not have their eyes or their smile, but I had 200% of their hearts."

Jennifer felt a rush of relief. This bit of luck opened the adoption door, but how should she march through? "What a beautiful way for them to describe their love for you. Would you tell me a little about your parents?"

Aubrey grinned. "My parents? They're Dreda and Perry Hanson. Such wonderful people, and I'm so incredibly lucky they chose me. I couldn't possibly want better parents."

"So, if Hanson's your maiden name, then Bishop...?"

"Is my married name." Aubrey sipped her iced tea. "Harley Bishop, my architect husband, a wonderful guy but a hopeless womanizer. We divorced three years later, but I kept his name because by then we had a son...a son who died when he was seven."

"Oh, Aubrey. I'm so sorry."

"A terrible bicycle accident." She closed her eyes a moment, remembering. "But back to my parents, my mother's in Montessori School management and teaches there and my father's a psychologist."

"They sound great." Jennifer stirred her coffee. "Have you ever wondered about your biological parents?"

"Occasionally, but I'm convinced my bio-mother had important reasons for deciding adoption was better for me than what she could offer. I think she wanted the best for me and, hard as it may have been for her, adoption was her gift. I feel comfortable with that understanding."

"What if an unlikely series of events made information about your biological family instantly available to you. What would you do?"

"Well... I guess I'd want to know. Information is information. But it wouldn't change the love I feel for my real... for my adoptive parents. Naturally, I'd be curious. Not curious enough to ferret out the information myself, but if it fell into my lap, sure, I'd look."

"I think it's fallen into your lap." Jennifer pulled out the copies Greg gave her. "Might you like to look at these?"

Aubrey locked eyes with Jennifer. "Is this a life-changing moment?"

"It's whatever you make it."

Aubrey hesitated, then extended a hand as Jennifer passed her the papers. She read them once, looked up at Jennifer and read them again.

Their food arrived. They concentrated on their meals as Jennifer waited for Aubrey to take in this startling information.

Aubrey touched one of the papers. "This says I have a *twin*?"

"An *identical* twin." Jennifer put her hand over Aubrey's. "But I'm so sorry to tell you, you *had* a twin. Sadly, she died recently, before you had a chance to meet her. Her adoptive parents named her Katherine, Katie for short." Jennifer described seeing Katie's familiar-looking face at the sale, seeing the obit photo of that face, visiting the funeral home, and meeting Katie's Aunt Jean.

Aubrey nodded. "This could explain why friends sometimes say they've seen me places around town where I knew I hadn't been. Where did she go to high school?"

"McLean High, according to her Aunt Jean."

"Imagine, she and I, both living in McLean, yet our paths never crossed. But we lived in different neighborhoods, which meant different schools and different friends. McLean has at least 50,000 residents. Was it fate?"

Jennifer gently touched her arm. "Or just coincidence. I'm so sorry you two couldn't meet, but when I saw you at the garage sale, I thought I'd seen a ghost. You and Katie look exactly alike. I didn't want you to disappear. When I learned you are a real-estate agent and Veronika wants to sell her property, it clicked."

Aubrey held Jennifer's gaze as she lifted the papers. "Thank you for telling me about this. It must have been hard for you to do."

Jennifer shrugged. "Yes, because I didn't want to upset you, but I had to take that risk to give you this important information."

"You did the right thing. I *should* know."

Jennifer hesitated. "Actually, there's one more puzzle piece."

"What do you mean?"

"Did you notice the names of your biological parents?"

Aubrey studied the papers again. "I don't recognize the woman's name at all but... wait a minute...this says Jason Shannon." She gasped. "Isn't that...your *husband's* name?"

Jennifer nodded.

Aubrey read the document again. Her eyes narrowed in disbelief. "Am I to understand this says my father is your husband?"

Jennifer leaned forward. "Apparently, he and Abigail dated all through high school. Then they went to different colleges, where they knew they'd have different experiences, and agreed to cool their relationship during that time. If it were meant to last, they thought they'd find each other again. But after the first few months, he didn't hear from her again. He assumed she'd met someone else, and eventually he did, too."

"You."

"Yes. But we met our sophomore year. This happened freshman year, before he knew me."

"This is huge. What a shock. But...you're okay with this?"

"Well, there's one T left uncrossed. Abigail was young, probably scared, and might even have had some other awkward reason for naming the father of her twins. Which is to say, she could have written any name as the father."

Aubrey nodded. "I see. This leaves two possibilities: we always wonder, or I get a DNA test."

Jennifer inhaled. "Yes."

"I don't know...too much too fast." She kneaded her napkin. "What's your husband's reaction?"

"He'll play any role you like: welcome you as a daughter and offer you more people to love you, *or* let you go, with his love, his blessing and his farewell. You make this decision."

Aubrey sat forward. "Where...where does one get DNA testing?"

Jennifer smiled. "Funny you should ask." She handed Aubrey a business card. "I used to work for this company. They're just up the road at Tysons. If you decide to take this next step, I'll tell them to expect you. We're willing to pay for this as an investment in your future, however you decide to shape that future."

Aubrey sagged back into her chair. "Sorry, I...I'm just completely overwhelmed."

"Aubrey, I couldn't think of an easier way to tell you this, and I apologize for bringing you such startling information. On the other hand, if later you decide you like the idea, I'm pleased to welcome you into our family as a new daughter."

Aubrey's tapered fingers covered her eyes. "This is...just too... way too much to believe."

Jennifer sighed. "I understand. I felt the same way when this wild situation revealed itself."

Their eyes locked, acknowledging this shared experience. "Then you're as shocked as I am?"

"Yes, but I've had an extra day to think about it."

Aubrey gave a mirthless laugh and spoke with resolve. "Look, I have no trouble making decisions, and I'm making one now. I'll get this test—this afternoon if my appointment finishes in time. If not, tomorrow. Please tell them to expect me. And paying for the test is something I need to do as an investment in my own future."

Jennifer patted Aubrey's hand. "In addition to your other talents, you're brave."

"Jennifer, it took courage for *you* to share this with me."

"If it were me, I'd want to know."

The waiter approached their table. "Would you ladies like dessert?" he asked.

Aubrey shook her head and Jennifer volunteered, "I think we've just had dessert."

Smiling at his confused expression, Jennifer paid the check. The two women left the restaurant arm-in-arm.

CHAPTER 56

WEDNESDAY

Arnie finished work at the grocery store and drove straight to the catering office.

"Hi, Arnie. Good to see you," Ginny said. "Tonight's catering event is a businessmen's cocktail party at a home in Great Falls. It's a big-bucks party so we're going all out. Rolf tells me you've done well serving and keeping the buffet table containers full. You already know the routine. But I like to coach new hires about diplomacy."

"Diplomacy?"

Ginny studied him. "It's what you do or say to build and keep good relations with our customers. The usual politeness and good manners. Call the men 'sir' and women 'ma'am.' Remember they've hired our catering company to provide a professional event to please everyone so much they'll want to hire our company again and recommend us to others."

"Uh...okay." Arnie shifted uncomfortably. "Do you have some examples of this diplo...?"

"Diplomacy." She thought about this. "Always be responsive to guest requests. If someone asks you to pass a certain appetizer again or asks for a special drink, provide it quickly. You can't serve liquor yet because of your age, but you can alert Rolf right away and point out the person wanting the drink. That way the customer gets fast results."

"That's easy."

"Another diplomacy bit: avoid getting drawn into conversations or expressing your opinion. If they ask what *you* think about a controversial subject, like politics or religion or race or sports teams, be diplomatic. Say something like, 'Your guess is as good as mine." Or 'I'll have to think about that.' Or 'I'm not sure I'm the best one to answer that.' You're polite but non-committal. Get the idea?"

"Yeah... I *think* so."

"Okay, here's your white shirt. Rolf speaks well of you, Arnie. I trust you'll do a good job for us tonight."

In less than an hour, the van of food, drink, linens, flowers and four servers pulled into the ample driveway of a large Great Falls home. Once inside, they efficiently set up the bar and food tables. Promptly at 6:30, the doorbell rang as business-suited men began arriving. The servers circulated with trays of appetizers and drinks. As the company expanded into the large home's many main-floor rooms, the boisterous buzz of conversation rose to a din.

As Arnie offered his tray of snacks to a small cluster of men, one of them turned to him. "Here's a smart young man. Let's ask him. What do you think about climate change?"

Diplomacy, Ginny called it. He flashed the guest a congenial smile. "Thanks for asking, but I'm just not qualified to answer that big question, sir."

Arnie moved smoothly among the guests for half an hour, but as he turned the corner from the living room to the den, he froze in his tracks. Was he hallucinating or in the group of men ahead of him, was that his *father*? As Arnie stumbled backward to withdraw, one of the men called him over. "Son,

I'd like another whiskey sour," the man said without looking at Arnie, as if the boy were an automaton. "And I'll have a scotch on the rocks," said his father, also not looking up. "And some more of those crab cake appetizers."

"Yes, sir," Arnie mumbled, backing away. He sped to the bar to report the drink requests and to load more crab cakes onto his serving tray. He wanted to run outside, to get away, but he needed this job. He made himself return to the den, approaching the group of men slowly, balancing his tray and listening to their conversation. They didn't notice him.

Deep into the topic, Arnie's father said, "Yeah, adopting a kid may sound good at the time, but it can backfire. Take my case. My wife lost a baby at birth, and nothing would do afterward but for us to adopt an infant. Bonding with this child worked miracles for her, but the truth is, I never could warm up to him. I always preferred the two who were my own flesh and blood."

A man entering the room nudged Arnie aside. "Hello, young man, I'll take some of those crab cakes. Any napkins to put under them? Good. How do you like the catering business?"

"I...I like it, sir," Arnie responded, aching instead to overhear his father.

"Have you one of their business cards for me? This is a great party and I'd like to hire your company for my own event next month."

Balancing his tray with one hand, Arnie reached into his shirt pocket for the cards Ginny placed there for just such an opportunity.

"Thank you. You represent your company well, young fellah."

"Thank you, sir." Why wouldn't this man leave him alone so he could hear his dad? "We'll look forward to working for you, sir." As he moved on, Arnie gave a slight bow and sidled near his father to pick up on the conversation.

"...my son Jim. But eventually it turned out okay."

Another man in his father's group interjected, "What about our new home-team football quarterback?" The crowd jumped on this topic as Arnie approached them, offering his tray. Several grabbed crab cakes mid-conversation and one man thanked him without looking at him.

Arnie answered, "You're welcome, sir."

His father looked up sharply. Total surprise blended with recognition that his son stood beside him. "Excuse me a moment," he said to his companions and guided Arnie to an alcove. "What the hell are you doing here?"

"I work part-time for this catering company."

"I haven't seen you around the house lately." He smiled. "Is it because you're enjoying that car?"

"The car's great, Dad. Thanks for giving it to me. But the reason you haven't seen me around is Magda made me move out."

"*What?*"

"Yeah, I'm bunking at a friend's house now. But Dad, I need to talk to you about two *important* things you need to know. *Please* listen." He didn't wait for permission but plunged ahead. "The night I moved out, I snuck into your office. I hid in the kneehole under your desk when the den door opened. It was Magda and a man she called Otto. She showed him the safe and said the money and guns were there. She said she didn't have the combination yet but expected to soon. She said as soon as you put her in your Will and on your bank accounts, they'll 'remove' you. That means killing you. They laughed about it, Dad. She said now that I was gone, she had complete control inside the house. You probably don't believe me, but I'm telling you the truth. Every time my cell phone rings, I'm afraid it's police telling me you're dead."

His father's stunned expression told Arnie his father didn't know. Dejected, the boy shook his head. "You never listen to me, but please, Dad, understand what I'm saying."

His father eyed him warily. "And the second thing?"

Arnie hung his head. "I knew you kept a pistol in your desk drawer and, well, I wanted to kill myself, so I took the gun. You might say I stole it, but I only borrowed it because I knew the police would give the gun back to you when they found my body. But then, I realized if Magda and Otto tried to hurt you, you might reach for that gun and it wouldn't be there. You couldn't protect yourself. But I was too scared to return to the house to try to put it back."

"Oh, my god." His father gritted his teeth.

"My life's changed now that my friend's family, like, took me in. And I have the car you gave me, and two jobs. I'm okay now. But if anybody finds the gun in my car or my dresser drawer, they won't understand. I want to give it back to you because now you need it and I don't."

His father appeared to age while Arnie relayed his news.

Rolf came over to them. "Excuse me, sir," he said to Arnie's father; then to Arnie, "We need you in the kitchen for a minute."

"Be right there. Look, Dad, can we meet somewhere tomorrow or very soon so I can return..." he glanced at Rolf, "that item? Do you even know my cell-phone number?" When his father shook his head, Arnie produced a pen from his pocket and wrote the number on a catering company business card. "Here it is. Please call to meet me tomorrow or, like, as soon as you can."

Arnie accompanied Rolf as they threaded their way back through the crowd. "Someone you know?" Rolf asked.

"Yeah, my dad."

"A good surprise?"

Dejected, Arnie sighed. "Hard to know."

CHAPTER 57

THURSDAY

Arnie hardly believed his ears when a familiar voice on his cell phone said, "Arnie, it's Dad. Could we meet for dinner tonight?"

The boy could not suppress a relieved smile. "Sure, Dad."

"Where?"

"Ah, how about McLean somewhere.?"

"All right. Could you come to Kazan at 7:00?"

"I'll be there."

"See you then." His dad disconnected, but Arnie stared at his phone, amazed.

After work, Arnie got a haircut. He donned his white catering shirt, the only non-T-shirt he owned. He changed his tennis shoes for the black Sketchers he wore to his catering job.

He arrived a few minutes early at the restaurant, surprised to find his father waiting for him, drink in hand, at a table in a corner of the upscale Turkish restaurant. This was the first time in Arnie's memory the two of them had shared dinner alone together.

With no idea what to expect, he steeled himself for some new level of rejection. His hands fidgeted under the table. "Thanks for meeting me like this, Dad. I...I appreciate it."

"No problem, son. Look, let's order first and talk afterward." He raised a hand. "*Waiter.*" The server materialized immediately. "Another scotch on the rocks and," he extended an open hand toward Arnie, "what do you want?"

"A Sprite?"

They studied the menu briefly and made choices. The waiter sped away.

"Arnie, it's time we talked about some things. Thanks for telling me about your experience with Magda. My lawyer told me to install surveillance equipment to record her activities and phone calls. Without a prenup agreement, unless I can make a case against her, under Virginia divorce law she could get half of everything I've worked my ass off to accrue. Before you told me what you overheard, I had some suspicions, but now I'll document what I need to know."

Their drinks arrived.

"So, tell me, Arnie, how did Magda make you move out of your own home?"

Arnie told the story, trying not to get too emotional.

His father listened intently. "I had no idea about this. I'm sorry it happened, son. You can move back any time you want. I'll make sure she doesn't crowd you this time. You may think I haven't been a good father." He took a deep swig of his drink. "And you'd be right. My parents were not warm, wonderful people. My father was never ...ah, approachable. So I learned early not to express many feelings, because he thought it showed weakness. This doesn't excuse my behavior, but...but maybe helps explain it. Your mother was the opposite, warm and gregarious. We complemented each other. When she died, I...I took a nosedive. I thought marrying again would make a home for you and balance my own life again. I apologize it didn't work out that way for either of us."

Wide-eyed, Arnie sipped his Sprite.

"How old are you now, Arnie?"

"Seventeen."

"And what year in school?"

"Senior next year."

"Any college thoughts?"

"Not really. I knew I couldn't afford it. Why want what's impossible?

"How are your grades?"

"Mostly A's."

"Have you a career in mind?" At Arnie's blank look, he narrowed the field. "What interests you now? What are your favorite subjects in school?"

"Basically, STEM."

"Stem?"

"Science, technology, engineering and math."

"Ah, *that* STEM." His father grunted an apologetic laugh.

"And I really like flying drones. I belong to a drone club at school, and my friends and I operate them for fun most weekends."

"Drones, huh? Well, I asked about your plans because you can count on me to fund your college education. Why not talk with your guidance counselor about college careers matching your interests and skills? To point you toward colleges offering that education. Once you know, they'll help you apply, and I'll pay any fees. In fact," he rooted in a pocket for his wallet and extracted some bills, "here's $500 in advance to cover those fees. I'm also seeing my lawyer tomorrow to put your college funding in my Will, so it's not contestable in case...in case anything happens to me."

Their food arrived and Arnie's father ordered another scotch. They ate awhile in silence.

Then Arnie leaned forward. "About that...that *item* we talked about in my glove compartment. It's in a box, so easy to move into your car when we go to the parking lot."

"Good."

"I...I hope you don't need it, but while she lives in the house with you..."

"Thanks for your concern, Arnie, but I think I can handle this."

The waiter approached. "Dessert?" He recited the choices and they each selected one.

Because of his catering job, Arnie noticed how efficiently their waiter handled every phase of the meal and how requested items arrived almost immediately. Now on the receiving end, he understood the impact swift, polite service made.

Following dessert, his father ordered a double brandy.

"Dad, at that party where we saw each other last night, I... uh, accidentally overheard part of your discussion with your friends about you and Mom adopting a baby."

Surprised at this segue, his father tried to recall the conversation, unsure exactly what he'd said. Remembering now, he wished he'd said nothing about adoption, never mind that his son overheard it. He downed half his brandy and thumped the empty glass heavily on the tablecloth. He stared into space, appearing to talk to himself, although he spoke the words aloud. "The stillbirth devastated Rachel. My god, she was..." his eyes filled with tears, "inconsolable. Then she got this idea that if she didn't have her own infant to love, she could heal her pain by mothering someone else's. Coincidentally, the adoption agency had babies available. They processed our application in only two weeks. And the result worked like magic. With this newborn in her arms, she became her happy self again. The baby was exactly the therapy she needed, and how she loved him."

Arnie shifted in his seat. "So, you named him James. My big brother?"

His father gulped the remaining brandy, studied the empty glass, and lowered it deliberately to the table.

"We named him Arnold."

CHAPTER 58

FRIDAY

After Becca left for the antique shop and Jason for his office, Jennifer processed her e-mails and, facing a hectic day, reviewed her day's to-do list:

8:30 Celeste cleans here
9:00 Grammy's movers arrive
Hamilton family moves in
Veronika - phone moral support?
Tonight - Dinner with Grammy & Veronika at Pebblebrook?
Aubrey DNA?

The doorbell rang. As Celeste entered, Jennifer couldn't resist. "You survived cleaning Hamilton's house?"

Celeste shrugged. "A *huge* job for only one day, but my team did it. Good thing the house was empty, but you were right. The place hadn't been cleaned for *years*. Every surface *very* dirty. Bathrooms and kitchen especially grimy. Lots of scrubbing.

Insects, nests and webs, strange spills of 'stuff' hardened like concrete. Dead mice, decayed rats, and a snake carcass. We had to clean each window at least twice."

"Oh, Celeste. After such hard work yesterday, are you up to tackling my house today?"

"Sure." She laughed. "I'm young, strong and determined."

Jennifer hugged her. "...and the owner of a successful residential cleaning business. I'm proud of you and what you've accomplished, Celeste."

At the sound of a loud, grinding motor, discernable gear shifts and squeaky brakes, they looked out the window to the cul-de-sac, where Grammy's moving van maneuvered for curb position. "I'm at Mom's if you need me." Jennifer grabbed a basket of prearranged goodies and some boxes, hurried across the street and rang the doorbell.

"Hi, Mom. Ready for your big day?"

"Yes, and they're right on time. Good start."

Jennifer handed her mother the basket. "Coffee thermos and fruit are for us, but the donuts are for anybody you choose."

"Thank you, dear. With these, the movers and I can face the day."

They took a quick look around the main floor. "You're well-prepared, Mom. Great job."

"Have you asked Celeste to clean here after I leave, so we can turn it back to the owners in good condition?"

"No, but good thinking. She's at my house today, so I'll arrange it before she leaves."

The doorbell rang. Before Grammy opened the door, she smiled at her daughter. "Here they come. Let the adventure begin."

"Good morning, ma'am. I'm Whistler, the guy in charge. Let me introduce my crew." He did. "First, we pack whatever goes into boxes. Then we wrap the furniture. Then we load it all in the truck." He consulted his clipboard. "Three wardrobe boxes and six large picture/mirror containers?" At Grammy's nod, he added, "Okay, just show us what we need to pack, and we'll get started."

With this underway and Grammy comfortable with the situation, Jennifer said, "I brought donuts for the Hamiltons, too. Remember they move in down the street today? Are you okay alone for a bit while I dash these over and come right back?"

At Grammy's confident nod, Jennifer drove her car down the block, where another moving van hugged Hamilton's curb. The front door of their house stood open as movers wandered in and out. She collected the donut boxes and rang the doorbell. An attractive redheaded woman appeared.

"Welcome to your new neighborhood. I'm Jennifer Shannon from six houses down the street that way." Since her hands held boxes, she pointed her face in the right direction.

"Hello to you. I'm Holly Hamilton. Hugh told me about you. Let me add my thanks for the advice you gave him. He *did* find some valuables and, using your other idea, he stored enough of my cousin's belongings to hold a garage sale once we're settled." She smiled, accepting the boxes. "Thanks also for these. Donuts will definitely help sweeten this busy day."

"Going well so far?"

"Movers arrived a few minutes ago, so it's just underway."

"I won't keep you. I know you need to tell them where to place every item they bring in."

They chatted a few minutes, said their goodbyes and Jennifer drove back up the street to help her mother.

CHAPTER 59

At that same moment at the antique store, Becca opened a box of new merchandise. Unwrapping each newspaper-clad item with care, she placed delicate cups on saucers, lined up fragile vases and unusual sterling silver bowls for display. She unwrapped the next item and stared in surprise: a Shang Dynasty ritual wine goblet just like her mother's and Veronica's. Feeling a thrill of excitement, she'd tell her mother about it tonight, in case she wanted another.

Examining the goblet, she turned it upside down and gasped. In the cleft where the three legs joined the goblet's cup was her sharpie mark. This belonged to Veronika! How did it reach the antique shop? Because of the woman's age and the confusion of moving, had Veronika forgotten she intended this as a gift for Jennifer? Had she sold it instead?

The next pieces Becca unwrapped belonged to a delicate china Royal Crown Derby tea set. Veronika owned just such a set. Was this also bought from Veronika's home?

"Mrs. Radner? Do you happen to know the source of this box of beautiful things?"

"Bobby brought them in last night. He buys antiques all over the place. He has amazing connections and brings our best merchandise. And look... here he comes."

The bell over the door jingled as Bobby strode in, a large rocking horse under one arm. "Hello, lovely ladies." He kissed his mother's cheek and Becca's too.

Mrs. Radner beamed at her son. "You seem exuberant this morning,"

Bobby flung his arms wide and emoted, "I love the smell of possibility in the morning."

Both women chuckled. He pointed to the rocking horse. "A great-great-great grandfather lovingly created this a hundred years ago and it's passed through family generations ever since. Now it waits for a discerning buyer who enters our establishment."

Becca admired the skilled carving of the animal's wooden body, the black horsehair mane and tail and the matching red saddle and bridle. "He's certainly handsome."

Mrs. Radner looked at her son and laughed. "And so is the rocking horse."

Bobby turned apologetically to Becca and gestured toward his mother. "She's my one-member fan club."

"You do find marvelous antiques." Becca's curiosity rose. "Like this box you brought that I just unpacked. Where did these come from?"

Bobby hesitated. "I bought these from a dealer yesterday."

Becca knew these items came from Veronika's house, but Bobby had planned to make offers on various items. Had Veronika sold them to him, or to this other buyer from whom Bobby said he bought them?

Half an hour later, Becca excused herself and, in the privacy of the shop's bathroom, dialed her cell phone. "Veronika, it's Becca. How's your move going?"

"Nice to hear from you, dear. Going well. Packers doing a fine job. Will I see you tonight at Pebblebrook when your parents come for dinner?"

"Yes, you will. I know you're busy, but two quick questions. Did you decide to keep the Chinese bronze wine goblet for my mother?"

"Oh my, now that you mention it, I think that's one of the things missing from my Oriental room upstairs."

"What about your Royal Crown Derby tea set? Did you sell that?"

"No, Becca, but I don't remember seeing it yesterday either. I told your mother I thought we'd had a break-in, but I can't find any broken windows or damaged locks."

"Did the teapot lid have a tiny chip in the base?"

"Why, yes, it did, but how could you know that?"

"Long story. I'll explain tonight. Happy landings with your move. Bye."

Becca disconnected and stared at her phone. Someone stole Veronika's goblet and tea set, and maybe more. Bobby? Or the person he said sold them to him?

Slipping out of the bathroom, Becca busied herself in the shop. When Mrs. Radner went back to the storeroom, Bobby sidled over to her, "Beautiful lady, will you join me for dinner tonight?"

Was this an unexpected chance to learn more about the theft of Veronika's belongings? "Why yes. Thanks, Bobby. But would tomorrow night do instead? My family's having dinner at my grandmother's new apartment tonight."

Bobby tapped a finger to his forehead. "That's right, I almost forgot. She and Veronika move to their senior residence today. Tomorrow's perfect for our dinner, lovely lady. Why don't we meet here at the shop to make my restaurant choice a complete surprise?"

She wrapped her mission in a flirt, "Okay. But only if you'll share some of your trade secrets."

He turned on the charm. "Ask and ye shall know."

"Where in the world do you find unusual things like this hobby horse?" She caressed its mane. "Or" she gestured toward Veronika's tea set, "that remarkable china pattern?"

He flashed her a disarming grin, stuck his thumbs in his belt loops like John Wayne. "Well now, little lady, if I told you I'd have to kill you."

Though his voice remained light and his face amused, she thought his smile didn't reach his eyes. She felt a wave of discomfort. Had she seen a glint of calculating coldness beneath his persistent charm?

Becca picked up the Shang Dynasty wine goblet. "I'm always alert for the unusual. This caught my eye. What can you tell me about it?"

He didn't hesitate. "It's a ritual wine goblet from the Chinese Shang Dynasty, made using the lost wax method so no two are exactly alike. This one came from a wealthy estate."

"Oh? How do you know?"

He studied her a moment before turning away. She couldn't read his face as he called back over his shoulder, "That's what the dealer said when I bought it from him."

CHAPTER 60

B ack from Hamilton's house and about to join her mother, Jennifer parked in her own driveway. She'd skirt the moving van and walk across the street to Grammy's rental. But first, she dashed inside to arrange a day for Celeste's team to clean Grammy's place after today's move.

Starting toward her mother's house, she realized she'd left her cell phone in the car. As she opened her car door, it rang. Recognizing Greg Bromley's number, she eased into the car to sit comfortably while they talked.

"Hi, Greg."

"Any update for me?"

"Yes. Jason took the news well enough, though he's sorry Abigail struggled through that experience without his help. Aubrey already knew she was adopted. Her parents told her from the start. But discovering she had a twin surprised her, although with Katie dead, she can't really pursue that knowledge. The good news—she agreed to a DNA test, so we should soon know if Jason's really involved. Once she has the results, she'll figure out how this may affect her life...as will we all."

Greg sighed. "Sorry, Jen. As I mentioned before, there's just no good way to share such info."

"True, but overall, so far so good."

"Well, if you're sitting down, there's one last piece of information I didn't mention to you until I knew how the earlier news settled out."

She lay back in the car seat and sighed. "You're kidding, right?"

He chuckled. "Afraid not. This connection comes from another 'unauthorized' note left in Katie's file in that same mystery person's handwriting. Without these notes, we'd never have imagined how these separate adoptions connect. Are you ready?"

Jennifer gulped. "I...I hope so."

"At age twenty-six, Katie Kalinsky had an out-of-wedlock child in Maryland, a state where Tri-State Adoption operated. But this child was adopted two weeks later by parents here in McLean."

"*What?*"

He repeated it.

"Does it name the parents?"

"Yes. A family named Anderson adopted the infant. They named him Arnold Foster." A silence. "Jen, are you there?"

"Yes...yes, I'm here. Just...digesting this." She gave a slightly hysterical laugh. "Are more revelations coming or is this the last one?"

"Jen, I apologize. Not fun being the messenger, but I couldn't know where this would lead any more than you could. And I know you always want the truth."

"You're right. Thanks for straight talk, Greg. I'm not ungrateful...just a lot happening fast."

"Call me if you need some support."

"Thanks, Greg, but I'm okay."

Jennifer ended the phone call, leaned on the steering wheel, and stared out the windshield as she processed this latest grenade burst of information. She shook her head. Would this disturbing chain linked to the woman at the garage sale never end?

She hurried across the street to her mother.

"Hello, dear," Grammy greeted her. "They expect to finish by early afternoon."

"When the van leaves, shall I drive you over to Pebblebrook to meet them?"

"Yes, dear. I made dinner reservations for us in one of Pebblebrook's lovely dining rooms at 6:30. Will Jason and Becca join us?"

Jennifer nodded. "They will." She gazed at the nearly empty room. "Mom, what stands out about today's move so far?"

"Their efficiency." She thought a moment. "How well the Pebblebrook staff smoothed this experience." Grammy chuckled with hands over her ears. "And now I know why they call the crew chief 'Whistler.'"

They shared a spontaneous laugh.

*****

Before dinner that night, the group gathered to see the newly furnished version of Veronika's and Grammy's apartments. As they entered Grammy's unit, she explained, "When the packers opened boxes, the Pebblebrook team put dishes and glasses on shelves, clothes in closets and food in the pantry."

Veronika nodded. "They even made our beds and hung towels and wash cloths in the bathroom. And they send maintenance tomorrow to hang pictures. What a pleasant way to end an otherwise difficult day."

Jennifer gestured. "Did they provide these flower bouquets in each of your apartments?"

Grammy grinned. "No, those came from Bobby Radner. Here, I'll read his card." She pulled it from a pocket. "'Grammy, wishing you happiness at Pebblebrook Manor and always.'"

Veronika produced her card, "Veronika, thanks again for the wonderful party. An honor to meet the Mistress-of-the-Mansion and see your fine antique collection.'"

Becca and Jennifer exchanged glances. Was Bobby a polite gentleman or a polished con man?

At dinner shortly after, in one of Pebblebrook's attractive dining rooms, Grammy said, "We've signed up for a play at the Kennedy Center next week. They bus us there and back so all we do is stroll inside for the show. How convenient is that?"

"And," Veronika added, "tomorrow night we attend a musical program right here in our own auditorium, when George Mason University music department grad students show their talents."

Jason laughed. "You've been here less than 24 hours and are already in the swing of your new lives. Amazing!"

Becca folded her napkin. "I'm afraid I have some bad news. Today at the antique shop two items came in that I'm sure belong to Veronika." She explained how she identified them.

Veronika's brow knitted. "Jennifer, I must have been right about the displays upstairs looking different. This proves someone took them."

Jason nodded. "And apparently unloaded them fast, if they were resold to your shop, Becca."

Jennifer patted Veronika's hand. "You were right about a theft. Should you involve the police?"

"But I'm just getting settled here..."

Becca observed, "The sooner they look into it, the better their chances of solving this crime." She wanted to speculate how this theft might link to Bobby's conversation that Arnie overheard in the stable, but Grammy held up a hand.

"Although Veronica and I agree our moves were easy, we're both weary tonight."

Veronika smiled. "Will you forgive us for fading early? And Becca, I'll follow through tomorrow with the police. Thank you for your alertness in discovering this situation."

Jason took Grammy's arm. "We'll walk you back upstairs to say goodbye."

"Let us know if you need anything at all," Jennifer said for the umpteenth time as they all hugged goodnight.

CHAPTER 61

SATURDAY

Feeling a paw touch his forehead at 7:00 a.m., Arnie looked into Toby's yellow eyes. "Thanks for the wake-up call, pal. Here, give me a minute to dress and we'll go outside."

As they walked into Gerry's back yard, a flash of red in the next yard caught Arnie's eye. He moved toward it but stopped short. Peering through a bush, he saw the red was a shirt worn by a teenage girl in Mrs. Ogelby's back yard.

Man, she was a knockout. Excitement stirred as he noticed how her long brown hair swayed whenever she moved her appealing figure. He stared, lips parted. Against her red blouse, she held a cat. He heard her talking to it but couldn't catch her words. Edging closer, he eased through the bushes and trees dividing the properties and stepped onto the Ogelbys' driveway.

Weeks earlier, he wouldn't have dared this, but he'd gained more self-assurance by working at the grocery store where Armand treated him, and the other workers, respectfully and fairly. The catering job further increased confidence that he could be sociable in ways he hadn't known possible. He no longer felt like the shy, despairing, unwanted loser he did while living at home.

His need for destructive behavior—when attention for bad actions felt better than no attention at all—had ebbed. He'd substituted positive attention from people who accepted him for who he was and what he did. And he better understood the reason for his father's coldness toward him. The man wasn't his real father, just the reluctant husband of the woman who insisted on becoming his adoptive mother, the person he knew had loved him. That was her gift to him. When she died, he thought he was lost, falling through life with no handholds. But now, he saw it differently. He felt as if he'd shed the skin of that person he'd become, and a different Arnie stepped out, the likeable person his mother always assured him existed inside.

"Hello," he said to the girl.

"Hello to you. We just moved in. I'm Heather Hamilton."

"Arnie Anderson. I'm, like, staying awhile with the Wilberforce family. Have you met them?"

"Gerry and his parents? Yes, yesterday afternoon."

"Toby is my cat's name. How about yours?"

"Cally, short for calico."

"Calico?"

She closed the distance between them. "See, she's white with orange and black spots, classic calico markings. Did you know calico cats are females?"

"Gee, no. That's, like, really cool."

"Cally, say hello to Arnie."

Cally meowed on cue, causing them each a surprised laugh.

"Guess what." Heather looked up at Arnie.

"Okay, what?"

"Today's my birthday. I'm 17."

"So am I. Well, like, happy birthday, Heather."

"Thanks, Arnie."

He thought fast. "Hey, I'm, like, going to the McLean Fire Station this morning for a tour. Want to come along?"

"We're really busy unpacking, but I'd like to. Let me, like, ask my parents. What time?"

"Ten. I'm driving there, so leave about, like, 9:45?"

"They'll want to meet you first."

As he gazed at this beautiful girl, Becca left his radar. "...who?"

"My parents."

"Ah...okay then, why don't I ring your doorbell at 9:30?"

CHAPTER 62

L eaving Heather, Arnie rushed to give his car a frenzied cleaning for a good impression on this incredible girl. He combed his hair, cleaned his fingernails, and put on clean clothes, before ringing the Hamiltons' doorbell at 9:30.

When Heather opened the door, flashing her enchanting smile, Arnie hoped his jaw hadn't fallen open in awe.

"Come in, Arnie. Meet my family."

Wanting Heather and her family to like him, he tried not to appear awkward. He used catering-event behavior—polite, smiling and upbeat. He shook hands with the parents and acknowledged the three sisters who gave their names: Helen, Hilda and Harriet.

Arnie scratched his head. "Wait a minute. Your names *all* start with 'H'?"

The sisters nodded and nine-year-old Hilda giggled. "And our mother's named Holly and our dad is Hugh."

Arnie's amazement showed. "Wow."

Heather's mother gestured toward her 13-year-old. "I hope you don't mind if Harriet goes along with you this morning."

"Yesssss," Harriet hissed, punching a fist into her other open palm.

"Ah... sure. Um, that's fine." Arnie hoped he hadn't gargled this disappointed answer. He wanted Heather to himself. Thirteen-year-old Harriet flashed a triumphant grin, following him and Heather to the door. As they started toward his car, Arnie waved back to those inside. "Nice to meet you all." So far so good...

When they settled into the car, Heather shrugged. "Sorry about the chaperone."

Arnie paused at a stop sign. "That's okay. She might even, like, have a good time."

Harriet snickered in the back seat. "Just give me any reason to get my sister in trouble!"

Heather sighed. "She's a little snot, but I love her anyway, don't I, Harriet?"

"You better," Harriet growled.

At the fire station, they asked for Nathan, who appeared moments later to greet them. After introductions, he said. "Come on, let's take a tour. We're open for duty 24/7/365. We're here to help protect community life, property and environment. Fire & Rescue responds to four basic kinds of emergencies: medical, fire, hazmat and rescue."

Heather looked confused and Arnie watched her flawless profile as she turned to Nathan. "What's the difference between medical emergencies and rescues?"

"Medical emergencies are things like chest pains, trouble breathing and sudden injuries."

"Like chainsaw amputations?" Harriet gave a mischievous grin.

Unfazed, Nathan agreed. "Exactly. Accidents just like that, whereas rescues are things like people trapped in elevators or lost in the woods or downed in a plane crash. Hazmat deals with chemical and gas leaks or spills, and so on. We also handle fire-alarm and sprinkler malfunctions, and we're first responders in dangers like earthquakes or floods."

Heather's mouth formed an O. "You have *earthquakes* and *floods* in McLean?"

"Earthquakes starting elsewhere in Virginia occasionally pulse through here, so we feel them. In August 2011 we felt a 5.8 magnitude that started in Mineral, Virginia. McLean got scattered structural damage from that one, and the Washington Monument closed for two-and-a-half years for repairs. We don't feel most small tremors, although seismographs record them. This spring, we had a flood in a low area of Kirby Road in McLean that required rescue and wiped out a chunk of road." Nathan continued show-and-tell about their equipment, uniforms and gear.

At last, Arnie shuffled his feet impatiently. "Did you want to, like, talk some about drones?"

Nathan nodded. "Arnie, they are amazing tools. How did you get interested in them?"

Arnie looked self-conscious, remembering. "My best friend's a drone-freak and it kinda, like, rubbed off on me. Once I learned what they can do, I was, like, hooked."

"Fire departments, like all drone users, must operate legally, which includes being respectful of citizen privacy. You can find what's legal at the FAA Drone Page to learn UAS rules and regs."

Harriet scratched her head. "FAA? UAS?"

Nathan opened his mouth to respond but Arnie beat him to it. "Federal Aviation Administration and Unmanned Aircraft System."

"Right," Nathan confirmed. "FAA has jurisdiction over anything we put in the air."

Arnie watched, riveted, as Heather opened her pretty lips to ask, "Does that mean a kite or balloon is a UAS?"

Noticing Arnie's attentiveness to Heather, Nathan gave him a chance to shine. "Arnie, can you answer that?"

"Anyone can fly kites up to 150 feet in open areas but, like, not near an airport or military base. Same for helium balloons. I think tethered balloons can go up 400 feet in open areas. Or you can request special FAA permission if you have some other reason to fly higher, like maybe a science experiment."

Nathan nodded.

Heather looked concerned. "My family just moved here from southern California. Besides earthquakes, we, like, also had awful forest fires there. Do they happen here, too?"

"Virginia Forestry Department fights those fires. Our climate's normally greener and wetter than southern California's, but we get occasional dry spells with fire risk in the Shenandoah forest and elsewhere. In Virginia, 98% of forest fires are caused by humans, so prevention is important. Speaking of forests, I read last week that planet-wide, we lose 1½ acres every second, or 15 billion trees a year. Reforestation is a problem."

Alert, Arnie turned to Nathan. "Have you heard about Bio Carbon Engineering's drone invention?"

"No, tell me."

"Man, it's a tree planting drone that fires biodegradable tree bullets into the ground. Each bullet has, like, soil, nutrients, and a tree-seedling. They use artificial intelligence to tell drones to fire the bullet the exact depth and position to grow. And get this: one drone can plant 100,000 trees a day."

"Awesome." Nathan pulled a small notebook from his pocket. "I want to write this down. You never know when info like this could make a difference."

As Nathan wrote, Arnie repeated the facts, adding, "Yeah, it's an Australian company. Who knew?"

"I'm impressed, Arnie. Have you thought about a future operating drones?"

"Not really, but someday I'd like that, because I work now for a grocery and a caterer. Kind of a waste drone-wise, huh?"

Nathan considered this. "I think you can learn something new from every job you do, but future planning's also good. When do you graduate?"

"Next year."

"Any college plans?"

Arnie's dad promised to fund his college, but could he count on that? "My school counselor says with my 3.8 average I should go to college, but I don't, like, have a specific plan yet."

"Well, get busy on that. You like math?"

"Yeah."

"Maybe aeronautical engineering to design and build drones?"

"Maybe..."

Sudden blaring sounds rocked the station, triggering fevered activity among the firefighters. Nathan backed away. "Uh, sorry kids, gotta go. Come back another time?"

The firefighters clambered aboard the engine and the shiny red truck pulled out of the station, siren screaming.

CHAPTER 63

Elsewhere in McLean, Jennifer worked at her computer when the phone rang.

"Good morning, Jen. It's Aubrey Bishop."

"Hello there."

"DNA results are back."

Jennifer's breath caught. "What...what did you learn?"

"Mine matches Jason's." A long pause. "Jen, are you still there?"

"Yes. We really appreciate your doing this for us, Aubrey."

"Well, I did it for me, too. Now we know the truth, I hope to get to know Jason better."

"He'll be glad to hear that. Would you like to have dinner with us? Maybe even tonight?"

"That's a wonderful idea. When?"

"How about cocktails at 6:00 and dinner after that. Any dietary restrictions?"

"Not a one."

"That makes it extra easy. Maybe Jay will grill something for us."

"See you at 6:00."

She hung up the phone, checked her watch and dashed out to her first garage sale. Once there, she nosed her car into a parking spot outside the address and walked up the driveway. After checking out the tables and grouped items like luggage, bicycles and sports equipment, she approached the furniture. A quick survey confirmed she wanted nothing there, until she noticed something short behind a chair. Walking closer, she realized this upholstered vanity stool looked familiar—a different color, but otherwise just like the one in Katie's bedroom. As she took a closer look, a member of the Seller's family, wearing a University of Virginia t-shirt, strolled over.

"Hello," she said. "This belongs...belonged to me. I spent many an hour sitting on it, looking into my vanity mirror and wondering if I'd ever be attractive."

Jennifer appraised the pretty college girl. "Well, you certainly reached that goal. You're a beauty."

The young woman laughed, caressing the stool's velvet upholstery. "But it was important in my life for another reason."

"What?"

"The treasure trove."

"The *what*?"

"The secret hiding place." She bent forward. "Behind this biggest tassel is a button. When you press it, the top releases. See?" She demonstrated, opening the top of the stool to reveal an empty cylindrical cavity inside. She sighed with nostalgia. "Over the years, I hid many things here. As my banker Dad might say, this was my safety deposit box."

Jennifer's face brightened in amazement as she felt a mental light bulb blink on. "That's it."

The girl looked puzzled. "That's... what?"

Jennifer grinned. "You just solved a mystery for me. Thanks so much."

Spontaneously, she hugged the surprised college girl and dashed back to her car. Inside, she dialed Jean's number. The phone rang until the answering message kicked in. "Aunt Jean, it's Jennifer. Please call me the minute you get this message. I may have some new information."

*****

A few hours later Jean returned her call.

"Aunt Jean, thanks for getting back to me. Are you on your cell phone? Good. Could you walk it upstairs to Katie's room to check on something? Wonderful. While you're on your way there, may I explain? Okay. Today I learned Katie's vanity stool may have a hiding place—and if it does, maybe we could find what's inside."

"I'm almost there," Jean puffed up the stairs. A pause. "Okay, I'm in her room. Let me flip on the light. All right. I'm ready."

"Look among the vanity stool tassels for one larger than the others. Take your time." Jennifer heard movement sounds as Jean searched the upholstered cylinder.

"This could be it."

"Lift the tassel and see if there's a button underneath. If there is, press it to release the top."

"Oh my...you're right, I heard a click and the top moved a bit."

"Okay. Open the top to see if anything's inside."

Silence. Then Jennifer heard a moan. "Aunt Jean? Is anything inside?"

"...yes."

Jennifer waited. At last, she prompted. "Aunt Jean, what did you find?"

"...a lot of things."

Fighting her impatience, Jennifer chose calm. "Could you please describe them?"

"Notebooks, jewelry, some...clothes, some pictures... various things. Sorry, I...I must sit down. Wait while I pull her desk chair over here...."

"Aunt Jean, do you see dates on any of the notebooks?"

"Yes."

"Is one of those dates for this year?" She heard shuffling sounds.

"Yes."

"Could you open that notebook and look inside?"

"I'm not sure I can do this, Jennifer. I'm not sure I want to know what's inside. I'm so uncomfortable. I..."

"Would you like me to come over to help you?"

"I'm not sure if anybody should look at things hidden by a dead person. I'm not a snooper. I respect people's privacy. How could I face Katie's ghost if I pried into her secrets?"

Jennifer tightened. "I could be there in fifteen minutes."

"Well, I...I don't know. I...guess you could, but...."

Jennifer *knew* she must act fast to take advantage of this unique opportunity.

"Okay. I'm on my way."

At Aunt Jean's house, she found the front door unlocked, hurried inside, and dashed up the stairs to Katie's room.

Jean sat on Katie's desk chair, gazing vacantly across her room.

Jennifer extended a hand. "I brought us each bottled water. Here, let's have a sip." Trance-like, Jean opened the bottle and drank.

"Have you been outside today? It's beautiful. Your crepe myrtle in the front yard is blooming."

Jean looked her way for the first time. "Oh?"

"Yes. Want to come over to the window for a look?"

Jean rose. Jennifer took her arm to guide Jean's robot-like walk to the sill. Looking outdoors seemed to waken her return to reality. "You're right. I see some blossoms."

"Want to take a little walk outside?"

Jean shook her head, as if removing cobwebs. "No...I'm okay now." She glanced at the vanity stool and shrank back. "But I think I'll wait downstairs while you see what's here."

"What's this pillow?"

"It was stuffed inside on top of those things."

"I see. To compress the contents against rattling around if the stool were turned upside down. All right, Aunt Jean. Careful on the stairs."

Jennifer knelt by the vanity stool and scooped the contents onto the floor.

CHAPTER 64

L ooking at vanity-stool array on the floor, Jennifer separated the items into like groups: photos, notebooks and miscellany.

Noticing dates on the backs of the pictures, she turned them all upside down to arrange those dates consecutively. Then, right-side up, they would unfold in chronological sequence.

The first photo, dated five years earlier, showed an antique-shop scene with a staged-looking grouping of Mr. and Mrs. Radner with Katie standing beside the wife. The next, dated six months later, showed Mr. Radner and Katie, smiling at the camera as if they shared a secret. Another, four years ago, of Katie and Radner seated smiling in a restaurant. He held her hand toward the camera, showing an antique ring on her finger.

A picture three years ago showed the two of them standing holding hands in front of an unidentified building. She wore unusual earrings, highlighted because of her blond hair, pulled into a ponytail. Two years ago: Katie and Radner focused on a table of antiques, his hand on her arm. One year ago, she smiled but he looked stern. The picture dated nine months ago showed both looking serious.

Then an abrupt change of subject. The photo from six months ago looked like a selfie. It showed Katie and Bobby laughing. The next three showed Katie and Bobby in front of different locations, apparently enjoying each other's company.

Jennifer put the photos aside to check the notebooks. They weren't identical in size, but each had a year written on the front. She flipped through several. Diaries! She wanted to start at the beginning if Jean allowed her to take them home, but Katie's aunt had become skittish. In case not, Jennifer needed to learn what she could now. She opened the current year, flipping to entries right before Katie's death. A few pages before the last entry, in what the dates showed as the days before her demise. Jennifer read:

"I didn't think I could survive when Rob broke up with me, but Bobby saved me."

"Are you coming downstairs?" Jennifer heard Jean's impatient voice.

"Yes...yes," she called. "Just gathering up." She whipped out of her purse the "emergency" Ziploc snack bag into which she'd squished two wadded-up plastic grocery sacks. These had proven useful in the past and soon bulged with the vanity stool's cache. She descended the stairs, praying Jean would let her take them home.

"Would you like me to look through these, Aunt Jean? I'll return everything once we know if it sheds any light on what happened to Katie."

Wringing her hands, Jean showed her anxiety. "I...I don't think so. Call me superstitious, but this feels like walking on a grave. I think Katie hid those things not wanting me or anyone else to see them. She can't protect her belongings now, but I can. I think I should burn them all."

Jennifer panicked. She must change Jean's mind to protect this critical information. Buy time, she told herself, until you think what to do. "Aunt Jean, you're right. This unexpected discovery feels overwhelming. Let's sit down a minute and take some deep breaths." They did. "Would you like a glass of water or anything from the kitchen?"

Jean shook her head, close to tears. Jennifer spoke gently. "These notebooks are diaries. I share your concern about Katie's privacy. But why did she record and hide this information if not to protect it? She could have written nothing and saved nothing. Instead, she carefully documented her life and kept these notebooks safe so someone could find them one day. That day is today."

Jean brushed her eyes with the back of her hands. She looked up, listening. Jennifer had her attention, but could she change Jean's mind?

"Finding them right now's important, Aunt Jean. If Katie wanted to live to raise her baby, someone snuffed her life against her will. This information she safeguarded for us could tell us who. And if someone took her life away when she wanted to live, wouldn't she want that person accountable? She left this information for us to answer those questions. How could we consider destroying what she worked so hard to preserve for us to find? And now's the time we urgently need this gift she left us. To find the truth she wants us to know."

Jean sagged in her chair. "You'd take good care of it?"

"Aunt Jean, of course I would. You know I would. This will all come back, for you to keep."

Jean was on her feet and moving toward the front door. "Then just take it...quick, before I change my mind."

*****

That afternoon Jennifer and Becca pored through everything in the bags. They studied the photos and, in a small box, found the ring pictured on Katie's hand and the earrings she wore in another shot. They found an expensive Hermes scarf and other probable presents from Robert Radner.

Jennifer indicated the stack of diaries. "Let's read the last diary first, the one likeliest to explain her death?"

Becca nodded. "It's also the shortest since she died in June. That's only six months of this year."

"Here's something she wrote a few days before her death. I started reading it in her room before Jean called me.

"*I didn't think I could survive when Rob broke up with me, but Bobby saved me. His attention and affection, his humor and kindness, helped me feel lovable again. But now that's all changed. He's leaving the country and can't take me along. He says we must end our relationship. I told him about his baby, to know he wasn't making a casual choice. He said he'd pay to get rid of it but otherwise runs from parenthood. I can't believe his attitude. I'd never harm a baby. Just like I didn't with my baby 17 years ago. Then I chose adoption because I knew I couldn't care for him, but this time I'll keep my baby. Even if Bobby doesn't want to, he'll need to pay child support because I must protect this child. If he doesn't agree, I'll have to go to court. How will Aunt Jean accept my motherhood? She doesn't like change—but I think I can convince her, and she'll soon fall in love with the baby.*"

Jennifer exchanged "the look" with Becca. "Homicide needs to know about this."

She dialed Adam.

CHAPTER 65

Aubrey rang the doorbell Saturday at six o'clock. Right on time. Jennifer and Jason met her at the door.

"Thanks for inviting me. As you can imagine, I have many questions."

They settled into the sun porch's rattan furniture. Jason brought their drink orders, saying, "To the beginning of a long, happy relationship." They sipped.

Then Aubrey added, "To my biological father, who I never expected to meet, and to his remarkable wife." They sipped again.

Jennifer's eyes twinkled. "Many people in the world feel lucky to have one set of parents. Now you have two sets."

"And three mothers, if you include Abigail." But no sooner had Aubrey spoken than she shrank back. "Is it all right to...to mention her?"

"Of course," Jennifer said. "We're all adults who know life springs surprises."

"Whew, I'm relieved you feel that way."

Jennifer stood. "Jay, why don't you and Aubrey get better acquainted while I get some appetizers? Do you like lamb chops, Aubrey?"

"They're a favorite."

"Jason uses a special marinade and grills them like the pro he is."

He shrugged, palms up. "Despite that build-up, keep a reasonable expectation."

Hearing their voices as she puttered in the kitchen, Jennifer caught occasional partial phrases from each, such as "and then I moved to..." and "got my degree in..." when she returned with an olives-cheese-and-cracker platter, her eyes flickered a bit wider at Aubrey's next question.

"Finding myself now on this unexpected new path, you might understand I'm also curious about my birth mother. The adoption agency's papers said her name was Abigail Pomeranz. Do you know if her family still lives in McLean? If so, maybe they'd know where she is."

Jason frowned. "I know where they lived, but that was about forty-five years ago. You're welcome to the information. I'm surprised I still remember the address. Here, I'll write it down."

"Were...were you and Abigail together long?"

Jason gave Jennifer a sidelong glance. "We met as high school freshmen at Langley. She was beautiful, like a movie star. We 'went steady,' as they called it then, all four years. We tried for the same college, but it didn't work out. Cooling it while we went to different colleges was Abby's idea. She said we could still see each other when we came home to McLean for holidays and summers, and if we were meant to last, we would."

Jennifer hadn't heard these details and followed his words as closely as Aubrey did.

Jason sipped his wine. "At first, we talked long distance every day, then every few days, then once a week and finally hardly at all. When I came home for Christmas holidays, her parents said she decided to stay at school—some ski trip opportunity with a dorm mate. I was disappointed not to see her but figured it was a nice trip for her. Then at Spring Break she scheduled another trip and that summer she stayed on for summer school. I wanted to drive there to see her, but she was too busy. She always loved horses and had a summer job working at the school's stables. With that and her studies, she said she didn't have enough free time to justify the long drive."

Aubrey and Jennifer stared at him, each wondering how an unplanned pregnancy fit those scenarios. Her refusal to come home surely covered her baby's arrival. Perhaps she stayed away even longer to avoid awkward questions while she got her act together again afterward.

"Her parents were confused, like me, but we respected her decisions. Back in college my sophomore year, I began dating again, met Jennifer, fell in love with her and the rest is history. Abby never contacted me again and I had no reason to visit her parents, so I lost track of them all." He polished off his wine. "Looking back, I must admit Abby's brushoff hurt at the time. I thought then we were solid, with a future together."

Silence filled the porch.

Jennifer asked brightly, "Time to grill the lamb?"

After a pleasant dinner, Aubrey left. Jason hugged Jennifer close. "Remembering those old days made me realize how lucky I was to find you." They climbed the stairs arm-in-arm.

Later, as they lay under the covers in their darkened bedroom, Jason snored lightly while Jennifer stared at the ceiling. What if Aubrey found her biological mother and this woman from his past reappeared in Jason's life? "Beautiful, like a movie star," he'd described her this evening.

She crept out of bed and into the bathroom. She turned on the light to examine her face in the mirror. No, her sixty-year-old wrinkles hadn't disappeared. She considered her body, no longer the sleek, firm 20-year-old coed he'd remembered Abby being. Jennifer frowned. He'd loved Abby once; might he love her still? Might the romantic sight of his dazzling first love eclipse forty-some years of routine daily life he'd shared with his now middle-aged wife?

When found, could Abigail threaten or even *destroy* her happiness?

CHAPTER 66

E arlier the same day in their McLean home, Sally Bromley reminded Greg, "Wonderful that they're joining us for dinner tonight. According to some of my friends, we're lucky our only child and his wife live so near, and that we get along well. One gal told me they hadn't seen their son for twenty years. What a heartbreak...."

Greg nodded. "And more luck, we're grandparents. Notice how little Zeland acts good-natured and intelligent...just like his grandfather?" He grinned.

"Is this your cue to lower your eyes shyly?" Sally giggled. He obliged. "But it's true," she said, "you and Z are both smart and friendly. And I don't have to risk earning the 'dreaded-mother-in-law' label, because Hannah's easy to love."

"...and so are you." Greg kissed her cheek. "I'm so grateful we found each other."

Sally nodded. "And I'm so grateful, for Jennifer's alert discovery about Adam that changed our lives."

"She's a natural at discovering things. I think we're in good company, being related to the Shannon family."

The doorbell rang. "Here comes the grandbaby!" Sally eagerly headed to open the front door, with Greg a step behind her.

*****

After a delicious roast-beef dinner, laced with good conversation, Sally and Hannah cleared the table, chatted in the kitchen, and played with Zealand.

Adam excused himself to the patio to answer a business call on his cell phone. As he finished and started back inside, Greg said, "It's such a pleasant evening, may we talk out here a few minutes?" They strolled across the stone pavers to look out over the expansive lawn. "Here, I brought you a snifter of Bailey's Irish Cream, in case you'll join me.

"Thanks." Adam took the glass. They stood quietly, sipping their after-dinner drinks.

"Thank you, son, for coming tonight and sharing your family with us." Another pause. "Is everything going well?"

Adam gave a wry laugh. "Could use more sleep, like any new baby's dad. Busy at work. On loan to homicide now, I see an even seamier side of police work. But I like my job and think I'm getting good at it. My personal life is great. Love my wife. We're settling into our new house, in a good location with a wonderful view. I didn't use to think about school districts, but Fairfax County's is outstanding, and Zealand will start first grade in less than six years."

Greg chuckled. "Having a son broadens your outlook, doesn't it? Ask me how I know...."

Adam caught his glance, remembering they'd only learned two years ago that they were related, thanks to Jennifer's detective work. This discovery could have gone either way, but luckily this accomplished man and his calm manner were easy to like.

Greg spoke again. "My life certainly improved when I learned you're my son. I thought I'd never be a father, making you the best surprise I could imagine. Not everyone who discovers a grown son has my good fortune."

"Fortune?"

Greg smiled broadly. "Well, you're accomplished, intelligent, responsible, a devoted family man and you're pursuing an important job you believe in. You're all I could hope for in a son."

"Thanks, Dad," he said seriously, and then laughed. "Guess now I need to live up to those generous words." He hesitated. "And I feel equally fortunate my father's a fine man like you."

Greg put a fatherly hand on Adam's shoulder. "Have you given more thought to my job offer? You're well-qualified, and by working on cases together, we could get to know each other better."

Adam hung his head, dreading what came next. How could he describe his dilemma without offending this kind man? Worse, might he derail their fledgling father-son relationship? "Dad, I've put off answering because this is awkward for me. Of course, I value the opportunity to work with you. And Hannah loves the idea of a bigger salary and less danger."

Greg indicated two chairs behind them. "Shall we sit down?" They did.

Adam shifted uneasily, "I admire you as a successful general-practice attorney doing family law like wills, trusts, pre-nuptials, divorces, adoptions, real estate and so on. But you're also a defense attorney. This may be hard for you to understand, but for a sworn policeman like me, working for you feels like going to the dark side."

Surprise etched Greg's face. Recovering, he said, "I admire straight talk, Adam. Please, go on."

"Police risk their lives and prosecutors work their butts off to get criminals off the streets...to make our community safer for the public. I've testified in court numerous times when we *knew* a perp was guilty as hell, but he got off because his defense attorney snowed the jury. How? To inject reasonable doubt for his client, the defense attacks the cop's character and record, then he attacks how the cop conducted the investigation. Last, he attacks the homicide victim, who's dead and can't defend himself. It's a dirty business. And if I'm that cop, and it ends with the guilty guy walking free, then it's a big professional *and* personal disappointment for me."

Thoughtful, Greg tapped a finger on his knee. "Adam, it took courage for you to explain this."

Adam shrugged. "Yeah, but there's more."

His father's eyes locked onto his. "More?"

The distress on Adam's face revealed his inner struggle. "Even if you concentrated only on family law, what would your chief investigator do? Shadow cheating husbands for divorce evidence? That doesn't light my fire. I'm sorry, sir, but much as I'd like to join your firm and work alongside you, I just...I don't see how it's possible."

Greg's silence lasted so long that Adam winced. Had he irreparably damaged their relationship by insulting his father's professional ethics? Yet what choice did he have? He *needed* to explain his caveats if they hoped to shape a future together, never mind a professional one.

Greg sounded thoughtful. "Would you agree big companies usually have some good employees and some bad ones?"

Adam wondered where this was going. "Yes, of course."

"And narrowing that further, among the good employees are very good employees and among the bad, very bad employees."

"True again."

"Do you think that applies to any large group, hypothetically, including the police force?"

Adam hesitated. "I guess."

"So when the bad cops cause trouble, as has happened in various police departments, what do the good cops do?"

Adam hesitated. "I see where you're going with this. Bad cops cause problems two ways: deliberately or incompetently. Good cops hate it both ways."

"No question in my mind that you're a good cop. But defense attorneys sometimes face bad cops who haven't done their job well or whose court reports aren't trustworthy or who plant evidence. Don't defendants in trials resulting from bad-cop case-handling also deserve justice?"

Adam shifted uneasily in his chair. "I understand what you're saying, but I can speak only to my personal experience in court."

Greg's voice was calm. "Good talk, Adam. You brought up things I needed to know. Now I understand a job to excite you would use your keen investigative skills *and* appeal to your strong sense of justice. If I can come up with something, shall we talk about this again?"

Adam looked up in surprise. "Of course. And thank you, sir, for..."

"Listening to my son? Isn't that just what you'll do with Zealand?"

"I...yes, sir. And this exchange just reminded me why I will."

CHAPTER 67

Elsewhere this same evening, Becca and Bobby finished a delightful dinner in nearby Tysons Corner at the glitzy Brazilian restaurant Fago de Chao. His debonair and knowledgeable banter during the meal again wrapped her in his spell, despite her attempt to remain objective.

Bobby grinned. "Instinct moves our bodies to Brazil's sultry, whispery music like 'Ipanema,' and now you see how their food served by costumed gaucho waiters makes our bodies sultry in other ways."

To defuse this sexual tension, Becca said, "Did they really carve seventeen different meats onto our plates from those swords?"

"For you, Becca, nothing but the best." He tipped the valet, guided her to his car and wove his way out of the Tyson skyscraper maze toward Vienna. At the antique shop, where she'd parked her car, he said, "Let's go inside a minute. I want to show you something."

She followed him into the hall, past the office and storerooms into the breakroom. "Come in," he said, and she joined him.

Relaxed on the couch with a large book in his lap, he patted the sofa cushion beside him.

"Want to see some family pictures, including yours-truly, nude on a bear rug?" Seeing her hesitation, he added, "I was six months old."

She smiled and sat beside him. As he turned pages, he progressed in the photos from toddler, kindergartener, grade schooler and soccer player to high school and college.

"My mother put this together. Calls it my Baby Book, even though she still adds to it occasionally."

Becca turned more pages to pictures of him in restaurants, at auctions and posing beside various antiques, and in conversation with well-dressed people. As the pages turned, his parents and others she didn't recognize appeared. She stared at the album, but he stared at her, reminded of the couch's convenience for romance. His hand rubbed her back.

Suddenly Becca stiffened at a picture of him with a girl... Aubrey? "Who's this?"

He looked, surprised. "I haven't seen this, but it's not important." He fumbled to close the book, but she forced it open.

"No, I'm curious," she insisted.

"It's...it's just Katie."

Alert now, Becca spoke carefully. "She looks smitten. You two are holding hands, and look at the way she stares up at you."

"Ah," he thought fast, "maybe because I'm the boss's son and she worked here?"

Becca knew better from Katie's diary. Deliberately, she turned the page. "Look, here are more of the two of you."

"Hell, I didn't even know they were there. My mother has a wry sense of humor to continue this album at all, never mind like this. It seemed amusing when she captured me as a kid, but this new stuff is nonsense."

"Looks like she deliberately linked the two of you."

He thought fast. "Nah, Mom just has too much time on her hands and I'm her only kid." He whisked the album away from her, plopping it on the coffee table. "Why don't we talk about the two of us instead?"

"The two of us?"

"Yes. I'm sure you've noticed we're remarkably compatible. Why not take that a step further? We have a convenient, private setting here. We're both adults. You have my full attention, beautiful lady." He embraced her and kissed her lips lightly.

Despite better judgment, she felt drawn to this handsome, suave man, this dream of a date. He was right about their being consenting adults. She responded to his kiss. But as he pushed her down on the couch, an unbidden realization flashed into her mind. This was the very couch where Radner senior and then his son had bedded Katie. The girl one of them murdered.

She pulled free and stood up, smoothing her clothes. "Thanks, but no thanks."

"You don't want me?"

"Not where your father and you used Katie."

"What?"

"You admitted your father's a womanizer. When he hired me, he put the make on me, too. Just like he did with Katie when she worked here. And *you* played a strategic role in there somewhere, because you're the father of Katie's baby."

He eyed her suspiciously. "Where'd you get that demented idea?"

"Her autopsy reports."

"What are you? Some nutty detective? Because, if your idea of a good time is insulting me, I don't see any reason why you should work here any longer."

"So you're getting rid of me just like you got rid of Katie?

"What the...what did you say?"

"Your affair with Katie, her inconvenient pregnancy. You told her you two were through. Then you drugged her, drove her home, parked in her garage, closed the garage door, left the motor running."

His eyes glittered. "Have you lost your mind? Katie killed herself. She was always shy and introverted and needy. Don't know what my dad saw in her except she was an easy conquest and right here at the store every day to enjoy. My dad had it down. She wasn't his first or best conquest, but she was certainly convenient."

Becca turned to leave. He followed as she edged toward the door and into the hall. "If she was your father's pet, how did *you* get involved?"

He shrugged. "Hey, let's clear the air here. I don't know why you're focused on Katie, but you're letting this spoil our evening. Look, Dad *is* a lecher and he carried on with Katie for years—a record for him. When he dropped her for his next flirtation, she took it hard. She was so pathetic even I felt sorry for her. I thought it was kinder to let her down easy instead of seeing her crash and burn. Believed I could boost her morale and save her self-respect. So I rode up on my white horse, though God knows it was a mercy move."

"You didn't even like her?"

"She was never my type. And old enough to be my mother. But hey, for a guy, poor sex is better than no sex. Fair trade. She felt desirable instead of discarded and I got some recreation. But after five months, I realized how mousy and dull she really was. I was more than ready to move on. I tried the gentlemanly approach, explaining work would soon take me away to other countries, so I couldn't continue the relationship. And it's true. I'm about to start an extended trip abroad. But she whined about loving me and then announced the baby. That clinched it. I have no desire to be a father or to marry anyone now, least of all Katie."

Becca pressed on. "What about the hush money you paid Katie's aunt?"

"The *what*?" He gave a humorless laugh. "How do you know about that? What's happening here? I just wanted a memorable evening with you tonight. This is nuts. But ...okay, I'll try one last time to clear the air. My father's not a nice man. He's an unfortunate combination of egotistical and obnoxious. We didn't know how Katie's aunt would react to her suicide and if she retaliated in some way, we didn't want the shop's name involved. Antique dealers depend on client trust. Nobody likes my father. Hell, I don't even like him. Certainly, Katie's aunt couldn't like him. I told my father we should give her a significant financial gift toward the funeral expenses, as a gesture of good will and compassion. By default, I became the delivery boy."

"The bronze Chinese wine goblet and Crown Derby tea set. They belong to Veronika. You saw them in her house during the picnic. Did you steal them?"

His brow wrinkled. "Geez, Becca, I told you the other day I bought them from a dealer who said they came from a wealthy estate. If they were Veronika's, he was right, because she owns beautiful things."

"So how *did you* react to Katie's pregnancy?"

"Back to that again? I told her I'd finance an abortion and even go with her for the procedure. Simple, practical, legal and gentlemanly. But Katie insisted she'd never hurt her baby. That decision, I reminded her, came with consequences. I'd help her end the pregnancy but if she didn't, whatever followed would *not* include me. She solved that by killing herself. Not an original idea, under the circumstances. Hey, are you the nice girl I think I know or some twisted undercover cop?"

She ignored his last comment, returning to Katie. "Since you admit Katie wouldn't hurt her baby, her suicide makes no sense."

"Hell, you're ruining our beautiful evening together. Where are you getting this crap?"

"My mother. She's...like a detective. She wants to help Katie..."

"Your *mother?* Wait, didn't I meet her at Veronika's party... Jennifer Shannon?"

Becca stepped back, wishing she hadn't revealed this. But it was too late. Time to go.

She picked up her purse to leave. He advanced to within inches of her face and spoke in a loud whisper. "Forget Katie. You and I are another matter. I wanted you the second I saw you and clearly, you want me." He grabbed her roughly, pinning her against the hallway wall in a passionate kiss.

For a fleeting second, she felt torn between physical desire for this handsome, willing man and disgust for the monster who likely murdered Katie.

"I'll take a pass." She pulled away.

"Oh, I don't think so." He pressed her hard against the wall. His hands began moving across her body. His lips sought hers, but she twisted her face away from him.

"*No,*" she shouted, but he was too powerful for her to push away. Frightened now that using all her strength wouldn't budge him, she screamed. "*NO.*"

When Bobby's weight shifted, she wrenched away from him, but he grabbed her hand and turned it sharply to twist her arm up behind her. She doubled over in front of him, crying out in pain. The more she struggled, the harder he jerked her aching arm. How to escape?

Desperate, she dug the point of her high-heel shoe deep into his leg. He groaned, momentarily loosening her arm. She squirmed from his grasp, knowing he'd recover any second, adding anger to his aggressive passion.

Afraid for her life, she couldn't wrestle her cell phone from her purse fast enough to call 911. Instead, she groped for the closest object she could find to smash the glass on the fire-alarm box. As the glass shattered, she realized she'd used the Shang Dynasty wine goblet. She pulled the fire-alarm handle seconds before Bobby grabbed her again.

Ear-splitting clangs filled the shop. She pulled away from him and ran for the front door, struggling to unlock it. But as she succeeded and pulled the door open, his powerful hand clamped onto her shoulder and squeezed a grip so hard the acute pain immobilized her. He jerked her back into the dark store and kicked the door shut.

Bobby growled, "You ingrate. We gave you a job and this is how you repay us? Watch what you say when they answer the fire alarm. I know your whole family from the picnic. You don't want something terrible to happen to any of them, do you?"

Her eyes narrowed as she spat out, "When police grab you, you won't do anything to anyone."

Livid now, Bobbie punched her down across an antique table, his fingers closing around her throat. Red-faced and gritting his teeth in a malicious grimace, he began choking her.

Becca's nails on one hand gouged his face before she realized her other hand still clutched the Shang goblet. She stabbed the three sharp, pointed legs against him again and again, feeling them strike flesh. Then, frantic to release his grip on her throat, she dropped the goblet to rip at his hands. The more she clawed, the harder he squeezed. Desperate for air now, she suddenly understood she couldn't escape. A strange acceptance filled her mind as she stopped fighting. Her fingers loosened. Her arms dropped lifelessly. A light brightened briefly behind her eyes, then darkened.

And then nothing.

CHAPTER 68

At the Vienna, Virginia, fire station, Nathan and the other firefighters applauded as a tenor from their crew sang the last notes of "Happy Birthday to You."

They all cheered. Nathan clapped his brother's shoulder. "Congratulations, Sam." He turned to the group. "Thanks for inviting me over here for my *big* brother's party. Sam's not thirty today; he's eighteen with twelve years' experience."

Through other male guffaws, someone shouted. "In dog years, you'd be dead now, Sam."

Another called, "You're only young once, but you can stay immature forever, eh, Sam?"

But their good-natured ribbing and laughter froze when the alarm sounded. They moved into immediate action, grabbing gear, and boarding the fire engine.

"Downtown commercial area," one called out.

"Just down the street," another said.

Nathan knew the drill well from his own McLean station. "What's the address?"

Hearing the answer, he recognized those numbers—the antique store where Becca worked. He'd driven by numerous times, hoping to catch sight of her. One day he had invited her to meet him for lunch in Vienna during her noon break. Another time he wandered into the store, pretending to be a shopper interested in antiques when she waited on him. They made it a game in front of the Radners. Nathan queried her about various merchandise and she answered as if he were a stranger visiting the store, not as his girlfriend of two years. Yes, he knew the address well.

"Could I ride along?"

The engine driver looked around. "Ah...sorry, no room this time. You could try following us in your car, but" he snickered, "you McLean guys get lost all the time."

"Watch out. I may beat you there," Nathan called back as the truck pulled out, siren blaring.

He didn't arrive on the scene first, but right on their heels.

He checked the time. Nine o'clock at night. The shop closed at six. Becca wouldn't be there, but if the shop went up in flames, she'd have no job tomorrow. He parked close by. No obvious smoke or flames. Maybe a medical emergency or a false alarm? He followed the firefighters into the building, where EMTs bent over a body, either unconscious or dead.

Nathan watched from a respectful distance as they took vital signs and applied an oxygen mask. Two techs exchanged looks. One shook his head. When they started CPR, the body shifted, and long locks of hair fell into view. Wait a minute. He recognized the hair and then the familiar dress. "My god. Becca!"

He elbowed his way closer, aghast at her chalky face and unresponsiveness. Two techs continued CPR as others brought a stretcher. "If CPR keeps her brain alive, maybe they can bring her around at the hospital. But I doubt it."

As Nathan pushed his way to her side, one tech said. "What do you think you're doing?"

"She's my fiancée," he lied, wishing it were true. "I must go with her."

Again, the techs exchanged looks. In respect for a fellow firefighter, one of them made the decision. "Okay, but hurry. We're on our way."

*****

At the hospital, Nathan watched closely as the EMTs passed Becca to the ER staff. He followed as they wheeled her gurney into the emergency room, where a nurse waved him out. "You...to the waiting room," she stated firmly, closing the door in his face.

At the waiting-room desk, he gave the receptionist Becca's name and information, and that he waited for her. Then he sat down, staring at his phone, and wondering what to tell her parents.

Instead, he called his brother.

"Sam, I'm at the hospital with her. What happened at that shop?"

"Cops are looking into it. Front door unlocked but nobody else in the store when we got there. Her car's the only one parked outside. I'll let you know if we hear anything. Maybe she surprised a burglar and he tried to kill the witness." Sam knew Becca from the many times his brother had brought her home for special family occasions. "How is she?"

"Don't know. She's in the ER now. I'm about to call her parents. Just wanted to know if there's more to add than what I saw."

"Okay. Good luck. Sending you vibes, Nate."

"Thanks, bro."

He ended the call and dialed the Shannons' number.

*****

Three hours later, a blanket-covered ICU patient stirred. Did she hear far-away sounds? What were they? Where was she? Her mind cringed in terror. Bobby! More danger? Should she look, or better not to know?

Her eyelashes fluttered and gradually opened. She stared. Nathan smiled down at her. At the sight of him, a welcome feeling of safety flooded through her. Dear Nathan. Could she smile back? She wasn't sure. She felt as if she'd wakened inside an unfamiliar body.

"Hello, darling. Welcome back to us." Nathan's voice. She tried to move her head, but the slightest change hurt too much.

Then her mother's face filled the space where she'd seen Nathan. "How do you feel, sweetie?"

Becca formed words with her mouth, but her throat couldn't say them.

Now her father's face appeared in the space. "Don't try talking yet, but the doctor says you'll be able to soon."

Could she move? She tried lifting a hand. It worked. She reached toward her father and mouthed, "Hello, Dad."

Then she felt pressure on her other palm. "Becca, this is Mom. I'm gently squeezing your other hand. Can you feel it?"

She tried to nod, but it hurt too much. She mouthed, "Where am I?"

Her mother's voice: "In the hospital, honey. But you're going to be okay."

Her lips formed the word. "Nathan?"

His face reappeared in the space. He beamed down at her. "I'm right here."

Becca smiled and closed her eyes, safe at last with precious, trusted people around her.

CHAPTER 69

SUNDAY

Next day, Adam, in police uniform, rang the Shannons' doorbell. When Jennifer answered, he greeted her with a quick hug. "How's Becca?"

"EMTs and ER saved her. The hospital may even discharge her later today. They recommend heating pads at home for her sore ribs from the CPR. She'll sound hoarse at first but should talk normally again in a week. Her concussion-type symptoms—blurry vision and nausea—should end soon. She's one lucky girl. Without that quick rescue, we could have lost her."

"If she comes home today, could Hannah and I visit this evening? If she's up to it."

"Of course. Now, I know you're in a hurry." Jennifer gestured toward the dining room table. "This is what Katie hid."

He looked at notebooks, photos, and miscellany in neat piles on the dining-room table. "Where should I start?"

Jennifer guided him, sharing what she knew about how items connected. Half an hour later, Adam put down Katie's diary. "This points the case in a new direction. The ME's report showed Robert Radner as father, without specifying Junior or Senior. This diary says it's Bobby, who has disappeared. Unless the BOLO brings him in, we can't question him about

Katie or charge him with Becca's assault, which we're calling attempted murder."

Jennifer tapped the diary. "Katie didn't describe her last day because she couldn't make an entry the night she died, so we still don't know who ended her life."

Adam thumbed through Katie's photo stack. "Both Radner men offered the same alibi for the night Katie died—that they went together for a pre-arranged look at antiques at a home in Maryland, but when they got there, nobody answered the door. They didn't buy gas or food along the way or use EZ Pass tolls, so no receipts prove the trip happened. They're each other's alibis now. Mrs. Radner agrees the two men left together that night, but she knows only what they told her."

Jennifer considered this. "If they didn't go to Maryland, they could have harmed Katie together or separately. Both had motive."

Adam gestured toward the laptop. "Anything helpful on her computer?"

"Haven't had time to delve back far, but the current stuff shows interest in baby furniture and infant care. This underscores her expectation to have the baby and raise it, not to kill herself."

Adam nodded, but then looked sheepish. "By the way, I want to thank you for the suggestion to dust for prints on Katie's garage side door. We shouldn't have missed that."

Her eyes lighted with interest. "Did it pay off?'

He looked at his watch. "Tell you about it later. I'm bringing the Radner parents into the station, one at a time, for another interview. Gotta go." He sniffed the air. "What's that aroma?"

"Chocolate chip cookies in the oven. It's the last batch. First two batches are on the kitchen counter. Want some for the road?"

"Does Pinocchio float?" He emerged from the kitchen moments later with a handful. "You may be the world's best mother-in-law."

He kissed her cheek and whisked out the door.

CHAPTER 70

A t the McLean police station, Adam stood, to end the interrogation room session. "That's all for now, Mr. Radner. Thanks for coming in. We'll check the name and address you've just given us for the antique owners you say you were to meet on your alleged trip to Maryland the night of Katie's death. Until we do, stay in town."

Rude as always, Radner sneered as he stalked out of the interrogation room. "Of course, I'm innocent. I'm an *antiquities dealer*. But what could you know about the finer things of life?"

"Right, sir," Adam sighed in resignation before closing the cubicle's door.

After the man left, Adam wiped off the table, restarted the interrogation room voice/camera recording equipment and went to the waiting room. "Mrs. Radner, will you please come in?"

A dignified Mrs. Radner entered the small, sparse room, Adam pulled out the metal chair to seat her. The stark setting and bright lights contrasted sharply with her expensive clothing, perfect make up, flawless coiffure and glistening manicure.

Smooth and sophisticated, she placed her designer purse in her lap and folded her fingers over it. Adam put bottled water in front of them both and sat opposite her.

She spoke in a composed, confident voice. "You said routine questioning?"

Adam wanted to get her talking, identify her comfort zones and hope for a "tell" if she showed unease. "Yes, to help us clear up some loose ends. Thank you for coming in."

Her hands lay motionless atop her purse. "All right."

He consulted a file on his desk. "Do you know where your son Robert Junior is?"

"No. But he planned an overseas buying-trip soon. I don't know his itinerary. Maybe he's gone."

"If he's still here, where would we find him?"

"His apartment in Tysons Corner? I think you have that address and phone number. But he also travels Europe and the world looking for antiques—attending wholesale events, big international sales and so on. He's worked for our shop in some capacity since grade school. During college, he worked summers as our buyer. Since graduation two years ago, he's full time on our payroll."

"Does he use a company credit card for business expenses?"

"Of course. He has two, in case one isn't useable for some reason."

"What about personal credit cards?"

"That's his private choice. At twenty-three, he's an adult."

"Since he's on your payroll, when he travels, don't you need to know what he does and where he goes? After all, you're paying him to do it. What if you have a new lead on an antique or instructions to buy or not buy?"

"We have complete faith in Bobby. He knows the business well. We give him a budget and general ideas, but we encourage his innovation. He never disappoints. He calls us if he has something to report, for example, to expect a shipment."

Adam tried a new tack. "Can you think why your son would attack Becca Shannon in your antique shop at 9:00 p.m. yesterday?"

She looked uncomfortable. "Shouldn't you ask him?"

"We will when we locate him. Meantime, we understand you're often in the shop, and we'd appreciate your insight on this."

Mrs. Radner studied her fingernails. "I don't know. Perhaps he caught her stealing money or merchandise from the store. Perhaps they had a personal misunderstanding..."

"Such as..."

"Well, they're attractive young people about the same age. Maybe they had some personal involvement."

"Did he tell you that?"

"No, just guessing. What did Becca say?"

He used this opening. "She said talking with him about Katie led to their altercation."

Mrs. Radner's lips tightened. Her fingers adjusted their position on her purse. A "tell"?

"Oh?"

"Yes. The autopsy found strong sedatives in Katie's system. She was three months pregnant. DNA evidence proves Robert Junior's the father. That's motive for him to silence Katie by staging the apparent suicide in her garage. He had method: the monoxide poisoning in the closed garage. He had opportunity: to drive her home and set up that final garage scenario resulting in her death. With this evidence, we could arrest him for Katie's murder when we find him, never mind Becca Shannon's attempted murder."

Mrs. Radner's eyes widened. Another "tell"? She opened her purse, retrieving a handkerchief. "We raised him to be a gentleman. I can't believe he would harm any woman."

Adam scratched his head. "If not your son, then who murdered Katie? Your husband?"

She couldn't hide a little gasp. "Why would you suggest that?"

"Katie told her aunt she'd had a four-and-a-half-year affair with your husband. Doesn't your store have an employee room with a convenient sofa bed?"

A slight tic pulled at Mrs. Radner's lips. Another "tell"?

"We do have a comfortably furnished breakroom." Avoiding mention of the couch, she blew her nose delicately.

"Mrs. Radner, our investigation reveals your husband has a long reputation for seducing women. Katie was just one of many. Given his documented involvement with her, he's also a suspect for her murder."

Mrs. Radner bit her lip. Adam couldn't believe his luck. He pressed on.

"And then there's Katie's diary..."

Mrs. Radner looked up sharply. "*What?*"

"Katie kept diaries the last five years. Quite detailed diaries."

Mrs. Radner stared at her hands.

"She described her gratitude for your sympathy when you found her crying in the store and urged her to tell you what was wrong. She mentioned appreciating your kindness and understanding when she told you about her involvement with your husband and, later, with your son, and about her pregnancy. She admired you. She wrote you offered to help her deal with her crisis."

Mrs. Radner's mouth narrowed into a straight line. She composed her words. "Katie's distress touched me. That my husband and son caused her distress," she breathed, "troubled me *deeply.*"

"And..."

"And I wanted to help her find a way through this experience. I pointed out abortion, though a difficult decision, deserved consideration. It was obvious she couldn't continue working at our shop, so she'd have no job. As a single mother, the best thing she could offer her child was adoption. On the other hand, if she chose the procedure, she could put this traumatic episode behind her, begin to heal emotionally, and start fresh with a new job and a new life. I reminded her, life always presents problems and our job is finding solutions."

"How did she react?"

"She listened." A long pause, which Adam did not interrupt. "Some...some people have difficulty making hard decisions. According to the police, her solution was ending her life." She glanced up, expecting Adam's corroboration.

But he pressed forward. "Except we found fingerprints on the garage's side door, a door not used by the home's residents, but a door used by the person who left Katie unconscious in the car with the motor running."

Mrs. Radner failed to disguise her shock. *"Fingerprints?"*

Adam pulled a report from his file and pushed it across the table. The page showed the comparison print identification, but Adam had blacked out the identified person's name. "Yes, we just got this report. Funny how that happened." Adam shifted in his chair. "The person who left Katie in the garage left no prints inside the garage or the car or its steering wheel. So those belonged to Katie, just as we'd expect."

Absorbing his words, she breathed through her parted lips as she studied the identically matched whorl-pictures on the fingerprint report.

"But when the killer left through the garage side door, his protection was gone, so he had to clean his prints off both doorknobs. To do this, the person's right hand held the wooden door steady while his left hand cleaned the inside knob. Then he steadied the door with his left hand to clean the outside knob. Since the owners hadn't used the door for years, this person left a complete set of prints from each hand on the sides of that door. This pushed us to cast a wider net for who might have motive, method and opportunity."

She locked eyes with Adam. "Whose fingerprints are they?"

CHAPTER 71

A dam acted puzzled. "Maybe you can help us out here. Who besides your husband and your son knew of Katie's predicament? Who offered her trust and the ability to solve her problem?"

Mrs. Radner's eyelashes fluttered in her otherwise composed face. Silence filled the small room for several minutes, during which she crossed, then re-crossed, her feet. She opened, then closed, her hands. Adam didn't move or speak.

Her voice changed to a whisper. "Whose prints did you find?"

"That's the surprise. They're yours, Mrs. Radner."

Her eyes shut tight. Her lips drew taut. Her upright posture sagged in the stiff metal chair.

Adam let her predicament's gravity sink in. One of her hands fluttered to smooth her flawless hair. She looked toward the ceiling, then down at the table.

Then, before she thought to ask for a lawyer, he pushed the advantage. "But I don't see how that's possible. How could your fingerprints end up on Katie's garage door?"

She stared at her fingers. "You...you can't begin to imagine what I've had to face...the years of hellish humiliation. At the start, I loved and trusted Robert. When I learned of his blatant infidelities, and still naïve to the core, I denied it. But indisputable evidence surfaced again and again, shattering any adoration for my husband. Unfortunately, by that time I'd created an appealing lifestyle in my community. I considered leaving Robert, but our marriage provided that pleasant life of social status, friendships, and related amenities. So, I... I made the *painful* decision to stay with him and tolerate the...the *grief* he caused me. I focused my attention on Bobby, a wonderful, bright boy, who grew into a handsome, capable adult."

Her face clouded. "But by the time he graduated from college, I discovered he'd become his father's clone with women. He used them without caring whom he hurt. A crushing revelation for me, leaving me with no one left to love. It broke the last fragments of my heart."

Adam didn't move.

She shifted position on the uncomfortable chair. "Katie's involvement was the final straw. As a woman, I sympathized with her predicament: jilted by the two weak, pathetic men in my family and pregnant besides. At first, I considered thinking of Katie as the daughter I never had and pouring my love into this grandbaby. I understood when she refused abortion as the simple way out. But then she said Bobby told her he had no intention of taking responsibility, that *she* alone must protect her baby. That meant child support. To get it, if necessary, she'd tell the court Bobby was her baby's father. Telling the court is like telling the world. I couldn't allow that."

She uncapped the water bottle, taking another delicate sip.

Was she finished? Would she lawyer up? Adam hid his relief when she continued speaking.

"I offered to pay her an equivalent amount of support, although quietly doubting I could swing that for eighteen years while the child grew up. And I knew she'd eventually want larger amounts, ostensibly for the child's needs, but in what amounted to blackmail."

She paused, remembering her struggle to explore all sides of the situation. "To me, my amoral husband was not the immediate problem, nor my disappointing son. Katie was the problem. Her revelation would rock their lives and my social world. Moreover, it would affect the respect antique shops need to attract and keep clients. Thus, it would destroy our income, the very thing that made my life-style possible."

Adam leaned forward, pretending sympathy to encourage her to admit more.

"Since Katie was the problem, making it go away meant eliminating Katie. I didn't want to...I liked her. But as you see, she gave me no choice." She looked up at Adam for validation.

Adam relaxed slightly. Her confession recorded—plus the fingerprint evidence and Katie's diary—made a good case. Now to frost the cake. "It's easy for me to understand your reasons, but" he feigned confusion, "help me out. How could anybody be skillful enough to accomplish that solution?" Would Mrs. Radner take the bait?

"I knew for days I must move quickly, but when? Learning my husband and son would go out of town investigating antiques on a certain night, I invited Katie to my home for dinner, just the two of us. I pulverized many pills from a powerful sedative my doctor had prescribed for me, to mix in her wine and in her food. During the meal, she ate and drank it all. When she started feeling woozy, I offered to drive her home. As she fumbled the keys out of her purse, she didn't notice me slip on gloves. I helped her into the passenger side of her car. I knew exactly where she lived from scouting the day before. At her house, I opened the garage door with the gadget on her visor, drove inside, left the motor running and closed the door behind the car."

Mrs. Radner appeared lost in the memory. "Pulling her behind the wheel from the passenger side was *much* harder than I expected. The console between those bucket seats made it nearly impossible. She was sound asleep by then and heavy. I couldn't get enough grip wearing my gloves, so I took them off and stuffed them in my pocket. Dragging her over to the driver seat took about twenty minutes. I began to worry I might also succumb to the monoxide fumes if it took much longer. At last, I straightened her up behind the wheel and pressed her limp hands onto the steering wheel as if she'd been driving."

"Did you worry her aunt might come to the garage?"

"No. She told me several days before, and confirmed again at dinner, that her aunt was a creature of habit who didn't come downstairs after retiring to bed nights at eight o'clock. But, if she *had* found us, I'd have explained driving Katie home because she was drunk. Her aunt couldn't know my real intention." A sardonic smile crossed Mrs. Radner's face. "In fact, she'd *thank* me for helping her niece."

"And then...?"

"Difficult. The automatic overhead garage light turning off surprised me, but so long as a car door stayed open, I had enough light in the black garage to see what I was doing. After I put Katie's hands on the steering wheel, I needed to close that door for the car to fill with fumes. The sudden darkness without the car's interior light when the door was open forced me to grope my way, hand-over-hand, across the front of the car to the other side. Nervous about breathing the fumes, I didn't take time to put on my gloves again. Just wiped off each place I touched with my jacket sleeve. On the other side of the car, I opened the passenger door for just enough faint light to study the locks on the garage side door. No barricade of locks and bolts like those on my own exterior garage door. This was a simple knob lock with an inside thumb-turn, plus a keylock on the outside. No additional bolt locks. Bad security for them, but perfect for me."

Mrs. Radner sipped water again. "Anxious about inhaling carbon monoxide, I had to hurry. I closed the passenger door and made my way in the blackness toward the side door. Without gloves, I again used my jacket sleeve to wipe any place I touched as I fumbled through the dark toward that door. When I got outside, before closing the door, I re-engaged the thumb-turn to "lock" and wiped both knobs clean. That way it would lock, seeming not to have been opened at all."

"What if that garage door going outside had keylocks inside *and* outside?"

Mrs. Radner gave Adam a conspiratorial look. "I anticipated that problem. Talking with Katie at the shop, and again at dinner that night, I pretended to flounder about the most convenient way to deal with my own garage doors to avoid juggling keys every time I arrived or left. Katie said at her house, she and her aunt used the garage door opener to get their cars in and out but always left the inner door into the house unlocked for easy access. They reasoned once that garage overhead door closed, it already protected the inside door to the house."

"So..."

"So my backup plan was to go through that unlocked door into the house and then slip out their front door. With Katie asleep in the car and her aunt upstairs, nobody would even know I was in the house. But, if her aunt *did* come down and find me, I'd explain that after knocking unsuccessfully on the garage door into the house, I opened it to come inside to find her. Then she would put drunken Katie to bed."

Adam couldn't believe his luck—a confession. But could he get more details? He managed a skeptical expression. "But wait a minute. How could you get home afterward?"

"I walked many blocks from their residential area to a commercial part of McLean and called a ride service with my cell phone."

After a lull, Adam asked, "Anything else?"

Mrs. Radner stared at the table and shook her head. "Yes. Robert and Bobby's dreadful choices left a mess I didn't want to clean up, but when they didn't do anything, someone had to. What a travesty. I'm the real victim of their mindless behavior, yet I'll be blamed while they go free. Chilling, isn't it?"

But she saw no compassion in Adam's stern expression as he stood. "Mrs. Radner, I'm arresting you for Katie Kalinsky's murder."

CHAPTER 72

The Shannon doorbell rang Sunday evening. Jennifer peeked out the door's glass, surprised to see Aubrey Bishop.

"Come in, Aubrey," Jennifer invited, noticing the woman's flustered look. "Having a busy day?"

"Yes. Sorry to come unannounced, but I'm in the neighborhood anyway on real-estate business. If you have a few minutes, may I talk with you and Jason about something in person, better than on the phone?"

"Sounds mysterious, but we're here and pleased to see you." She called up the stairs, "Jay, Aubrey's here to see us."

From above they heard a muffled, "Be right down."

"We'll be on the sunporch," she called again, and turning to Aubrey, "Coffee? Tea? Something stronger?"

Aubrey glanced at her watch. "It's six o'clock. Maybe a glass of wine?"

"Come to the bar and select what you'd like. Reds on the shelf, white in the small fridge below."

When Jason arrived a few minutes later, Jennifer explained, "We're starting the cocktail hour. I poured your favorite red, there by your chair."

"How much happiness can a man take?" he chuckled and lifted his glass. "To two charming women and a vintage wine." He lifted his glass even higher. "Together again." Their glasses rang clear tones as all joined in the toast.

Aubrey turned serious. "Today I played detective, trying to pick up Abigail's trail. Following your clue, Jason, I talked with her parents, still at the address you gave me. They seemed doubtful about my story, but when they read the document copy you gave me and saw your name, Jason, they seemed to consider I might really be their granddaughter."

Jennifer sat forward on her chair. "A huge surprise for them. How did they react?"

"They were understandably cautious at first. I could be anybody—most likely, someone wanting something from them. But when I showed them I'm a successful real-estate agent and life-long McLean resident, rather than a drifter with mysterious roots or motives, they decided to tell me her story. Would you like to hear it?"

Jason tapped a finger on the table. "Yes. I'd very much like some closure for that chapter of my life."

Jennifer encouraged. "Of course, we would, Aubrey. Please."

"Abby finished college, and then asked her family and friends to call her Gail, a different contraction of Abigail than Abby, which had always been her nickname. They agreed. Soon she met and later married a man they liked, named Victor Laviano. So she became Gail Laviano and lived with her husband in North Arlington, next to McLean. There she took a job in a company's headquarters and stayed *thirty-seven* years, until the company closed."

Jason sat forward. "What company?"

"One with a main office in Fairfax and branches around Virginia, Maryland and Pennsylvania."

Jennifer and Jason exchanged searching looks, unable to identify the company.

Aubrey supplied the answer. "Tri-State Adoption Agency."

Astonishment crossed both their faces. Jason broke the silence. "You're kidding."

"No. I suspect the company made no connection between their hire, Gail Laviano, and Abby Pomeranz, who'd given them twin girls for adoption years earlier. And get this: she worked in their records department for nearly four decades, obviously a valued employee."

Jennifer hoped her voice sounded casual. "So...ah, where is she now?"

"She died last year. Her husband was a military officer. He predeceased her, so she's buried with him at Arlington Cemetery."

Jennifer hid a flicker of relief. Then a new idea crossed her mind. "Do you suppose she's the mysterious employee who left anonymous notes in certain file folders? She surely meant it as a way to connect her children, don't you think?"

Jason stroked his chin. "You know, that makes sense. As son-in-law Adam might say, she had motive, method and opportunity."

Jennifer factored this into something else she knew. She touched Aubrey's arm. "If this is true, she left one more note you don't know about. Greg Bromley told me just today."

Aubrey's face clouded. "Oh no, please. I'm still reeling from his last shocker. Should I gear up for another major jolt?"

Jennifer smiled. "Only you can decide the impact. Want to know?"

Aubrey considered, finally giving a reluctant nod.

"Your sister Katie had a baby when she was twenty-six and unmarried. She gave the baby up for adoption through Tri-State. That little boy was adopted by a McLean family. He's seventeen years old now and currently living with a friend down this very street. You're now Aunt Aubrey, since he is your sister's child."

"Oh, no." Aubrey's hand covered her mouth. "My little boy was born when I was twenty-six. If he'd lived, he'd also be seventeen now."

Seeing Aubrey fight tears of memory, Jennifer tried to lighten this tense moment. "Well," she chuckled, "remember, you and Katie are *identical* twins."

"Yes, but..." Aubrey shook her head in disbelief. "you're *sure* about all this?"

Jennifer gestured with her wine glass. "As sure as possible without the boy taking a DNA test, which he'll probably do if we ask. Another touching lead Gail Laviano left in the files."

Jason and Aubrey exchanged looks.

He nodded. "It fits."

Jennifer leaned forward. "Especially since Greg Bromley says these mysterious—and illegal—notes in Tri-State's files were all in the same handwriting. In those days, agencies pledged to unwed mothers that their information would remain secret. Laws were passed to that effect, so it was illegal to reveal any compromising information. The agency issued new legal birth certificates for adopted infants, showing their true birthday but listing the new adoptive parents as mother and father. Neither those new parents nor the child was ever intended to learn anything about the true biological parents."

"I'm surprised," Aubrey said. "Even with sperm banks, the company reveals the donor's characteristics so a prospective mother can choose."

"But that's different. Adoptive parents accept all the characteristics from both biological parents when they accept the baby. The adoption agency might share vague generalities describing mother, like blond-hair/blue-eyes, but even that was mostly frowned upon. Homes for unwed mothers, in this case one also owned by Tri-State, took infants from their mothers at birth to defuse attachments that made the separation even harder."

Aubrey sipped her wine and smiled. "You say I'm an aunt. When can I meet this nephew?"

Jason cautioned. "You know about him now, but he doesn't know yet about you *or* his link to our family."

Jennifer stood. "I have an idea. Becca's still in the hospital until we pick her up in two hours, but we have her cell phone with Arnie's contact info. I'll get it while you two…"

"…in the hospital? What…"

As Jennifer retrieved Becca's phone, Jason described his daughter's harrowing experience.

Jennifer returned with the phone to hear Aubrey say, "I'm *so* sorry to hear about Becca. Thank goodness she's going to be okay."

Jennifer tapped Becca's phone screen numerous times, pressed "call," and put her finger to her lips for quiet.

"Hello, Arnie? This is Mrs. Shannon from down the street."

She heard a pause on Arnie's end of the line before he said, "*Who?*"

"You know, Becca's mother."

"Uh…okay.

"I wonder if you might drop by our house for a few minutes. We have something to tell you and someone who'd like to meet you.".

"You mean, like, *now?*"

"Yes, if it's convenient for you."

She envisioned Arnie trying to process her out-of-the-blue request and felt relief when he said, "Ah, okay… I guess. Sure. So, see you in, like, ten minutes?"

"Wonderful. Oh, and by the way, Arnie, I'm just curious—do you have a middle name?"

"Yeah…Foster."

"Thanks. See you soon, Arnie."

CHAPTER 73

A rnie disconnected the phone call. Passing Mrs. Wilberforce as he left through the front door, he said, "Thanks again for that great dinner. Going out for a little while. Back in about an hour."

As he walked down the sidewalk toward the Shannons' house, he shook his head, perplexed at their odd invitation. Adults—almost all of them—totally weird. When he got old like them, he'd never fall into that trap....

He wondered if Becca would open the door. Since Heather had captured his attention, he'd re-ordered his world with Becca as a casual friend instead of the acutely unattainable object of his affection.

What could the Shannons possibly want with him? He mentally replayed their phone call in his head. Something to tell him and someone to meet? Becca knew of his interest in drones. Maybe a friend of theirs who operated them? Or, uh-oh, maybe her cop brother-in-law. Fear scratched a warning. Was this the Ogleby show-down he'd dreaded for so long?

He rang the doorbell, anxious now about what awaited him.

Jennifer opened the door. "Arnie, thanks for coming on short notice. Please join us on the sunporch."

He followed her uneasily. Once there, he recognized Mr. Shannon and that real-estate woman from the catered party. No sign of the cop. He relaxed slightly.

Jason stood. "Arnie, have you had dinner?"

"Yeah."

"May I offer you something to drink? Coke? Iced tea? Sprite?"

"Sprite sounds good. Thanks"

"Anyone else want something? No? Okay."

When he left to get Arnie's order, Jennifer said, "You already know Jason and I are Becca's parents, but have you met Aubrey Bishop, who's a real-estate agent in McLean?"

Arnie looked at Aubrey. "Yes, ma'am, I saw you at that catered party but didn't know your name. Uh, good to meet you."

When Mr. Shannon returned with Arnie's drink, Mrs. Shannon said, "Arnie, we've just learned about some things that involve you. We'd like to tell you a story to explain."

"Ah...okay." This had to be the Ogleby confrontation. He tried not to cringe. Why had he come here? What an idiot he was. He took a nervous sip of his drink to camouflage his discomfort.

"Have you ever been to a garage sale?"

Where did this come from? Arnie shook his head.

"Well, I ask because our story started at one." She described the familiar-looking woman at the garage sale, the obit photo giving her a name, meeting Katie's Aunt Jean, learning about Katie's adoption, asking an attorney to investigate Tri-State Adoption records and discovering Katie's identical twin. "Because someone at that adoption company tucked a secret note into Katie's adoption file, we learned that Aubrey is Katie's identical twin."

Arnie exhaled. While this irrelevant story killed time, he felt palpable relief that this wasn't about Mrs. Ogeleby.

"But then this story took a surprising turn. The attorney discovered from the adoption records that Jason," she nodded toward him, "is the father of those twin girls because of a high school romance he had long ago with a girl named Abigail. He knew nothing about these twins for over forty years—until this information surfaced recently."

Arnie began taking a tiny interest in this odd story.

"And then that attorney learned from another secret note in her file that Katie had a baby when she was about 25 years old. She wasn't married, and since she couldn't provide for this baby, she put him up for adoption. Her baby was adopted by another family in McLean, who named him Arnold Foster Anderson."

Arnie's mouth dropped open. He looked as if he'd been hit by a brick. This weird story about strangers had somehow circled to point at *him*.

He shook his head as if dislodging cobwebs. "So...what exactly does this mean? I...I'm all confused."

Mr. Shannon smiled. "You're absolutely right, Arnie. The story is confusing, but bottom line, it means I'm your biological grandfather. Abigail was your mother and Aubrey is your mother's identical twin sister, making her your biological aunt."

Arnie looked around the group, trying to reorient these near strangers into family members.

"Man...I...I don't know what to think."

Aubrey leaned forward in her chair. "Think about discovering you have a whole new family who welcome you to join them. I understand you live with your adopted father, and you're probably very happy there, but I live alone in a big, empty house in McLean and you'd please me very much if you'd like to visit—or even live with me. And Arnie, there's more. When I was married years ago, I had a little boy, who died at age seven after a dreadful bicycle accident. He would be exactly your age, seventeen, if he had lived. Having you in my life would be a double delight...as a nephew and like a son."

Jennifer unfolded her hands. "Jason and I, who you know now are your new grandparents, also offer you our home and our family and our love, any time you'd like to be with us. You may have noticed at Veronika's party that we have a big family, and all of us welcome you to be part of us."

As Arnie sat before them, they saw complex emotions cross his face and alter his body language. At last he leaned forward, his hands covering his face, as his body began to heave with sobs.

CHAPTER 74

For a moment, the others froze, disarmed by the weeping boy's reaction to what they'd told him. Then Jennifer hurried over to touch his shoulder. "It's a lot to process," she soothed.

When the crying stopped, Arnie wiped his face with his shirt. "Sorry," he said, his eyes swollen with tears, "to snivel like a baby, but you...you just offered me a lifeline out of the... the terrible life I lived at home."

Jason placed his hand on Arnie's knee and said gently, "Would you please tell us about it?"

The boy struggled for composure. "I...I grew up okay. My older brother and sister were, like, long gone, since my mom called me her late-in-life surprise. My dad was," he gave a wry laugh, "and still is, a cold guy. But my mother loved me a *whole* lot. Then she got cancer and was sick a year. I pretty much took care of her since my Dad was—and still is—away all the time on business. When she died, I felt like I did, too."

"How awful for you," Aubrey consoled.

"I thought since it was just the two of us then that my dad and I would get closer. But instead, six months after Mom died, he married Magda. I didn't meet her until she walked in the house as his wife. She hated me from the start, and I didn't want her trying to take my mother's place. With my dad away most of the time, she and I were always at it. Because she had Dad's ear and I didn't, I couldn't tell him what was going on. Worst of all, she said she had cat allergies and was mean to my cat, not just to me. By that time Toby was my only family left who cared about me. During school I had to be away from Toby most of the day, but when school was out for the summer, I knew he needed protection."

Jason didn't like where this was going. "What did you do?"

"I mailed a letter to Dad at his office, asking him to buy me a car. He did and then I got a job. All this time I got angrier and angrier about my sick life. At least I could take Toby with me in the car to keep him safe. But when I got the grocery store job, I needed a safe daytime place for Toby while I worked, so he wouldn't die in my hot car."

Jennifer asked, "Were you able to solve that?"

"I...I asked Mrs. Ogleby if he could stay in her garage daytimes for a week while I worked at the grocery store—until I could figure out a long-term plan."

Aubrey looked concerned. "Did that work?"

"She said no, and I didn't know what to do. But then a miracle happened."

"What?" Jason asked.

"Gerry's family said they like cats and would keep Toby at their house while I worked."

Jennifer smiled. "What a nice thing for them to do. And what happened at home during this time?"

"Magda already rationed my food, wouldn't let the maid clean my room and gave me just Saturdays to do my own laundry. Then one day she said she was going to make my room a guest room and I had to get my stuff out or it would disappear forever. I, like, packed up everything in boxes and loaded them in my car. I didn't know where to go. But then another miracle happened. My friend Gerry's family invited me to live a while with them, so Toby and I moved in."

Aubrey studied her glass. "And that's where you are now?"

"Yeah. I mean, it's temporary, until I can figure out what to do next. But what you said about being adopted. I just learned that I was a few days ago."

Jason urged. "Would you mind telling us how?"

"Well, you already know I work part-time for a caterer, because I first saw all of you at the party we catered at that mansion. At one evening catering job, I bumped into my dad. Before he noticed me, I overheard him tell some other men that he never could warm up to his adopted child, who he thought of differently than his own children. We...he and I talked about that a few days ago and he told me for the first time that kid they adopted was me." Arnie paused and drew a ragged breath. "Actually, that helped me understand better why he ignored me so much. Up to then, it was a mystery. I had always figured he just thought I was worthless."

Jennifer brushed aside tears of her own. "Oh, Arnie. We're heartbroken you had to go through this. Now you have people to love you, and at least two welcoming places to stay. The bad stuff's behind you."

He grimaced. "You're wrong. The bad stuff isn't all behind me. I live in daily fear of what I did at Mrs. Ogelby's house."

The others exchanged guarded looks.

Finally, Jason broke the silence. "You mean when the drone you and Gerry operated found her body upstairs?"

Tears formed again in Arnie's eyes. "No, earlier that day, when she asked me to stack boxes in her garage and I begged her to let Toby spend the days there until I could make another safe plan for him."

At the three caring faces focused on him, Arnie again fought tears. What did he have to lose now? Why not just tell the truth and get it over with? "I *had* to protect Toby. And I was mad at the world and I knew Toby's safety depended only on me. I love Toby and I couldn't let him down. When Mrs. Ogleby told me to stay on the porch while she went in the house for money to pay me, I stepped into her kitchen and took her set of keys. That way, if all else failed, I could sneak Toby and his food and litter into her garage daytimes while I worked."

Aubrey spoke compassionately to Arnie. "You just wanted to protect the pet you love."

He nodded, grateful to have that horror off his chest with people who understood. "But when our drone found her dead upstairs, I thought the police would arrest me for stealing the keys and maybe even think I killed her. It's been a nightmare. I was even scared to come here today in case your policeman relative might try to arrest me."

Jason wanted to allay Arnie's fear. "Just as you protected Toby, now the three of us will protect you."

CHAPTER 75

MONDAY

E ven with Becca retrieved from the hospital and recovering in her own bed, Jennifer went to bed troubled. Events sparked by the woman at the garage sale roiled through her mind. After hours tossing-and-turning, she finally crept out of bed, took the fanny pack from the nightstand, and padded down the hall to the large windows overlooking the street below. Her watch read 2:00.

The lone cul-de-sac streetlamp illuminated the black night enough to make out the circle of road below, ringed by sidewalk. She studied the shadowy Donnegan house across the street. A real-estate For Sale sign reflected their intention to sell it now that her mother had moved out.

She unzipped the fanny pack brought from the nightstand. No need to strap it around her waist now. But she'd worn it, or had it at her fingertips, day and night, since Veronika's vision of danger for her family. Funny, nobody around her asked why she wore it every day instead of only for weekend hands-free garage sale shopping. She prepared to explain that it held her cell phone and purse "stuff," creating the bulky look. She wouldn't add that Veronika's loaded weapon contributed to that bulk.

But she'd struggled with another issue from the moment Veronika's Derringer entered her life. A gun brought responsibility. Would she shoot to kill? Adam described this dilemma for every policeman and gun owner. When only disabling an opponent, you risked his grab for a hidden weapon, with which he would *not* return your no-kill restraint. He'd zap you.

Moreover, an opponent's torso presented a large target, one his extremities did not. In the excitement and pandemonium of a life-and-death situation, you'd need to act faster than you could think. The consensus advice, supported by state law, was to use deadly force only in fear for your life, but then shoot to kill. Her shooting-range trainer reinforced this.

In the past, Adam had also reminded them that justice should fit the crime. Self-defense meant shooting to protect your life. But just as in a court of law, where punishment for trespassing or purse snatching wasn't a death sentence, similarly the justice you dealt should fit the crime happening at that moment. You must decide if and where to draw the self-defense line.

She rolled scenarios in her mind but couldn't know which might fit unfolding circumstances if the Radner threat loomed. If that moment came, would she know what to do?

A car circling the cul-de-sac below startled her. Odd at this wee hour—maybe someone lost? But odder yet, the car rolled to a stop in front of her house. The driver climbed out, eased open the trunk and pulled out something the size of a small suitcase. He lugged it to the front of her house, opened the gate and *walked up her sidewalk.*

Quietly, she lifted the window a few inches, adding night insect sounds to the scene below. But then she heard something else. Splashing water? She eased her cell phone out of the fanny pack and removed the pistol.

From the open window, a familiar sharp smell assaulted her nostrils. Gasoline! She backed away from the window and hurried down the stairs, dialing 911. "Someone's splashing gasoline on my house. Please send help before he lights a match. *Hurry!*" She gave her address, dropped the cell phone, grabbed the flashlight kept in the foyer's corner and jerked open the front door.

The man, hauling another gas can, halted midstride, attempting to shield his eyes from the blinding beam of light she shone in his face.

In her most commanding voice, she demanded, "Who are you and what are you doing?"

"I'm Robert Radner, a name you'll never forget, and I'm burning down the goddam house of the person who ruined my life. Now you're going to suffer the way I've suffered. You're going to lose everything tonight, just as I have."

Her anger mingled with fear. "I...I have a gun. Stop this minute or I'll shoot."

He sloshed more gasoline against her house. In the flashlight's beam, she saw him reach in his pocket. She couldn't let him ignite a match. A house fire could burn Becca and Jason alive as they slept upstairs. This fit a life-and-death situation. She moved out on the porch, pistol in hand. "I say again, *stop or I'll shoot.*" She watched him lift a lighter and heard the scratch of flint as he tried flicking on the flame. She cocked the antique silver pistol's hammer, aimed, and squeezed the trigger.

The man fell to the ground, bellowing in pain and clutching his mid-section. "You *shot* me. *What the hell?*" he screamed. "Haven't you damaged me enough, you meddling Cretan?"

As Jennifer advanced toward him, he hugged his body with one arm, using the other arm and his legs to crab his way along the ground toward his car. At her sidewalk gate, he pulled himself upright and lurched toward his vehicle at the curb.

"Police are on their way." Jennifer shouted the warning. But where were they? She felt panic. Did he have a gun in the car? Should she shoot him again before he got inside his vehicle? How should she direct the *one* cartridge left in the pistol?

"*Stop* or I'll shoot again," she cried.

Ignoring her, he fumbled to open his car door.

Should she shoot him? Or dare she gamble, firing again but not at him? Would the noise of her weapon's explosive second shot scare him into thinking she meant business, or should she aim again for his body? "I have five more bullets here, all with your name on them," she called before lifting the pistol, cocking the hammer and firing again, this time at his vehicle's front wheel.

As the shot cracked the air, Radner flattened himself against his car. "*No*, don't shoot. *Please* don't shoot me again."

She gulped a breath. He seemed subdued, but what if he changed his mind? He couldn't know she had no more bullets, although she was terrifyingly aware. She consoled herself with the desperate thought that at least he couldn't drive far with a flat tire.

Sirens pierced the night. Help on the way. Thank god....

Radner clung to the side of his car. Blood pooled down his shirt around the hand pressed against his chest as he snarled at her, "Before Bobby left, he told me how you instigated my family's disintegration. My business is ruined, my wife's in jail for murder, my son can never come home again after assaulting your daughter."

He began whimpering as he clung to his car door. Was haughty, rude, callous Robert Radner cowed at last? Straightening suddenly, he whined, "Everything that's happened to me is your fault for meddling in that girl's death."

Upstairs, wakened by shots and realizing Jennifer wasn't beside him, Jason leaped from their bed and rocketed down the stairs so fast he nearly lost his balance. He rushed through the open front door in time to hear Radner's accusatory words.

In the front yard now and grasping the gasoline's implications, Jason advanced on the antique dealer. "You got it wrong, Radner. Everything that happened to you is *your* fault. And you're going to have a long time in prison to figure that out."

Radner began to weep.

With the wounded man convulsed in sobs and not an apparent threat, Jason cradled Jennifer protectively against him. "Are you okay, my love? Did he shoot at you?" Only then did he notice the pistol in her hand. His jaw dropped. "Jen, where...where did you *get* this? What *happened* here?"

But before she could answer, blinking blue-and-white lights, accompanied by blaring sirens, jarred the dark night as two police cruisers and a fire engine screeched around the corner toward the house.

CHAPTER 76

After the police cruiser left, a cop accompanied Radner in the EMT van to the nearest ER for treatment before his ultimate destination: jail. Meantime, the firefighters worked non-stop.

Their lieutenant in charge asked Jason, "Is your water heater in the basement?"

"Yes, two of them. It's a big house, where five kids showered and bathed."

"Gas or electric?"

Jason thought fast. "Electric."

"Lucky, because a gas-operated pilot light could ignite the vapor."

"Vapor?"

"We're less concerned with the gasoline than its vapor, which is the flammable part. That vapor is heavier than air, so it tends to make its way into basements, especially since our investigation found that some gasoline splashed into these front two window wells. I sent two firefighters down there with a four-gas-meter to measure the percentage of volatile compounds in the air against the likelihood of explosion."

"Explosion?" Jennifer whispered anxiously.

"That's why we're taking those fans to the basement and setting others atop the window wells. We want to extract any vapor-laden air from the lower level. The downstairs fans blow it out and these reversed fans on top suck it out."

Jason pointed. "What're they doing over there?"

"Putting absorbent material on that puddle of gasoline. Works like cat litter. Then we shovel it up and take it away. Runoff isn't a problem here because the gasoline soaked into the soil along the front of your house."

Jason frowned. "Will the gasoline kill all these bushes?"

The firefighter chuckled. "That's above my pay grade, sir."

Sniffing the air, Jennifer wrinkled her nose. "What about the smell? How long will it last?"

"Depends on various factors. Likely a day or two."

Jason glanced toward the front door. "Is our house in danger during that time?"

"By the time we leave, it shouldn't be. Do you have a garden hose with a power nozzle handy?"

Jennifer turned toward the fire engine. "Is ours better than your firehose?"

The lieutenant smiled. "For this purpose, yes. If you had no water source, we'd use ours. But since your hose serves this purpose well, our water source can remain ready for our next call."

Jason pointed. "Good. Our hose is around the corner, on the side of the house. Want me to get it for you?"

"Yes. We'll start washing the gasoline off the house at this end. By the time we get to the other end, we'll shovel out the puddle-absorbent material and hose down that wall, too."

Jennifer noticed an animal leashed by the truck. "Your mascot doesn't look like a Dalmatian."

"He's not a mascot, ma'am, He's an accelerant detection canine, trained to look for ignitable liquids like gasoline, kerosene or fuel oil. Turns out, we didn't need him here, but he's particularly good at what he does."

Jennifer shook her head. "I didn't know you could train dogs to do that."

"We also have explosive detection canines in the Fire Marshal's Office to identify explosives like TNT or gunpowder. Yeah, we have a few little tricks up our sleeves. Tonight was easy, compared to some."

Trying not to reveal how shell-shocked she felt, Jennifer managed a smile. "We thank you for coming so quickly and knowing exactly what to do."

"Just doing our job, ma'am."

Later, as the crew prepared to leave, Jennifer asked the lieutenant, "Would you mind...may we offer you and your crew some chocolate chip cookies I baked this afternoon?"

The firefighter knew grateful citizens sometimes needed to express gratitude for life-saving rescues. "Ah...okay, ma'am. Thank you."

Jennifer dashed into the house, returning quickly with a heaping cellophane-wrapped platter. "No need to return the dish. I buy them for practically nothing at garage sales for gifts just like this." She smiled. "Our thanks again to all of you."

As the motor revved and the big truck eased away from the curb, the Shannons waved from their front yard.

The lieutenant had accepted their gift out of politeness, but as the fire engine started down the street the other firefighters heard him say, "Hey guys...cookies! Let this party begin."

CHAPTER 77

TUESDAY

"What do we have here?" asked Homicide Detective Adam Iverson, as he viewed the body lying at the bottom of the stairs.

The patrolman beside him consulted his notes. "The maid called 911 at 8:33 this morning to report finding her employer dead. Doors, windows locked. Maid has a key. Cleans once a week. She's over there, when you're ready to talk to her. We checked the house. Nobody else here, just this guy on the floor. Looks like small caliber gunshot wound in the neck plus injuries consistent with a fall down the stairs. A lot of dried blood. Maybe the bullet nicked the carotid artery? ME's not here yet, but the body looks a little ripe, like he's been here a few days.

"Thanks. Send the maid over to me."

The woman approached, wringing her hands as anxiety distorted her face.

"What's your name?"

"Rosa Chavez."

"How long have you worked here."

"Five years."

"Who else lives in the house?"

"Just the Missus."

"She's not here?"

"I don't know. When I see the Mister here dead on the floor, I call 911 and stay right here."

"Okay, I want you to show me through the house and tell me if you see anything unusual in any of the rooms."

"We use the backstairs to go up? That way we don't touch nothing where he fall down?"

"Good. Show me."

Upstairs, the maid watched the detective open doors with gloved hands. "These are guest rooms. This is the office for the Missus. There is the bedroom for Mister and Missus."

As they entered the room, the maid's hand flew to cover her mouth. "Oh, looks like somebody pack for travel. Suitcase over there and clothes on the bed. Not like every day."

Adam verified. "Nobody else lives here?"

"The boy lived here but he moved out about a week ago. The Missus, she change his old room so now it is for company."

"Do they have a lot of company?"

"I don't think so. Just family on holidays."

"Okay. Now show me the downstairs rooms and whether anything is different than usual."

When they finished, he asked her. "What's the name of the family?"

"Mister and Missus Anderson. "Here, I show you a picture." She led him toward the office and pointed to a photo on the desk. "See, these two visit this house sometimes. The Mister calls them Jim and Anne."

Adam pointed. "And is this the Missus?"

"This is the old Missus. She die about a year ago. Cancer." Rosa pointed to an elegant oil painting portrait on the wall. "This is the new Missus. I think she is from another country, but I do not know which one."

"Thank you. Please give me your contact information in case I have more questions."

Rosa nodded. "Here. I already write it down for you."

Seeing her on the brink of tears, Adam asked, "Are you okay?"

"Okay, yes, I think okay. But very sad. And now also no job."

"Wait." Adam pointed to the desk photo. "And who is this one?"

"Nice boy who move out. Arnie."

Adam did a double-take. Wasn't this the same kid who lived with the Wilberforce family, down the street from his Shannon relatives?

CHAPTER 78

FRIDAY

"What a crazy month," Jason sighed as they crawled into bed the following night.

Jennifer leaned back on her pillows and closed her eyes. "Amen."

A few minutes later, Jason noticed his wife's pensive expression. "Uh-oh. That's your thinking look."

"You're right, Jay. So much to absorb. Mind talking before turning on TV?"

"Ah...okay, I guess." He dropped the remote on the blanket. "What's up?"

"Jay, you know how people try to understand what's going on around them. They look for cause-and-effect or other patterns to relate things. They try to figure out what's random and what's connected. And if it is, why it is. But how do we explain chance events that start a domino roll that will change our lives forever?"

He chuckled. "Whoa, where did *that* come from?" But she looked serious, so he considered her question. "You mean like expecting you'll drive to work but instead having a serious accident on the way?"

"Like that. Or going to a garage sale and seeing a woman I never met who changed our lives and our family even after she was *dead*. What's the chance of that happening?"

"Miniscule."

"Because of that woman at the garage sale, I met Jean and learned Katie's story, which led to proving her death wasn't suicide."

"That wasn't chance, Jen. Your imagination and your...ah, *persistence* made that difference."

"Then Greg showed us how Aubrey is your...*our* new daughter, and Arnie, our new grandson."

He shook his head as if to clear it. "Yeah...we were dealt some wild cards there. But Arnie's DNA match solved any doubt about our blood connection."

"And Greg could cross-reference Tri-State's files only because someone working there put notes in files connecting Katie, Aubrey and Arnie."

Jason nodded. "And that person must have been Abby."

"Yes, and on top of all the rest came the horrible shock about Arnie's father's murder. Adam says the stepmother skipped to her home country, but we have extradition there, so she'll come back to stand trial for murder. Arnie's eager to testify at the trial to get justice for his dad."

"Fortunately for Arnie, his dad's Will provides a generous college fund for the boy and then divides his remaining estate among his three children. Unlikely the stepmother will contest it since she'll be tried for murdering her husband."

Jason adjusted his pillows. "Didn't you tell me Aubrey has offered the boy a permanent home with her?"

"Yes. She thought any chance for a child in her life ended when her own little boy died. Now she hopes to adopt Arnie, if he's willing. Makes double sense since he's her sister's child and homeless, on top of being an orphan now. And isn't it another weird coincidence that if Aubrey's own boy had lived, he'd be Arnie's age?"

"Yeah, uncanny, even if Aubrey and Katie *are* identical twins. At least Arnie knows he has a home with his aunt any time he wants it, adoption or not. And we're backup if that doesn't work." Jason stated this as a fact, but now looked expectantly for Jennifer's reaction.

"Absolutely. Our house becomes an empty nest soon, and while I'll love private life with you after all these years, home will seem strangely quiet."

"And," Jason marveled, "during this whole crazy process, you settled your mom and Veronika at Pebblebrook Manor. They love the place."

She grinned. "What luck, Jay. She's independent, safe, and not lonely because of Veronika. Just think, three months ago those two hadn't met, and now they're like sisters—on a new adventure."

Jason smiled. "Were you surprised Becca announced her engagement to Nathan?"

Jennifer sighed. "Yes, but they haven't set a wedding date yet. Although they seem to us like a great match, I'll believe it when I see it. Funny how it took Bobby's dreadful assault on her at the antique shop to trigger her engagement decision."

Jason sat forward. "And speaking of decisions, what about Adam opting to work for his father? Tough for him to leave the police force next month, but he's excited about his new job with Greg's firm. And what about the clever way Greg drew him in. He'll discover and reopen cold cases of wrongly convicted people, to free them from prison, some from death row. That's something Adam can really sink his teeth into."

Jennifer nodded. "Ingenious, yes. Now Adam will help bring overdue justice for them. As he explained it to me, the attorney's office does the work, including all forensic and other investigations, gets the innocent person released, and so earns a percentage of any money the victim recovers as damages from the state wrongfully imprisoning him. Win-win. In the meantime, he'll use his detective skills for justice in the murder of Arnie's father."

Jason shook his head. "That's an awful situation for a kid like Arnie to face. And speaking of awful, what about Becca's attempted murder where she worked? Thank God she survived, and now she's home, talking and expected to fully recover. Who'd imagine a part-time job could turn out like that? Did they finally find that guy who tried to choke her to death?"

Jennifer squirmed in guilt. So far, Becca hadn't mentioned her mother's part in the antique-shop spying scenario. To Jason's question, she said, "You mean Bobby Radner? No, he disappeared. Adam expects, with his international connections, he'll be hard to find. But Becca says wherever he is, she thinks he sports some deep scars on his face from her stabs with the Shang Dynasty goblet."

Jason chuckled. "Hey, without you, the rest of us wouldn't even know such a goblet exists. Now we have two of them, since Veronika gave you hers after police arrested her security guards for selling merchandise they stole from her house."

"That's why Adam says security companies must vet employees so carefully—to avoid sending a fox to guard the henhouse. At least they caught the guard and the security cronies working with him."

"And all because Becca realized Bobby brought some of Veronika's antiques into Radner's shop. Bobby's at least on the hook for fencing stolen merchandise but may also belong to their burglary crew. And that added to his attempted murder charge for harming Becca." Jennifer looked perplexed. "And speaking of Becca, what about her odd message I'm supposed to give Veronika?"

Jason frowned. "What message?"

"...she's asked to wear Veronica's ankle bracelet a while longer. She wants the amulet's protection to get through any PTSD from Bobby's attack."

Jason shook his head in disbelief. "Did you say amulet? Are you serious?"

"I am."

"So much for our daughter's modern scientific college education."

They shared a wry laugh.

Jason's brow furrowed. "About that Derringer. You *are* going to keep it locked in our safe, right?"

"Of course. But admit it. Veronika's vision and her pistol saved our home and our lives. What if insomnia hadn't kept me awake to see Radner douse our house with gasoline? Even if the three of us miraculously escaped the fire, we'd have lost everything. Amazing, don't you think?"

"What's amazing is Radner's survival to rot in jail for a long time. Did you aim for the right side of his chest or is that another coincidence?"

"I aimed for his torso. Pure chance the bullet landed on the right side, away from his heart and major blood vessels. Doctors say his wound is not life-threatening, so he will do slammer-time for trying to burn down our house with us in it."

Jason gave a mirthless laugh. "And his recovery means you won't be tried for shooting someone in self-defense."

Jennifer gave him a sharp look. "Yes... but given the circumstances, don't you think any jury would acquit me?"

"Probably, but a relief not to face that. Unpredictable juries sometimes confound logic." Now Jason's face looked thoughtful. "Jen, have you noticed none of our neighbors face the situations we do?"

"What do you mean?"

"They lead more normal lives than we do, which isn't a bad idea."

"Maybe those people spend their whole lives waiting to start living."

Jason gave a dry laugh. "But how about the other side, Jen? The peace-and-quiet side. We haven't had a summer this exciting since just last year when that Civil War fanatic and his band of mercenaries tried to kill us during a family picnic at Hannah's house."

Jennifer knew where this headed. She tried a spin. "But remember how we discovered the Civil War treasure he wanted and donated it to the museum for the public to see and study."

"Or the summer before, when terrorists kidnapped our grandson because you discovered their diamonds...diamonds we now own by default but can't discuss with anybody without risking madmen from another country trying to kill us in revenge."

Jennifer tried another spin. "At least, we used several of those gems to fund our vacation trip last fall. Nice little windfall, wasn't it?"

"Because that's what Homeland Security suggested we do after your terrorist adventure. Or the summer before that, when a stalker kidnapped you and later came after our family?"

Understanding this conversation's uncomfortable direction, she knew Jason correctly worried about safety for her and their family. Like him, she never wanted to put her loved ones at risk. Could she help it if her inquisitiveness took her down paths that seemed entirely safe but often weren't?

Artfully, she changed the subject. "Adam says detectives don't believe in coincidence, although the entire woman at the garage sale incident, and everything following it, seems like a string of crazy coincidences."

Jason scratched his head. "Well, if not coincidence, then what? Design? And if so, why and how and whose?"

Jennifer mused. "Even if the dominos fell spontaneously after I saw her, surely spotting the woman at the garage sale was random chance."

"Jen, isn't why-things-happen one of those unanswerable questions? Right now, I'm too sleepy to figure it out."

Her distraction strategy had worked...at least for now.

"Me, too." She turned off her bedside lamp and slid under the covers. "I love you, Jay."

"Love you too, my dearest Jen." A pause. "But..."

She rolled on her side, facing him. "But...?"

He gave a deep sigh. "But not every husband is, ah..." he chose careful words, "lucky enough to learn the woman he married is a... ah, closet detective."

Jennifer smiled. "Not every woman who is a closet detective is lucky enough to go to bed at night with an irresistibly handsome, talented and successful engineer."

He gave an appreciative chuckle. "Well, when you put it that way..."

He clicked off his own bed table light and settled under the covers.

In the darkness, his strong hand reached for hers and their warm fingers curled together...and then their arms.

The End

ACKNOWLEDGMENTS

Capt. Steven Avato, Loudoun County Fire & Rescue, Virginia, with 40 years in law enforcement: 27 of that with Bureau of Alcohol, Tobacco, Firearms & Explosives (ATF), specializing in fire and explosion investigations; eight years in the Philadelphia Police Department; and more than four years with Loudoun County Fire Marshal's Office, described the implications of residential gasoline spills.

Sgt. Jim Baker, Drone Operations Coordinator, Collier County Sheriff's Office (Naples, Florida), gave me an impressive drone demonstration and insights about law-enforcement tactical support drone-use as well as restrictions. Sgt. Baker has 28 years' experience with Collier County Sheriff's Office, six years of that time as their subject-matter expert for drone operations.

Attorney Fred J. Getty of Getty & Associates, P.C. in Locust Grove, Virginia, graciously provided innovative legal insights for this story.

Battalion Chief of Special Operations Justin Green in Loudoun County, Virginia, provided useful information during a phone interview.

Holly Henderson, Ashby Ponds (Ashburn, Virginia) Sales Staff member with 25 years' experience in the senior-residence business (15 of them at Ashby Ponds), described how seniors become residents at this Erickson CCRC (Continuing Care Retirement Community) and described residential life. She enjoys watching the positive difference a CCRC can make in senior lives. (www.ashbyponds.com)

Sibyle Jenks When this friend of 30 years heard me lament coming up with a good name for this story's senior residence, she immediately volunteered "Pebblebrook Manor." The minute she spoke, I knew it was "right." Thanks, Sibyle.

Dr. Daniel Kaplan, Board Certified in Family Medicine and Geriatric Medicine in Naples, Florida, advised me about drugs, throat trauma and other medical questions pertaining to my story.

Detective Michael (Mike) Lamper, with 32 years in law enforcement (the last 23 years assigned to investigating Major Crimes and Crime Scenes in northern Virginia), gave me several excellent ideas for my story from his personal experience, including information about police lingo and procedures.

Bruce B. Rosenblatt, senior housing expert and *Naples Daily News* columnist with 30 years' experience in senior housing facility consulting, shared his knowledge with me. His **Senior Housing Solutions** business helps eliminate guesswork in choosing the right senior living community to meet elder needs and preferences. He offers knowledgeable advice about senior communities, plus follow-up afterward. (www.seniorhousingsolutions.net)

Detective William Szuminski, **Fairfax County Police Department**, Crime Scene Section, Cyber & Forensics Bureau, with 21 years in law enforcement, shared his personal and professional knowledge and vision for police drone use, as well as other police insights for this story.

Rich Utting, professional locksmith certified by Division of Criminal Justice Services, who has worked 18 years for **Spencer's Safe & Lock**, 46000 Old Ox Road, Suite 100, Sterling, VA, helped me understand how certain locks work. (703) 471-9022 (www.spencerslock.com)

Jim Webb of **Silver Eagle Group** (Shooting Range/ Sales/Training/Events) in Ashburn, Virginia, is a retired intelligence office at the CIA and longtime firearms enthusiast. He shared detailed research information and photos of Derringer pistols dating back to mid-1800s. Phone: 703-723-5173, (silvereaglegroup.com)

Scott Wolf, a gun enthusiast since receiving his first BB-gun in kindergarten, for a total of 58 years owning, using and appreciating firearms and their responsible use. He first acquainted me with antique Derringer pistols.

Richard "Pete" Velde, a member of the District of Columbia Bar and former official of the U.S. Department of Justice, introduced me to Shang Dynasty Brass Ritual Wine Goblets. He acquired his goblet in the early 1970s from the National Palace Museum in Taipei, where it was hand cast from the original Shang object, using a form of lost-wax casting done by expert curators at the museum. The minister of justice gave

Pete special access to the museum's 500,000-piece collection, and this goblet was a personal gift from that minister. Pete provided me with literature about the goblet and let me borrow his while writing this story.

OTHER BOOKS IN SUZI WEINERT'S *GARAGE SALE MYSTERY SERIES*

If you have not had the chance to read Suzi Weinert's other books, you can learn more about Jennifer Shannon's thrilling adventures springing from her garage sale shopping. These exciting tales are available from BluewaterPress LLC online at www.bluewaterpress.com and will keep you on the edge of your seat.

GARAGE SALE STALKER -
Jennifer lives in secure, affluent Mclean, Virginia, where she stumbles into danger lurking in places she thought safe. Her passion for weekend treasure hunting at local garage and estate sales pulls her into a twisted world of crime, child abuse and murder. When she's forced to match wits with an antagonist bent on revenge, her family's safety and her own desperate situation hinge on her intelligence and resourcefulness. Nothing prepares her for the ultimate discovery, producing a startling climax

GARAGE SALE DIAMONDS -
Jennifer discovers hundreds of diamonds hidden inside an innocent garage sale purchase. Terrorists, furious at their treasure's accidental inclusion at the sale, must seize these diamonds back in order to fund their explosive plot against America. From the strife-torn Middle East to the comforts

of McLean, conflicting philosophies clash with devastating effects. As danger to Jennifer and her family escalates, she must rely upon her ingenuity and inventiveness to hurdle frightening obstacles thrown across her path.

GARAGE SALE RIDDLE -

Jennifer buys an old painting at an estate sale, discovering a mysterious map and riddle hidden beneath the backing. Flying to Naples, Florida, to rescue her aging mother from a devious criminal preying on seniors, she sits on the plane beside William Early who "always gets what he wants, whatever it takes." Moving her mother from Florida to Virginia presents serious challenges as Jennifer protects her from predators, while researching riddle and map clues to an apparent Civil War treasure. But William Early lusts after the rare valuables she seeks. Marshalling his vast resources, he's determined to wrest the treasure away from Jennifer, by any means, including murder. Can she outwit him to save her mother, her family, herself, and the historic treasure?